Stick Figures

from

Rockport

Jennifer M. Lane

Cover design by Leigh M. Morrow – plotbunnies.net

Copyright © 2018

Published by Pen & Key Publishing

Jennifermlanewrites.com

ISBN: 978-1-7334068-3-3

ACKNOWLEDGEMENTS

Thanks to Alia, Leigh, Sunyi, Essa, Meghan, Sayword, Lauren, and CJ.
Especially huge thanks to my editor Cheryl Murphy
and to Leigh M. Morrow – cover designer extraordinaire.

DEDICATION

To Felix for taking me to inspiring places.
To Penny for allowing me to write.
To Matt for encouraging my art.
And to the Writer Alliance – for everything.

CHAPTER ONE

Tamsin filled her lungs with cool Minnesota air and faced her mother's door. It was metal with faux woodgrain, the kind that came with every house built in the nineties, painted a drab tan and scratched. Grease or sealant of some kind leaked from the small, fan-shaped window at the top of the door. It oozed down like slow-flowing honey. Beneath the faux brass door knocker was a name plate. *Mrs. Eliot* scrawled in her mother's neat print. From the ground to about knee height were stickers of super heroes, faded to varying degrees by the sun. Some scraped away so nothing but the paper backing remained. Her nephews' doing and undoing. Curtains covered the sidelights, and from within, Tamsin heard the romp of young nephews and her sister's shrill voice, an admonishment she couldn't discern but unmistakable in its gravity.

She took in one last moment of peace, a deep breath of autumn air. Dry and cold. She held it in and warmed it.

She didn't want to come. Not because cleaning out her mother's house seemed hard. Her mother had thrown away most of the past after her father died anyway. And not because her relationship with Margaret had been strained since they were kids, although it had. And not because Tamsin was unwilling to see her sister, her last remaining family member, as

1

anything more than a judgmental, condescending entity she was bound to by duty. The real reason, though Tamsin wouldn't admit it even to herself, was because closing the door to her own house and stepping away for more than a day of work required her to face the fact that she was alone. She'd been alone since Owen died. Since an aneurysm made the coroner take him from the house on a gurney, leaving behind a ding in the trim around the door. She swore that there would be one door in her world that wasn't damaged in some way. Someday.

Every door in Tamsin's life was dinged or chipped, abused by clumsy exits and hasty entrances. Even her mother's door out here in Minnesota wasn't spared. Tamsin faced it, knowing it was the last time she would step through it. She wasn't ready to sift through it all, to take what she wanted, help her sister box up everything else, and put her mother to rest.

Tamsin was an expert at grief. When her father, the man she admired more than any other, slipped from earth, she grieved for weeks, wearing black and pouring over photo albums. He left behind a trove of paintings treasured by collectors, a wife who threw it all away and moved to Minnesota, and two daughters more than a thousand miles apart in every type of distance. Tamsin was still wearing those scars when Owen died, and they ripped wide open again. Margaret had sent a sympathy card and called once, a chat that ended in an argument when Mags suggested Tamsin get on a plane and visit her and her mother when she was over it. Tamsin didn't get over it. She clung to the grief, her constant companion, in the farmhouse they bought to fulfill their dream. A dream she would never let die.

By the time she lost her mother, Tamsin was a professional. She shed a few tears until the day after the funeral, and then she packed it all away.

Tamsin loosened her grip on her suitcase. She'd squeezed it so hard the pattern of the handle was etched into her hand, five red lines stretching across her palm like sheet music without any notes. She rubbed them to soothe the ache. All the way through the airport, collecting her bag, all through her Uber ride, Margaret's expectations were the soundtrack. Once she opened the door to her mother's house and faced her sister, she would have to display the appropriate amount of grief, collect what she wanted to keep, box up the rest, and give an emotional goodbye to the house she barely knew before closing the door with its stickers and slime for eternity.

She would also have to face her sister's persistent protests against her happy childhood, playing yet another round of didn't-it-seem-odd-that-Dad-wasn't-around. She pressed the lever of the screen door with her thumb and warmed at the memory of a different screen door. The one to her childhood home. It had been one of those metal screen doors from the fifties. Aluminum. Steel, maybe. The bottom panel was an unpainted hammered metal plate, and the pane of glass in the upper half had shattered into a million slivers when she hit it with a softball. It had been her father's fault for aiming her in that direction. The handle had been a textured, black plastic button and pollen from the giant oak trees would bleed into it. Her mother would clean it with a rag and Windex, like it was neighborhood blight. Her mother.

Those memories of her childhood door brought a dozen more. The sound of it slamming behind her father when he came in from painting, the sound of his boots on the floor and the rustle of his green waxed oilcloth coat with its brown collar as he threw it on a hook. Being in college, watching a nature show about New England marshes and calling her father from her clear plastic telephone. She still had the urge to call him at times, to dial one of the few numbers she knew in a world where everyone was an avatar in a cell phone. Moments arrived like softballs, shattering glass everywhere. At least this door, defaced by stickers and oozing sealant, wasn't her childhood door.

3

She'd only stepped through this fiberglass front door of her mother's five times. Thanksgivings and Christmases. She'd been too raw to help her mother move. Too wounded from finding out that her mother had thrown away her childhood memories. Too jealous that she chose to be closer to her Margaret, who had a whole family, and further from her. On the other side of this door was nothing but stuff, things Tamsin didn't recognize and had no feelings for. But if something she cherished had survived her mother's purge, it was worth finding. Even if she found nothing of the past, she had an obligation to her sister, who had reminded her that she couldn't have her half of what the house was worth until they put it on the market, and they couldn't do that until Tamsin flew out there and helped clean it out, as if it were the money that mattered. Besides, Margaret had two kids who put stickers on everything, and she could really use some help around here.

There was a button for the doorbell. A little orange rectangle, dimly lit. Pressed by people she'd never met who came to visit her mother. Her book club. Some people from church. Tamsin had never met any of them. She ran her finger over the little plastic button. If she rang it, she would be asserting her place as a visitor in her mother's home. At best, Margaret would consider it a deferral to her decisions. Margaret did live closer and had seen their mother every day. But Tamsin would probably be interrupting some organized sorting of eighty-year-old dishes in the basement, sure to anger her and bring forth a fresh batch of why-do-I-have-to-do-everythings and what-took-you-so-longs and at least one just-open-the-door-like-you're-family.

Tamsin put her hand on the doorknob, and her purse fell from her shoulder. Tip. She'd forgotten to tip the Uber driver. Was she supposed to tip an Uber driver? She hoisted her purse and spun on her heel. Down the mulch path to the curb where the driver sat, looking at his phone. She dug through her wallet and waved a ten-dollar bill in the air. Better safe than sorry.

Behind her, the door flung open. "Jesus, Tamsin. Did you just get here?" Margaret. Hands on her hips like passing judgment was a full-time job and her burden to bear.

Tamsin yelled over her shoulder. "I gotta tip the driver. Wait a second."

"I've been waiting all day."

"Yes, I had a swift chat with the airplane and told it to fly really slow just to piss you off." Tamsin passed the bill to the driver and thanked him. The car pulled away from the curb, and she made her way back toward the house, suitcase grinding along the sidewalk behind her. "You know, Mags—"

"Margaret."

Christ. Tamsin had to change her mood or the next few days would be horrible. Finding the humor in her sister's oppression was the only way to survive it. "Yes, your highness. Margaret. I have a job. I can't walk away from it. I would have been here two days ago, but they pay me for the privilege of my company, and they'll stop paying me if I deny it to them."

She trailed her sister into the house and stopped halfway down a row of boxes that lined the wall. More boxes and bags covered the chairs, stuffed with afghans and doilies, throw pillows and books. Somewhere down the hall, her two nephews ran and shot at each other with Nerf guns. Their footsteps rattled glasses in the china cabinet. Tamsin lifted a towel from an open box, just a normal bath towel. If someone had asked her what color her mother's towels were, she would have guessed blue. This one was mauve. She grabbed the corner, a thick square of hemmed terry cloth, and balled it in her fist. It smelled like Gain. Her mother had always used Tide. Everything had changed after her father died. Tamsin saw a glimmer of hope among the tall stacks of boxes. With so much already packed away, perhaps she could head home early. She wanted nothing more than to steer her suitcase back to the airport, back to the farmhouse, to the quiet and predictable isolation of her home in the Pennsylvania countryside.

"Your Aunt Tam is here. Come say hello." Margaret yelled down the hall and four heavy feet ran past her. When they were little, she had been cool. Now she was just a stranger they had to hug at Christmas.

"I'm sorry I haven't been here." Tamsin threw her purse on the sofa and rubbed her eyes with the heels of her hands, wiping the travel away. "I can tell you've done a lot of the work. And you were closer to Mom. I'm sorry I've been distant."

Margaret clutched Tamsin in a hug that begged to be accepted rather than returned. "I have been falling apart, Tam."

"I know. I would have been here to help with all this but I—"

"That's not what I mean." Margaret moved a box from the sofa. It rattled. Candlesticks, maybe. Picture frames. She sat with her hands in her lap. "I could have called you sooner. We could have done this weeks ago. Months ago, when you were here for the funeral, but I couldn't let go of the house. I have so many memories here. I used to come by every day, dropping off the boys, and picking them up again. Mom and I would have tea, coffee. She'd talk about her book club, and I'd talk about the kids."

"Mom loved decaf."

"She thought the caffeine was something they added." A puff of air, the start of a laugh, escaped Margaret. Tamsin hoped she could keep her sister in a good mood, but the smile fell, and Margaret played with the knotted tassel of a crocheted afghan. "How long does it take to stop feeling this way?"

"After loss?" Tamsin filled her lungs with air. The air from her mother's house. Air that floated over her mother's things. She pulled in particles of her mother's life, the things she loved, the things she'd chosen to keep.

Aerosol potpourri and conflicting candles. Things in boxes and bags and piles, evidence of her mother's presence on earth. The last trench she'd dug in the war of life. How long does it take to stop feeling after loss?

Tamsin let the air escape, taking its sharp bite with it as it departed. "How long does it take to do what? To live again? A year. More. You have to make new memories to cover up the old ones. Not that the old memories ever leave. They just get new company. Happier company, I guess."

"How long did it take to get over losing Owen?"

Tamsin lowered herself onto the edge of an old recliner, its back faded by the sun. "I don't think I'll ever be over Owen. And stop. Give me a call the day you wake up in your perfect life next to Philip, and he doesn't wake up next to you."

Margaret plucked at the afghan. "I'm sorry. I wasn't trying to pry."

"Yet somehow, you just do."

"You never got over losing Dad, either, did you? I bet he's still on your mantel, and you talk to him all the time. How do you go on like that?"

"You just can't help yourself, can you? Why do you keep poking at things?"

Margaret had a way of unearthing old hurts and burrowing deeper when she didn't get the reaction she was looking for. Like a sand crab, never happy with the quality of the air at the surface. It was almost as if Margaret was jealous and took any chance she could to find Tamsin's weaknesses, to pick at the scabs. How dare Mags remind her that her only close relationship was with loss and ask her to unearth all that hurt, undo all the work of pushing it down.

Margaret dropped the afghan, and her hands clutched her knees. She looked small, like she had when she fell off her bike as a kid. "I'm not trying to be difficult. I'm just trying to figure out how to live without either

7

one of my parents. You're the only family I have left. But it's nice to know that nothing's changed, and we get along as good as ever."

Seeing her sister grip her knees, her knuckles white and eyes pained, reminded Tamsin that grief may be her devoted life partner, but it could stop and visit anyone. Even Margaret, with all her harsh edges and cold words, could be vulnerable. "Everybody's different. No, I didn't get over losing Dad, but I'm not reminded of him by every little thing anymore. I can drink tea or go for a walk in the woods and smile at a happy memory instead of feeling like I'm drowning. Comes with time." But. There was a but when it came to Owen. Time hadn't changed a thing. There was still a constant empty ache. Tamsin brushed dust from the arm of the recliner. "Owen was different. I was there for all of it, and you never forget those details. The coroner at the door and me in my pajamas. The guy at the foot of Owen's gurney-thing smelled like peppermints. It's a different kind of hurt, not just because he was my—" Calling Owen her boyfriend always felt strange, so Tamsin let it drop. Nothing ever felt right. Partner? Soulmate? Margaret would only remind her of her status as "not really a widow" anyway.

"I shouldn't have said anything." Margaret stood and folded the afghan, placing it back in the box. "I set some stuff aside for you back here. Things I found that you might want. Come on. Bring one of those empty boxes and a Sharpie. You'll have to start packing things you want to send home. I'll ship it to you."

The light was off in the hallway. Tamsin passed the bathroom that still smelled like that cleaner with the green crystals her mother used every Sunday after church. Past the den where her mother penned lengthy letters on yellow legal paper with red felt-tip pens. She'd received at least one a week for her whole adult life, folded into a tight rectangle and shoved in an envelope with return address stickers that came free from the Veterans

Affairs or whatever charity sent them with a request for money. Then into the bedroom, where the closet doors stood open, the bed strewn with clothes in piles. Slips, panty hose, balls of socks, and underwear.

Margaret pushed hangers aside. Brightly colored jackets and floral dress shirts danced from one side of the closet to the other. Black dress pants and khakis followed. Metal hangers scraped against the rod, the empty ones clanging together, singing out their vacancy. Margaret stepped aside, and Tamsin's heart stopped. Memories swam to the surface, gasping for air like neglected fish in a pond. Her father's coat.

She took the edge of a sleeve. Dark green with a plaid lining. Waxed oilcloth with a brown collar. He'd worn it everywhere. She reached into the closet and lifted the hanger, careful not to rouse the symphony, and laid it on her mother's bed. It was zipped and snapped, the flaps of its pockets still shoved inside, the way he always wore it.

"I'll take this." Tamsin heard the words escape, knowing that her sister wouldn't put up a fight. "I always wondered where his coat went, but I was afraid she threw it away."

"There wasn't even any dust on the shoulders. Mom must have kept it for you."

Tamsin widened her eyes and blinked, trying to absorb the tears before they fell into a puddle on her father's indestructible waterproof coat.

CHAPTER TWO

Tamsin buried her past in packing peanuts and stretched tape across the top of a box, sealing away books, photographs, and a serving tray. The tape gun echoed in the empty dining room. Next to her, Margaret pushed a stack of blankets into a box and reached for the tape. "He wore that thing everywhere. In every memory I have of him, he is wearing that coat. I don't know if that's true, but it seems that way."

Tamsin kicked the boxes against the wall and dropped into a kitchen chair. The table was notched with letters and numbers, the ghosts of homework past. She traced the letter K with her finger. "Remember Mom yelling at him for wearing it at the dinner table? Was that Easter?"

"I think so. Do you remember him waxing it? Scrubbing at it with a brush in the basement?" Margaret pushed a full box aside and started another, pulling glasses from the china cabinet destined for Goodwill. Everything Tamsin hadn't claimed was destined for charity.

Tamsin's thick, brown hair slipped out of her pony tail when she stood. With her hair down, she could be mistaken for her sister. She pulled it back again and added the last box of to-keep items to the stack by the front door. Small mementos of special moments and mundane life.

"You'll ship this to me? It's gonna cost a fortune."

"I'll send you the bill."

"Why not just take it out of my half of the house?"

The set of Margaret's jaw and the roll of her eyes told Tamsin that the idea was deplorable. "Why can't we just keep the accounting simple? You know, you haven't made a lot of effort here. You could try to make this easy for me."

"You chose to be the executor of the will, Mags. You decided to take this on. It's not a big deal. I'll just pay you for the shipping." Tamsin turned her back to her sister, grabbed a Sharpie from a shelf on the entertainment center and labeled the short stack of boxes with her name. They were objects rescued from the trash rather than relics saved for the nostalgia, but they were the last care package she'd ever receive from her mother. Far removed from the snacks and letters she got in the mail in her college days. "Speaking of paperwork, would you mind if I take one of Mom's red felt-tipped pens? You don't want them, do you?"

"Go ahead. You can go through the filing cabinet, too, if you want, but I've already dug through the files. Do you know how much work this is? The taxes had to be paid. I had to file a bunch of paperwork to get a certified copy of the deed to the house. I had to cancel her cell phone and her Netflix subscription. I didn't even have a list of people who were taking money out of her bank account. I called five banks and had to tell strangers over and over that my mother was dead, and then I had to prove it to them after listening to their fake sympathy. That woman kept terrible records. Before I could close out insurance policies to get the money to pay the tax bill on this house, I had to fill out forms with doctors to get her records, so I could fill out more forms. But by all means, go get a pen from her desk."

Silence landed between them, separating them like distance had in their adulthood. Tamsin shoved her hands in the back pockets of her jeans and looked down at her shoes.

"Why do you do this? You have to be in control of everything. If someone tries to help, you push them away or tell them they're not good enough. I told you on the phone that I would do anything you need me to, but you treat me like the most incompetent person in the world."

"You're not incompetent. You just don't care. Your time was too precious to spend helping Mom move out here, you were too busy to come out here for holidays and spend time with your family, and you sit out there in your perfect little farmhouse and think God knows what about the rest of us."

"That's not how I feel at all."

"Then why don't you tell me how you feel, Tamsin? Tell me how you could sit there at the funeral and not shed a single tear and then rush home without even saying goodbye."

"I did say goodbye. I went to your house, and we stood in the kitchen, and I said goodbye to you. Maybe you were busy seeking attention from everyone else and didn't notice I was in the room."

"No, I remember clearly. You walked in, poured yourself a cup of coffee, and made some weak apology about how you had to get back to work."

"That wasn't it at all." Or was it? Was work the excuse she'd used? All Tamsin remembered from her mother's funeral was the suffocating anxiety of being away from the farmhouse, away from what was left of Owen, and the clawing need to get back. It had nothing to do with her mother or Margaret or the funeral. It had everything to do with the grief and loneliness. They weighed a ton, and the only place she could put them down for a while was at home.

She set her jaw and pressed the cap of the marker into her thumb. It was clear to Tamsin that Margaret wasn't going to back down. It would take an excuse more potent than work to escape to the comfort of home this time.

"You don't even miss her do you?"

Tamsin slammed the pen down on top of the boxes hard enough to leave a dent in the flap and loosen the tape. "Stop. This isn't a grieving competition, Mags."

"Stop calling me that. I hate that. It hardly seems fair to me that I have to do all this work, and I'm the only one who misses her."

"That's absolute bullshit, and you know it."

"I took her to the grocery store. I took her to every doctor's appointment. You talked on the phone."

"So that means I loved our mother less than you did? You know, you could ask me how I feel instead of telling me. You could ask me what it feels like to live so far away. To miss everything. To stand outside that door and know that when I walk in here, everything about me will be picked to shreds, from my clothes to my hair, to whether or not I loved our mother enough to justify whatever stage of the grieving process you've decided I'm in. First you tell me I'm not grieving enough, and then you tell me I don't even deserve to be sad."

"Can you keep your voice down? The boys will hear you." Margaret folded her arms, her fingers digging into her skin. "Why do you always have to fight with me?"

"Well, I don't know, Mags. After all these years of practice, you're so good at starting arguments that I wouldn't want you to think you were an underachiever. I could point out that you could use some pointers in the apologies department, but I don't want to be an unsupportive sister." Tamsin grabbed her purse from the edge of the sofa and slung it over her shoulder. "I'm gonna head back to the hotel, yeah? Settle in for a bit. I'll see if they have a business center so I can ship these boxes from there. Then you won't have to worry about it."

"I can take care of it—"

"Well, just imagine how much easier life would be if you didn't have to." Tamsin pulled her phone from her back pocket and requested an Uber back to her hotel. Some guy named John and his Prius were fifteen minutes away.

"Come on. Don't be like that."

"No, Mags, it's okay. It's no big deal. I came here to help get rid of this stuff, so the least I can do is ship it to myself. I'm gonna head out. I'll meet you here in the morning." She faced the door, her hand on the doorknob. Where did her mother go the last time she turned this doorknob?

"You know that I'll just keep adding stuff to your boxes. I'm gonna find more of Dad's stuff you'll want, even after you've gone home. Let me send them to you. Why don't you come over for dinner. The boys—"

"I think I'm just going to turn in. Check my email, order some takeout, and—" Tamsin picked at the trim. White glossy trim with a notch taken out of it, a splinter hanging by a thread. Bare wood peeking through. The frayed seam of a house that had seen a tussle. All of Tamsin's doors had dings. "When did this happen? Do you know?"

Margaret raised an eyebrow. "What? The chip in the trim?"

"Yeah. Is it new?"

"Philip did it when he carried that set of shelves from the den. I'll paint over it."

"The shelves Dad had in the garage?"

"You said you didn't want it, so we put it in our basement. Kids toys are on it."

"I don't want it. I just...I just noticed the chip, that's all." The strap of Tamsin's purse slid down her shoulder. Her mother had always told her she had skinny shoulders. Margaret would have called them useless. Tamsin shifted her purse and picked the splinter from the trim, rolling it between her fingers. "I wasn't here for any of this. I don't recognize these things. I

15

have no connection to this sofa other than sitting on it a few times a year. I have no memories of that coffee maker. I don't know where the dings in the trim came from. It hurts, Margaret. I do have a heart, you know. It's just not exactly where yours is."

Tamsin tugged the door open. It gave way, setting her free. She didn't look back at her sister. "Dinner is at six?"

"Five thirty. Six. Somewhere in there."

"I'll be there."

* * *

Tamsin faced another door. Her sister's this time. There was little sense in standing on the front porch, building a case against every criticism Margaret could levy against her, so she pushed her way in without knocking. She moved through the entry with its vinyl flooring and past the central stairs, which were covered in toys and one stray sock, pausing to raise an eyebrow at the disarray. Down the hall and into the kitchen, she dropped the paper bag on the counter and the bottle of wine inside landed with a thud. Her mother's voice in her head told her to make nice with her sister. Family obligation meant spending a tense night smoothing over a rough day with her sister, but nothing said either of them had to be sober for it. Tamsin dug through a drawer full of loud utensils before she realized the bottle had a screw cap.

"Margaret! I'm pouring wine."

The house was quiet. No running boys. No car in the driveway, either, now that she thought of it. "Margaret?" Nothing.

She looked back over her shoulder at the door. Growing up, they'd always taped notes there. Going bike riding. Went to the movies. A pink Post-it lay face down on the floor among the toys. Tamsin left her glass of cabernet sauvignon on the island and walked to it, pushed at the pale sticky strip with her finger, but it didn't lift. Cheap knock-off Post-its. Their sticky stuff never worked. "Taking the boys to Philip's mom's. BBS."

Tamsin shrugged off the chaos, stepped over a stuffed Shrek, and returned to the kitchen. No sign of dinner. Crayons and construction paper were strewn from one end of the table to the other, and colorful links of paper taped together in a chain dangled from the table to the floor. Scribbles that exceeded their boundaries trailed onto the table. It was easy for Tamsin to overlook the clutter. She didn't have to live with it. How her picture-perfect detail-oriented sister could live with it was the bigger question.

She sipped wine and cleared a spot at the table, where she made a little gray walrus from plasticine bars she found in a zipper storage bag. The dough smelled as terrible as she remembered. She formed creases in his flippers with her thumbnail, pausing only for a moment when Mags showed up, her arms full.

Everything fell to the kitchen island in rustling plastic bags, and from them, Margaret extracted a bucket of KFC's fried chicken and Styrofoam containers with plastic lids. After all that talk about family, the last thing Tamsin expected Margaret to serve as a family meal was greasy chicken from a paper bucket.

"Philip's working late, and the boys have a field trip in the morning. His mother said she'd take them and pick them up so I could finish boxing up all that stuff for Goodwill. I rented a van for Thursday so I don't have to make fifty trips."

"Might as well get it over with, huh?" Tamsin made two little white plasticine disks, the whites for the walrus' eyes. "Like talking about our fight this afternoon."

Margaret lined up containers and popped off their plastic lids. Gravy spilled on the kitchen counter, but she didn't seem to care. "I'd rather not. You're tired from traveling, and I'm exhausted from trying to do too much at one time. Let's just have dinner and be pleasant. Can we."

"Yup. Fine by me." Tamsin applied two little black eyes to the walrus. "What's left to do at Mom's?"

"Everything small will be out of there by the end of the week. Next week, that estate sales woman is coming by to pick up the last of the big furniture."

"When does the house go up for sale?"

"Whenever I get around to it."

Tamsin lifted the little walrus into the palm of her hand. "Look what I made."

Margaret only glanced. She pointed to a cabinet across the kitchen. "Adorable. Grab plates?"

"Geez. You don't appreciate good art." Tamsin pulled two chipped plates from the cabinet. The closer she looked, the more chips she found in Margaret's perfect life. With two young boys, plates were probably the least of her sister's concerns. Tamsin wiped the counter with a paper towel and took a drumstick from the bucket. It looked like the kind of thing that would set her up for stomach trouble. "What's with the fast food? I haven't had this stuff since we were kids."

Margaret pulled a drawer open and metal serving utensils crashed to a halt. A potato masher, a garlic press, spatulas. "I was going to order out, but I passed the chicken place on the way to drop off the boys and couldn't stop thinking about it." She tossed a nutcracker on the counter. "Why do we even have this? We never use this." She dragged it back into the drawer and threw two spoons on the counter. "Here. Go to town."

Tamsin served mashed potatoes and biscuits. She skipped the gravy for herself, but the smell brought back memories of racing through dinner in their Halloween costumes, eager to save room for candy and get out the door. "Remember how excited Mom was when they finally built one of these?"

"I was seven, maybe? First grade, I think. She bought all this food and put it on the fancy plates. Years of seeing commercials on television, but the closest one was a billion miles away."

Tamsin fought back the urge to wrinkle her nose. She didn't have the heart to take the stroll down memory lane away from her little sister. "Now they're everywhere. It used to be special."

"Do you want something else? I wouldn't blame you." Margaret didn't look that pleased with the spread, either. "We can eat something else if you want. There's a salad place that delivers."

"Not a chance. Pour yourself some wine, and let's eat some greasy chicken."

"Wanna sit at the dining room table like we're adults or just stand here in the kitchen?"

"What do you mean *like an adult*? I want to be where the wine is. And your kitchen table looks like a summer camp exploded on it. What's going on in here, anyway? This place is a disaster area. Toys all over the stairs. There's a sock in the hallway. I've never seen your place look like this."

Mags waved it off. "It's not always like this. Philip's father has been here with the boys, and they play rough. It'll be cleaned up before Monday. It'll have to be because that's when the housekeeper comes, and I can't have her thinking I live in a messy house."

"Of course not. How could you?"

"What about that farmhouse. Anything new?"

"Nope."

"I don't know how you can still live there. Did you repaint anything yet? Move any walls?"

"Nope. Everything's the same. I moved a few things around. Decorative stuff." Snow globes. A few weeks after Owen died, she moved the snow globes from the living room to the den, but it still hurt to look at them, so she put most of them in the bedroom on the top shelf of Owen's wardrobe, sealing them behind a closed door. Relics safely stored in the inner sanctum.

"Rearranging furniture always feels good. Like living in a whole new space. Throw any amazing parties in that backyard of yours? I love that porch. Of course I only got to see it one time—the day you moved in."

Of course, Margaret would bring up the day they moved into the house. The day she stood drenched in sweat on the back porch, surrounded by friends and family, while Owen got down on one knee and said that the house was their dream come true, and it would all be complete if she would just marry him. She said yes, and when everyone left, she turned him down, terrified to break what wasn't broken by making it apply to outdated rules. Owen completely understood. He was happy to live with Tamsin and make house their home, but Margaret and her mother never let them live it down. Unless Tamsin changed the topic, she'd have to hear, again, how her status as an unmarried widow made her a lesser class citizen.

"Too bad it was raining, and you didn't get to sit back there. It's pretty. We stopped mowing that big field. It's mostly wildflowers now. Owen was going to start keeping bees but never got around to it."

"You never built a new barn back there like you talked about. Did you ever tear down that old stinky shack next to the house?"

"I love the old barn just the way it is." Tamsin stopped short of denying it was stinky. She'd abandoned the goal of a new barn the moment Owen died. What she did with her home was none of Mags' business, and she didn't need unsolicited advice.

"There must be something that keeps you so busy." Margaret looked down at her plate of crispy fried chicken skin and mashed potatoes, her jaw clenched. "Otherwise you'd have been here, right?"

Tamsin knew that her intentions ran deeper than mere curiosity. "Of course. I feel so helpful standing to the side while you do all the work and tell me how inadequate I am."

"Jesus, Tamsin."

"And now you're pissed that I know what you're getting at."

"No, I'm pissed that you always make a conflict out of everything."

"I didn't start this. You did. There's always conflict with you." Tamsin didn't need a fork to pull the chicken from the bone, but it felt good to stab something. "You just hide it under throw pillows and get mad when people sit down and find it. Why don't you just spit out what you have to say? I don't meet your expectations or ridiculously high, constantly shifting standards, and it makes you feel good about yourself to find fault with me."

"Maybe if you talked to me, and I didn't have to drag everything out of you—"

"What do you want to know so bad?" Tamsin regretted asking. If her sister wasn't satisfied with the façade she built over the last five years, she wouldn't be satisfied with the truth.

"I wanna know what happened to you. You used to be so happy all the time."

Owen happened. Waking up next to Owen happened. Owen not waking up next to her happened. Having the perfect life and having it ripped from underneath her happened. Margaret never experienced loss like that, or the stifling, smothering, suffocation that came with it. She could be forgiven for not understanding, but if it had been Philip instead of Owen carted down the stairs and out the door on a stretcher while she stood there in her pajamas, if Tamsin were sitting at that table with a widowed sister struggling to raise two kids with all that heartache, things would be different between them. Tamsin wouldn't capitalize on every opportunity to sharpen the knife. Besides, if Margaret's life was so wonderful, she wouldn't need

Tamsin around so badly.

Tamsin set down her fork and picked up her glass of red wine. Darker than blood, thicker than water. It washed over her tongue, leaving it dry. "It's a self-fulfilling prophecy, isn't it? I know that you're going to find fault with me the second I walk in the door, so I can find the fault in our conversation before it even happens."

"It probably doesn't help that you have the perfect life. Maybe you do fail to meet my expectations."

"Gee, thanks."

"No, listen. I expect you to come here and gush about your gorgeous farmhouse, how quiet and peaceful it is. How you lounge on your porch and sip mimosas, and you don't have to clean up after two screaming boys and an adult man baby who leaves wet towels on the floor. I'll never get to go to a third of the places you went to. London. Scotland. Germany. Venice. Two weeks in some cottage in the Cotswolds. The most romantic thing Philip's done for me is empty the dishwasher and put the cups somewhere close to where they were supposed to go."

"I never gloated about any of the things I had or places I went and things I saw. You were always welcome to come and stay with us, but you never did."

"I have two kids. They'd destroy everything in your house."

"It's not my fault if your life is different than mine. You can do the same things I did whenever you want."

"I can't, though. Maybe when Philip retires, and the kids are grown. I chose this. I'm not saying that I regret anything. I'm just—"

"Jealous that I don't have anything holding me down?"

"In so many words, I guess."

Her sister did what all the other women in their family did. She deferred enough dreams and aspirations to look longingly at the future. And when the future finally came, they skipped into the sunset. Their introverted mother threw it all away and bought a townhouse close to her grandkids. Started joining book clubs and drinking tea with strangers. And their grandmother ran off to Luxembourg right after her grandfather died.

Tamsin refused to live that way. "Do you remember Grandad's funeral?"

Mags dumped chicken bones back into the empty bucket. "In Rockport. Yeah."

"We took a limo back to the church after the burial. You and Mom were playing tic-tac-toe on the back of a program."

"What's that have to do with anything?"

"Grandmom was so excited about going to Luxembourg. I didn't even know it was a country. She sold everything. Gave it away. Threw it in the trash just like Mom did. Then she got on a plane and moved to Luxembourg to live with her sister and see Europe. She told Dad that she wanted to be a ballerina and had it all lined up to go to Europe before she met Grandad and settled down to have kids. Now that she was free, she was going to Europe to do what she always dreamed of doing."

"You want me to move to Luxembourg?"

"No. And you can't move in with me, either. I guess I mean that you always have the chance in the future. Like the rest of them did. There's, like, some kind of second life out there."

There wasn't a second life for Tamsin, though. She hadn't deferred enough life, hadn't left enough meat on the bone to have a second go at it.

The plates fell into the sink. No wonder they were chipped. Margaret refilled her glass and set her jaw at Tamsin.

"I'm sure you didn't mean it that way, but I love my kids. I chose my kids. Even if I hadn't and they'd been a surprise, there isn't anything about having kids that makes you regret what you didn't get to run off and do. I'm sure Mom didn't think she put anything off and neither did Grandmom. Maybe you have to be selfless enough to have kids in the first place to understand."

"I didn't mean it that way. It just seems that it's impossible to have it all."

"Well, you'd know."

"What's that supposed to mean? That doesn't even make sense."

"You don't even do anything anymore, do you?"

"What I do, or don't do, isn't any of your business." Tamsin did a quick scan of the scene. Dinner was mostly cleaned up, scraped into the bucket and tied up in the bag. She downed her glass and reached behind her chair, digging into her purse for her phone, and requested an Uber. All she could think of was home. "You know, I've got an early morning. I have to get back home in time to prepare for work."

"I thought you were here for the whole week."

"I never said that. I don't know why you would think that. I'm sure I told you I have to get to work on Monday."

"No, you didn't. What time does your flight leave?"

"I can't remember what time it boards, but I have to be there at seven." It was a lie. Another lie she told her only living relative so she could avoid telling her the truth. Margaret would never understand.

"Let me take your back to the hotel then."

She waved her phone. "I already got an Uber."

"Why don't I drive you to the airport tomorrow? I'll pick you up at six and we can stop at Starbucks on the way."

"I can just get an Uber."

"That's stupid. It costs money."

"Starbucks costs as much as an Uber to the airport."

"Please? I swear, Tam. If we don't try to end on a happy note at least once, the only two people left in this family won't be talking to each other at all."

Tamsin's purse strap dug into her shoulder. Traveling always weighed her down. Leaving behind the comfort of home always weighed her down. "Fine. It's fine. I'll see you at six. Thanks for the ride."

* * *

Tamsin dragged her suitcase behind her, plastic wheels grating and bumping over rough and uneven concrete slabs. The airport parking garage smelled like urine and cigarettes. Beside her, Margaret matched her step for step. They could have been twins if they hadn't been born two years apart. The same long, brown hair, same shoulders and stride. Their similarities ended with genetics. Tamsin tied her hair back in a ponytail, and Margaret's tumbled down her shoulders in curls secured by some magical product. Their entire lives had been a series of departures. Coming apart at the seams and coming together again, like a constantly repaired garment.

"You don't have to follow me to the actual airport, you know. I'd have been happy with the ride."

"Can you just accept that I'm trying, here?"

Tamsin yanked the suitcase to a heel and stopped by a pillar, beneath a no smoking sign. The yellow and white stubs on the ground showed no respect. "I know you think Mom was the glue here. It's not like we're never going to see each other again."

"When *will* I see you again?"

"The next time you buy a plane ticket and figure out how to use Uber to get to my house." She adjusted her father's coat over her arm, the waxed oilcloth stiff and rustling.

"Funny. You know I can't lug Philip and two kids to Pennsylvania."

"Fine. Thanksgiving, then. I'll be here for Thanksgiving. Unless...I'll work something out. We'll do something before then. You can always visit me alone, you know. I assume Philip can handle two boys on his own."

"There's not a chance I'll leave Philip alone with those two boys. Do you know what my house would look like?"

Tamsin pulled Margaret in for a hug. The prospect of getting home was putting her in a better mood. "I'll make the effort. I'll come to you."

"Call me when you get home. Let me know you got there okay?"

"I will."

"Dad's birthday is next month."

Tamsin didn't need to be reminded. Her calendar was full of birthdays and anniversaries that she celebrated alone. "I know."

"You've got it from here, huh? Don't need me to walk you to the hangar?"

"You mean the gate? This isn't 1950, Mags. I have to go through security first. They need to look at the soles of my shoes."

Margaret's lopsided smile told her that the goodbye might hurt this time. "You've always been better at travel than me. I don't know when I'll get out there to see you, but I'll try. I promise."

"We'll play it by ear." She patted her sister's arm. "Say goodbye to Philip and the kids for me."

Tamsin turned toward the airport. The suitcase wobbled on its wheels, and she leveled it into submission.

"Tam," Margaret called from behind her. "You know now that Mom's gone, there's no one left to ask about—"

"Not this again. Why do you do this? There's no big family mystery that destroyed your childhood. Dad was busy. He worked. He traveled. He sold paintings. You're so dramatic sometimes. Why do you try to make it sound like you had such an unhappy life? " Tamsin knew why. Margaret was jealous of her happy childhood. That instead of sulking indoors, hanging on

26

their mother's apron, Tamsin's childhood had been fields of wildflowers and romps through dense, perfumed forests while her Dad painted vivid scenes of New England. Margaret chose to be unhappy, jealous of anything Tamsin had, and she went out of her way to make up stories. Anything to tarnish Tamsin's view of her past and drag her down with her.

"I didn't say my childhood was unhappy. There are unanswered questions. Don't you see that? Mom took the truth with her, and we'll never have it."

"Stop. I don't want to hear any more about this imaginary mystery of yours, and I don't wanna fight. I gotta go. I'll see you at Thanksgiving."

"How can you completely ignore all of that evidence?" Margaret begged. "It's right there in front of you."

"I'm gonna miss my plane. I'm not letting you do this to me. You don't get to crawl inside my head, plant these little seeds of yours. For once, let's just have a conversation that doesn't involve you trying to make me feel bad about something." Tamsin grabbed the handle of her suitcase and turned away, toward the airport. She waved goodbye over her shoulder as the suitcase wheels scraped the concrete. She hoisted it over the curb, cursed the architect who put it there, and handed it to the baggage handler. The faster she could get home, back to her sanctuary, and away from a sister who sought to diminish her happy childhood and their father's memory, the better.

CHAPTER THREE

Tamsin lowered herself into a molded plastic seat as the list of boarding planes ticked through gates, delays, departures, and arrivals. Like a giant board of anxiety counting down the moments until she could finally get back home. Across from her, next to a mountain of carry-on bags, a mother played movies on a tablet for kids who weren't watching. Tamsin checked the time on her phone. Marlow would be at work by now, scraping yogurt from its tub and chewing on granola. Marlow had a direct line to the company owner by virtue of being his sister, making her the perfect person to have on the other side of the office wall. Tamsin heard enough to know that big news was coming.

Tamsin sent a text. *How's work? Any news re merger/sale?*

Rumors. No news.

She looked forward to returning to her routine. *Any need for me to come back early?* She hoped so.

Lol. No. Fam not so fun?

Never. Might come in Mon. Will let you know.

Another tick of the screen and first class passengers filed by. They pulled laptop bags onto their shoulders, tugging on the straps, sliding into a line, with boarding passes in hand. Business people hovered over their phones. A young couple stood close together. Seven years ago, that was Tamsin and Owen. Off to France, flying first class.

He was the adventurous one, and he traveled well. Calm at the right times, never obsessively checking the departure board or fretting that he was at the wrong gate. And when he arrived, he seemed at ease, befriending the concierge and navigating public transportation like a local. He ate whatever they put before him. Gorgeous seafoods in rich sauces, raw meats with rice, handheld treats from carts. He soaked up the world like he knew his time was short, and Tamsin, who never aspired to travel, found it exhilarating. She felt his absence in her unease, in the empty seat to her side. She dropped her father's coat into the empty chair and waited her turn to board.

When they called for coach travelers, Tamsin slid into line behind an impatient young man who smelled like a brewery. His sense of urgency in boarding the plane was only tempered when he reached his seat and brought the line to a halt, searching his bags for a sweater, a pen, a tablet, a book. Tamsin waited. She had nowhere else to be. She stashed her father's coat in the overhead bin along with her small carry-on bag, apologized to the man in the aisle seat, and slid past him to sit by the window. By the time the engine roar from takeoff faded to the high-pitched whine of flight and air vents, Tamsin's head was propped up on a five-dollar pillow she bought from the flight attendant, and she drifted off into a vibrant dreamworld. Her recent experiences were thrown into a blender, mixed with the past, and mashed into a colorful stew.

Her mind swam with images—her mother, her father, her sister, the coat—swirled in a jumble of time and places. Walking along the hallway of her hotel and the pattern of the carpet faded to stones. She followed the rocky shore, scrambling along giant rocks that separated Massachusetts from the mighty Atlantic Ocean. Water beat the boulders with so much force that the air seemed made entirely of sound, pushing against her eardrums, ringing between her ears. Behind her, her mother slipped on a rock, stumbled, and cried out. When Tamsin turned, her father was gone. She yelled ahead to Margaret, begging her to wait.

Then the landscape changed. Acadia. Lush pines and trails of colorful leaves. She bent to collect them in her tiny hands. She held one by the stem and twirled it in her fingers. Red and orange on one side, mottled with paint on the other. Every leaf was painted, thousands of little van Goghs scattered on the forest floor among twigs with tips like brushes. She sat on the forest floor among them and gathered them in her little fist until her fingers—the chubby fingers of a child—could hold no more.

She looked at her father, where he sat on a stool at his easel next to her. Sunlight streamed from behind him, and she blinked away the blinding sun. Tamsin crawled into her father's shadow. He swept a paintless brush across a field of white.

"Daddy, there's no paint."

"But you see, Tam, in a painting everything is important. Even the empty spaces hold important things that you can't see."

"If you can't see them, how do you know that they're there?"

"They call to you. They speak to your heart when you're ready to see them." Her father whisked his brush along an empty palette, and with deliberation, dabbed at the canvas.

She held up her fist, clutching the painted leaves and twig brushes, presenting her prizes. He took them, reached into his coat, unzipped a pocket—a hidden compartment near his heart—and sealed them away inside before returning to his canvas, again sweeping a paintless brush across a field of white.

"These are very important," he said. "I'll hold your dreams right here."

"Pretzels? Chips?" An elbow nudged hers. The airplane window was cool against her forehead, but it was hard as a rock. The man next to her, a grandfatherly figure who smelled like toffee, wanted an answer. "Psst. You told me to wake you. Pretzels or chips? She wants to know."

In the aisle, a woman in an uncomfortable looking blue skirt gave her a painted-on smile. The poor woman had to wear panty hose. Like there wasn't a full-on battle for equality raging outside the airplane. Tamsin tried to crack her neck and shake off the feeling of the dream. It didn't work.

"Pretzels, please."

She thanked the woman and reached out for the little bag of window-shaped carbohydrates. They reminded her of Lincoln Logs. Cabins in the woods. The cries of loons and the smell of pine. When the man next to her headed for the bathroom, she collected her father's coat from the overhead bin. She spread it across her lap like a blanket and found the zipper that secured the compartment over his heart. Dry pretzel stuck in her throat. The pocket from her dream was real?

Behind the zipper was an envelope, soft and creased, yellowed with time. The red postmark from Massachusetts, from the small town of Rockport, was smudged, its date illegible. Inside was folded paper, thin and browned. Wide ruled, like a page sacrificed from a child's schoolwork, and on it, a stick figure drawing in crayon. A boxy coat in green and brown. Tan legs with blue boots. A man, her father, posed on a rock, stick hands on nonexistent hips. Above, a blue line of sky stopped at a bright yellow sun, like a wedge of cheese in the corner of the page, and hovering in the ethos, in a child's scrawl, was *Ida loves Dabby*.

Dabby. The way children write before they can discern the letters. Flipping the Ds and Bs, mixing up the twos and fives. Who the hell was Ida? There were no cousins. Her father was an only child. Her mother had a sister who died in the 1970s, unmarried. There was no Ida in her circle of friends or in Margaret's. There was a Jill. A Mandy. No Ida. No reason for a lost letter to be collected and tucked, unforgotten, into a coat. Who was Ida? And why did her father keep her drawing? There had to be an explanation.

She folded the drawing along its creases and returned it to the envelope, the dusty scent of ancient paper caught in her dry throat with the pretzel pieces, the envelope shaking in her hand. She sealed it back inside the chest pocket. A pocket she didn't even know existed until her father showed it to her in the dense forest of a dream. How was this even possible?

Was Margaret right when she visited Tamsin in college and slobbered her childhood trauma all over the bathroom floor in a drunken sobbing heap? Their father's long absences and mother's excuses. Tamsin had held her sister's hair and told her to shut up. Stop destroying everything, wrecking her toys and stealing her clothes, making fun of her boyfriends. Margaret tried to demolish everything Tamsin had, even her happy childhood.

But what if Margaret was right?

Outside the window, the land stretched toward the sea. Ahead lay Rockport and the cottage loved by her grandparents and her great-grandparents before them. The cottage her father inherited. The leaves of her family tree had shaded generations of painters who depicted the scenes of Rockport and its rocky coastline, pummeled by a relentless ocean. And then her father had sold it. He'd said it was too expensive to maintain, and he used the money to support his dream of being a full-time artist. It was an abrupt end to an Eden. Somewhere out there, maybe in Rockport, was someone named Ida.

CHAPTER FOUR

The front door to Tamsin's farmhouse was at least two hundred years old. Solid wood, with no windows, arched at the top, it must have weighed a thousand pounds. It soaked water from the air and swelled in the frame when it rained, when it was humid. The old door had seen a lot. It held in everything Tamsin loved, everything that made her feel safe and gave her a sense of place in the world. She turned the key in the lock, leaning against it for solace and comfort, and pushed it open with her weight. Her suitcase thumped over the wooden threshold and wobbled to a stop inside the front door. Leaving her father's coat on the back of a chair in the dining room, she turned and faced his urn on the mantel.

"Who the hell is Ida?"

The urn had nothing to say.

"Everything is important. You used to say that. When I was trying to draw and wasn't half the talent you were, you told me all I could see was the stuff in front of me. That I didn't look at the space between things or what was in the background, that I didn't have enough perspective. I need some background, here. I need to know who Ida is and where this drawing came from, and now you're just ashes on a mantel."

Tamsin turned her back on her father and went to the kitchen to pull a bottle of water from the fridge. "If you weren't stuck to the paint, I'd put you in a closet. You know that, right?"

She turned on the radio. An ad for a car dealership filled the kitchen with standard features and MSRPs. Steep discounts. She adjusted the volume so the prattle filled the downstairs. It preceded her into the living room, where she grabbed the handle of the suitcase, half carrying, half dragging it up the stairs, stopping by the den long enough to leave the Rockport envelope on her desk. It landed between two snow globes with the rest of her bills, like a tax to be paid against the value of a family.

Ida.

With the flip of a toggle, music filled the second floor. The Beatles in a "Yellow Submarine" drowned the silence upstairs. In the isolation she craved.

Fist after fist of laundry went from the suitcase to the washing machine behind the bathroom door. She stood in the darkness, piling clothes into the washer, counting every neighbor they had, every childhood playmate. She uncovered no Ida and no woman who could be Ida's mother. Is this the secret that Margaret insisted died with their mother? An affair? She steadied her hands on the edge of the machine before pressing the buttons to start the load. No. It couldn't be. She couldn't even imagine her father showing affection to a woman who wasn't her mother, but the Rockport postage mark burned into her brain like a neon light in the darkness.

Out of habit, she opened the medicine cabinet. Nothing there was hers, but relief wrapped its warmth around her at the sight of Owen's razor, his aftershave lotion, the small pair of scissors he used to trim his sideburns. The door closed with a click and she faced herself in the mirror. Her brown hair and brown eyes. Her cheeks a little fuller than Owen knew them.

Her phone rang six times before she found it on the window ledge. Margaret. She pressed the green circle and accepted the call, wincing at the regret.

"I told you'd I'd find more stuff to send. I forgot to ask if you want paintings. There are at least three dozen of them in our basement, and I need the room to store the boys' stuff. These kids accumulate so much crap."

Tamsin picked at a stray thread in a washcloth. "I'll take anything you want to send. Any of the paintings you don't want, send to me. Just don't throw them away."

"I won't. I know I'd never hear the end of it. They'll come separate from the stuff from Mom's. Maybe next week. I'm sending the boxes from Mom's tomorrow. Did you know you can ship stuff from Staples?"

Tamsin chose to ignore her sister's dig. "Yeah. Send them to my work."

"Why not your house?"

Tamsin's brown eyes blinked back at her in the bathroom mirror. Some other set of eyes out there, somewhere in the world, belonged to someone named Ida who drew a picture of a man and called him Dabby. And she couldn't tell Margaret. Telling Margaret would open the hatch, and the truth about everything would come spilling out. Owen and life and love and loss. Truths she probably hadn't told herself. She stepped into the hall and faced the closed door to her old bedroom. The bedroom she shared with Owen.

"Hello? Are you there?" Margaret sounded exasperated. As usual.

"Yeah. Sorry. I'm trying to do some laundry. It'll be easier if you send them to work. Then I know they aren't sitting on the porch all day while I'm not home."

"Hoodlums in the neighborhood?"

"Can't trust anybody anymore."

"Okay, well, text me the address. I have to get off the phone before these boys destroy everything. They're slaying dragons in castles they built from my clean sheets. Call me when the boxes get there?"

"Yeah. I'll call."

Tamsin ended the call, turned her back on the door, and returned to her office, to the envelope from Rockport tucked between two snow globes—one from London, one from the Bahamian island of Eleuthera. Presents from Owen. She'd received a dozen of them over the years, each in a decorative box with a set of plane tickets and no itinerary. He liked his travel without restrictions. Most snow globes he bought, but some, like one for Eleuthera, he made from small mason jars and trinkets. She shook the snow globe from the island and winter fell on paradise.

She'd been warm and happy on those pristine beaches. At least she thought she was. Things seemed perfect then, but maybe they weren't. Maybe she was wired wrong. If Margaret could sense this discord in her childhood, why couldn't she? Was she designed to gloss over reality with white picket fences? She used her sleeve to wipe dust from the snow globe, shaking it and setting it down again. No, it was just Margaret's negativity sneaking into her subconscious again.

The distant voice of a radio announcer ran through traffic and weather. Tamsin studied the envelope. No return address. Just a blurry postmark from Rockport over an old peeling stamp, sent to a post office box in the town where she spent her summers. There was too much coincidence. Why was it in her father's coat pocket? A pocket she didn't know existed until it appeared in a dream? She turned the envelope over and peeked inside, to the tea-colored paper within. Margaret couldn't be right. Her childhood *had* been happy, and there was no mystery to unfold. Or was there?

The sky was starting to clear in the Eleuthera snow globe. Tamsin shook it again. How was she supposed to look at her father's ashes on the mantel while her life clouded over, wondering if he also belonged to someone else? To someone she never met. A storm was descending on her family, on Rockport, and the only one who could clear it, the only one who could prove Margaret wrong and save Tamsin from a life of what-ifs, was Ida.

The washing machine churned on the other side of the wall, the water ebbing and flowing through the machine in a mechanical tide. She shook the London snow globe and winter piled around Big Ben, but Tamsin's mind was in Rockport, holding Margaret's tiny hand at the water's edge so she didn't fall, watching gulls break clams against the rocks. When did they stop going to Rockport? Early teens? They went to Maine a few times after that. Scrambled through forests along the coast. Sometimes with Dad. He traveled a lot on business. At least that's what her mother said. Art shows. Work trips.

Her father had a letter opener. Unadorned. A flat metal handle with a hole in the end. He'd kept it in a ceramic mug full of pens and pencils on his desk, where he sat on Saturday mornings while cartoons crashed and banged and popped down the hallway. The envelope from Rockport looked just like the envelopes he tossed in the trash on Saturday mornings, slit across the top with the flap still glued shut. Scraps of paper with grapefruit rinds and empty V8 cans. But this one he kept. By mistake?

The internet wasn't much help. No one named Ida lived in Rockport as far as Google knew. Her father's name generated a lot of hits, but she expected it to. And her grandfather. He once owned a small shop on Bearskin Neck Road and the cottage on North Road. Her family had painted the town for generations. She got lost in Google Images, pausing only to shuffle the laundry to the dryer. Nothing ever changed in Rockport. Same little art shops, coffee shop, the wharf. Narrow streets with delivery trucks parked outside restaurants. A haven for tourists who took photographs of Motif Number 1. Driving all that way to take a picture of something that masters painted. The way people used to send postcards to say *I was here, too, once.* The dryer buzzed, and she closed her laptop.

Her childhood had been happy. It had. Nothing Margaret could say would change that. Nothing in the Rockport envelope could change that. Tamsin threw open the drawer to her filing cabinet where she kept a hanging folder with pieces of family history, tucked between receipts for house repairs and appliance manuals. It was full of letters from her grandmother with their European postmarks and birthday cards from her mother sent from Minnesota, greetings from women who left their past behind to chase the aspirations they postponed. Tamsin already lived the life she wanted. Now it was home repairs and appliance manuals and laundry.

But it didn't have to be.

She could go to Rockport. Pack a suitcase like Owen would have done. Find the artist Ida. Figure out what she had to do with her father, how she fit into the puzzle that challenged Margaret for so long, and prove to herself that it changed nothing. That she did have a happy childhood. She could prove to Margaret that she was wrong about the blinders and no amount of trying could destroy the past.

CHAPTER FIVE

Tamsin had her choice of keys. One set went to her Mini, with its rattles and leaky sunroof, good enough for short drives to work, but not her favorite for a five-hour road trip. The tiny metal key to Owen's classic truck was next to it, but that wasn't an option. It was locked in the barn, and she hadn't opened that door in half a decade. She grabbed the keys to his old Cherokee, an old friend, as much a part of their relationship as the home they shared. It was twenty years old, dark blue with patches of faded paint and missing clear coat. She called it Smurf. More Owen's friend than hers, it was a conspirator in his search for adventure. After the loss of Owen, she considered it a partner in grief.

She pulled the back door shut, and the panes of glass rattled. She didn't want to go. Owen held her there, safe and predictable. She'd avoided a lot of hurt by staying close to home, immersed in his memory. Going to Rockport alone, without him, was a leap into the unknown. But like her father had taught her, everything was important, even if you couldn't see it clearly yet. If she handed it over to Mags, she would lose control of the whole thing and miss her chance to find the truth on her own terms. Staying home would bring nothing but regret, and the questions would haunt her forever. Just a few days, a week at the most, and she could return to the routine of work and making dinner and waking up in refuge.

She thundered down the creaky stairs, across the drive, to the barn and the old Cherokee. She threw her suitcase onto the back seat and slammed the tailgate. If it was good enough for grocery runs and hauling mulch, it was good enough for the trip to Rockport. Her purse and father's coat landed on the passenger seat. After a rough start that faded to a smooth idle, Tamsin and Smurf kicked up gravel on their way down the long drive.

"It's been a long time. We've never had our own adventure together. I'm a little more prepared this time. Promise."

In the early days, Owen would call her on Friday afternoon and tell her to pack a bag. He wouldn't tell her where they were going or what to wear, and she'd climb into the Cherokee unprepared and return home sunburnt or windblown. Once she learned to ask the right questions, travel with Owen was escapism at its best. His trip planning bordered on performance art, with destinations worth the trip and enough spontaneity to keep her on her toes. Even when the plan was falling apart, the journey was worth the detour. Overheating at a gas station next to a diner with the most amazing blueberry pie. A coastal town with one inn that served homemade turtle soup, an exotic yet inhumane consideration for Tamsin who was slow to learn that eating like a local was a reward for leaving home. Diversions and unplanned delays wove into the travel like critical threads of an elaborate tapestry. From beneath a blanket, they watched every star in the heavens make a slow dance across the desert sky, and she swore that the Cherokee only broke down because it was his accomplice.

Tamsin didn't need a map or GPS to navigate her way to Rockport. She knew the route by heart. She skirted Boston and headed east on the Yankee Division Highway, entering Gloucester at Grant Circle. By the time she left the town at Blackburn Circle, just a few miles from her destination, she knew she'd broken her promise. She was ill prepared again. No sweatshirt to fend off cool air from the bay and no idea how to look for Ida or what to say to her if she found her. It all seemed ridiculous, chasing a woman who drew a picture decades before, and she wasn't even sure she wanted to find her.

She rounded the turning circle and almost headed for home, for an end to the impetuous idea of stalking a stranger, but the truth was unmistakable. Her mother's silent agony swelled to a scream. Her sister's unsolved mystery grew to desperation. And her father's absences. They weren't adventures. They were the deepest of betrayals.

Tamsin rounded the circle again and aimed for Rockport, for answers, for truth. She was tired and hungry and far from home. Far from Owen, who would have known what to do. Outside of her comfort zone and desperate for rest, she recalled a motel at the end of the Neck, just before the road ended at the sea. An out-of-place motor lodge among cottages and summer homes.

She pulled into its empty parking lot.

The lobby seemed abandoned, but for a bell on the desk. She made herself a cup of complimentary hot tea and drank most of it before a disheveled man showed up and stepped behind the counter, eyeing her and her suitcase with a suspicion that made Tamsin question whether the motel was still a motel.

"Not many people here this time of year. You come for something special?"

"Um." She tucked the tea tag under her thumb and sipped the lukewarm dredges, waiting for a little white lie to come to mind. "Just enjoying the town."

"There's not much happening. A lot of places close up earlier now, since school's starting, and the tourists are gone. There's a festival in a few weeks, but that's about it."

"That's okay. I don't need much. I can entertain myself."

She shrank under the weight of the man's side-eye, while he shuffled papers and logged her stay into his computer.

"Eliot, huh? You related to that painter?"

"My father did a lot of painting around here, yeah. And my grandfather."

"Hm. Your father was quite the artist." The man clicked away at the keys, frowning at the monitor while the computer went through its paces. "Was a time everybody here knew him. I was young, but if I recall correctly, he just left one year and didn't come back."

"He was well liked."

The printer spit out a piece of paper, and the man tugged it from the tray. "Was he, then? If you say so. Never knew him. Only heard of him. Been a long time since an Eliot stepped foot around here, though."

"I'm no painter. Not like them. I'm just here to see the sights."

"Rockport has low expectations. Sign here." She decided to see past the insult and signed her name to the paper. She exchanged a credit card number for a grunt and a key, which he extended like a hard-won prize she didn't deserve, and slinked to her first floor room. The suitcase smacked into the backs of her heel, propelling her forward, away from the man and his critical stare.

Her father had been loved. His work had been everywhere in town, in shops and galleries and hanging in restaurants. People from town would come to the little cottage for tea and wine, and they would talk about abstract things that Tamsin had been too young to understand. But she knew her father had been loved.

Rockport was like any small town, and it's people had every right to be protective of it, especially of its secrets. If this was the reaction to her checking into a motel, it could be a bad idea to wander around, asking if anyone knew a woman named Ida. Wandering around, prying beneath the floorboards wouldn't put Tamsin on anyone's good side.

The key stuck in the lock, and she pushed the door with her hip. It opened to a small room. In another context, it might be right at home along Route 66 in a dusty somewhere. One room in a long building attached to a diner that served greasy carbs and just enough nutrients to metabolize large quantities of beer. But the room at the motor lodge wasn't cold and impersonal, nor was it attached to a diner. It was cozy, painted in ocean-tumbled shades of green and blue, clean, comfortable. The view of Back Harbor and Rowe Point reminded her of her childhood and long days of summer that seemed like they would never end. But they did. And the last time she left Rockport, she hadn't known it was for good.

A small café table with two matching chairs sat at the foot of the bed. Cute enough to draw you in and intolerable enough to make you leave. It wobbled when she placed the suitcase on it, so she hoisted her luggage onto the bed, dropped her father's coat on the back of one chair, and threw her foot on the other to retie her shoe.

Everything in Rockport was in walking distance. With the streets emptied of tourists, a scattering of residents enjoyed the autumn air. Tamsin wished she'd brought her running shoes. She walked past the Cherokee, still pinging a cool down from its Boston traffic workout, and turned right, retracing her path into town. The streets were lined with closely-packed shops, wood-plank siding in various colors, if they were painted at all. Art galleries ruled Rockport. Pottery, painting, photography. Tourist shops that sold general wares rubbed shoulders with snack shacks and restaurants. Nothing had changed, though it all looked smaller, the way places from childhood do. The sidewalk was nearly flush with the street, making polite the mixed company of pedestrians who walked in the middle and the occasional car. Tamsin kept her head down and stuck to the edges, wishing herself invisible. She could hear the inevitable *Welcome to Rockport*, followed by the traditional *What brings you to town*. She didn't know the real answer, let alone the white lie.

The immediate need was dinner. Half the restaurants specialized in lobster, so it didn't matter where she landed. She followed the street to the top of the hill, where it forked. She turned left, following the road around the harbor and found a small restaurant. A grill. She opened the glass door to lobster heaven, and a reflection of light caught her eye from the sidewalk.

Tucked between slabs of concrete was a pin, a decorative pin, fallen from someone's sweater or bag. Tamsin dug it from the sidewalk and turned it over in her hand. The post was bent against the back of the pin. She ran her thumb across the enamel as she turned it over, brushing away a layer of silt. A red lobster smiled up at her. It swam in a silvery snow globe.

Time stood still. A man pushed through the door and Tamsin moved aside when he stepped onto the sidewalk. A message from Owen? What did it mean? Keep going? Go home? She pushed at the post with her thumb, but it wouldn't budge, wouldn't bend back or break free. The lobster was scuffed. There was a sadness to it. Tucking the pin in the front pocket of her jeans, she stepped into the restaurant.

Past a display case of sandwiches and drinks, she followed a woman in a blue waist apron to a table in the back. A blue dining room with a wall of windows that overlooked Rockport Harbor. Unfussy. No table linens or fancy cutlery. It was local, honest, and it soothed the ache of traveling alone. She yearned to spend the last of the daylight with a bright red lobster, a tub of melted butter, and a view of the red fishing shack known as Motif Number 1. Her father painted and sketched the shack a thousand times from the same angle, as had her grandfather, and she found comfort in the timelessness of the buoys that dangled from the side, a chain of history connecting artists and lobster fishermen to the sea.

"Just you?" The waitress held out a menu, waiting for Tamsin to take it.

She anchored herself, filling her lungs with the scent of the dining room. Bread and sauces and seafood. It wasn't crowded, and it smelled divine.

"Yeah. Just the one menu, thanks." Tamsin couldn't meet the woman's eye. She took the menu and locked her gaze on the list of lobster dishes. She'd never grown comfortable eating alone. No amount of exposure to solitary dining had managed to unseat Owen from the empty chair she faced.

"We have specials, if you wanna hear 'em."

"I'm okay." She extended the menu, returning it. "Just a lobster and a glass of white wine. Pinot grigio?"

"You get two sides with that."

"Surprise me." Tamsin offered her a smile, but she wasn't committed to it. It faded as soon as the waitress looked down to jot shorthand on a mint green notepad.

"I like the way you eat. I'm Deb. Scream if you need me."

Deb turned away. Tamsin slouched into her seat, weary from travel, and dug the pin from her pocket. She wiped it clean with her napkin. Being in Rockport was nothing like traveling with Owen. It felt empty and aimless. He would be chatting up a local, looking for the best cup of coffee, the best desserts. Once he had them talking, he would ask about the sites and the history, dig deep into what the place meant to the people who lived there. Somehow, Owen would have stumbled upon a path to Ida, and everything would have fallen into place. Tamsin knew enough of the history, and she was well-heeled in the lesser-beaten path. She didn't need to ask a stranger, and she didn't want the attention. She wasn't even sure she wanted to find Ida, to unearth what was buried there. At least she'd have a snow globe pin to remember the trip by.

Deb dropped a lobster at her elbows. "Plate's hot, hun. Careful."

"Thanks." She set the pin at the foot of her wine glass and covered her lap with her napkin.

"That's cute. Is it broken? There's a jeweler down on the left who might be able to straighten that out for ya."

"It's not mine." She felt like it was. "I found it out on the sidewalk."

"Ah. Some tourist trinket. They're probably a dime a dozen. Sorry. I didn't mean that as a bad thing."

"Don't worry about it. It's not a bad thing." Tamsin drowned her lobster in butter. "That obvious, huh? That I don't live here?"

"I've lived here for fifty-seven years. I know everybody in this town. It's less a look thing than a familiarity thing. Need anything? You good?" Deb truly was a local. Her vocabulary had no Rs.

"I think so. Thanks."

"I'll be back to refill that wine in a bit."

Tamsin smiled, nodded her thanks, and pulled the lobster to pieces. Her mother had hated them. Hated getting her fingers gooey. Hated seeing them in tanks, restrained and unaware of their fate. Her sister couldn't be bothered to work that hard for food. Her father dug into them so gracefully that his hands seemed destined for the task. She plucked at claws and tugged at the meat until she was no longer hungry, turning her attention to her wine glass, drenched in sweat and still full. The pin on the table next to it, a comical smiling lobster trapped for eternity in a wintery cage. She tucked it back into her pocket, another sign from the universe in a language she didn't speak. But something told her to keep swimming.

Her hands clean, her fingers sore from fighting claws, she nursed her drink as the sky turned dark behind the famous red fishing shack. The whole thing seemed ridiculous. Driving five hours to Rockport. Why? What was she looking for? Did she even want to find it? The whole thing seemed like something Margaret would chide her for.

"You all done here?"

Tamsin lifted her chin and forced a smile. She piled dirty silverware on her plate. Deb collected the stack, balancing it with fodder from other tables.

"What brings you to Rockport off-season? We don't get many visitors this time of year. There's a festival at the end of next month that brings people from the mainland, but the start of school drives people home, I guess."

Outside tourist season, people came to Rockport for a reason. What was Tamsin's? To prove her sister wrong and hold on to her happy memories? To find Ida first so Margaret couldn't stake claim on the fallout? To hide from her father who sat on the mantel, unable and unwilling to give up his secrets? She wiped a drop of condensation from the foot of her wine glass and locked on to Deb's mention of the start of school. It was the perfect excuse, so she didn't have to lie. "It is easier to travel once school starts. And quieter."

"That's the truth." Deb leaned closer, divulging a secret. "Never been one for kids myself. You been here before?"

Harmless question. "I spent many summers here as a kid. My grandparents owned a house down on North Road. But that was a long time ago."

"Cute cottages down there. I been on trips like that. Places you used to know. Everything looks smaller than it does in your memory, doesn't it?"

Tamsin slumped in her seat. "That's the truth."

"That's usually what I'm looking for when I head out like that, visiting the past. The truth."

In the front room, the air conditioner rattled and settled. Utensils scraped food from plates into a trashcan in the back somewhere. "Do you ever find it?"

"You know, I think I've found the truth every time I went looking for it. Wasn't always what I thought it would look like. Sometimes I didn't know I had it until I got home and unpacked. The truth takes a while sometimes to let itself be known. What kind of truth you looking for?"

Tamsin searched the clean tiles of the drop ceiling, the recessed lighting. "The kind your family leaves for you to unravel, I guess."

"Ah, breadcrumbs. You think another glass of wine will help you find it?"

"Couldn't hurt to look. I've found a lot of lost things in glasses of wine." She swirled the last sip of liquid gold before downing it.

"You got it." The waitress reached out and took the empty glass. "Welcome back to Rockport, by the way. Stop by anytime while you're here. A lot of people come here to stare at that fishing shack. If you ask me, it's not the shack that gives them the answer, it's the sitting still for a while."

Sitting still. It was the last thing Tamsin wanted. Her feet ached to run.

CHAPTER SIX

Tamsin woke before the sun. If she moved fast enough, she could greet it when it rose behind the fishing shack, as she had throughout her teenage years. The insomnia she shared with her mother drove them there some summer mornings to stand among the lobster traps stacked taller than she could reach. Throwing pebbles into the water, making plunks and ripples.

Sleepless, a dull headache from the wine and the constant drone of the air conditioner, she threw the covers off, pulled on her clothes from the day before, and fought the clock. Overnight rain had washed the streets clean and left puddles at the curbs. She dodged them. Running in the wrong shoes was like treading through pudding. The run was short, her muscles and lungs out of practice, so she landed on the dock out of breath, just in time to watch the sky burn orange and make silhouettes of the birds that waited their turn to pick food from the ocean. Her stomach growled, but she decided to stay until the shadows gave way, revealing the red painted planks of Motif Number 1.

Running wouldn't clear her head or make sense of her impetuous decision. The whole time she was helping Margaret clean out her mother's house, she'd wanted nothing more than to be at home where she felt safe. Margaret always thought that something wasn't being said, that her family was hiding some secret. From society, their friends, from their place in the world. From their reputation and their own children. Ida. One stupid, thirty-year-old drawing sent her on a five-hour mission to a place she hadn't seen since she was a kid. Alone, without proper footwear.

Going home, hiding in the farmhouse, shredding the drawing, and hiding it from Margaret would only create a new set of secrets. A new stack of lies. Tamsin knew the truth, no matter how much her heart wanted it to be fiction.

Ida wasn't a cousin or the artist of some missent mail.

She was a sister, and she deserved to be found.

Boats swayed. Ropes slapped against the masts, calling their crews to the sea. Tamsin's stomach growled again, and she set course for coffee and breakfast from the café across from the motel. The bent post of the pin in her pocket jabbed into her thigh. She retrieved it, tried to move the post, to break it free, while she walked to the coffee shop. Owen never had a plan, just a destination and a sense of direction. Somehow, the right way to go would always come to him. All she needed was a little faith.

The coffee shop was small and narrow, more shack than shop. Built for tourists and frequented by fishermen. They had fresh coffee before the sun, hours before any of the other shops opened. It smelled like heaven, and it was an excuse to eat a chocolate-filled croissant for breakfast. Tamsin took the bag, a buttery stain bleeding through the paper, and a cup of coffee that was a quarter cream. Turning to leave, she bumped into a dark sweater.

Tamsin jumped back. She held the coffee away from her jeans, trying to avoid the spill. The lid held, and she gave the owner of the sweater a relieved smile. An older man. Clean shaven. Ready for a day that clearly did not involve Tamsin or wearing coffee.

"Hey, I didn't know you were back." His eyes were fixed on his own cup, his hands busy securing the lid.

"Oh no, I'm just visiting. Do I look like someone?" Could finding Ida be this easy?

He looked up at her, but it was just a glance. He turned, took a planner and manila folder from a high-top table.

"No, no. I'm sorry. It's just me." He held up the paper cup. "Haven't had my coffee yet."

Of course not. "Sorry for bumping into you."

When he turned to take napkins from the dispenser, papers slipped from the folder and fluttered to the floor. Drafts of glossy brochures with printing marks in the corners. Tamsin crouched to pick them up, the pin sticking her in the leg as she stood. Her eyes fell on the oval logo of the Rockport Historical Society.

"There's a historical society here?"

"Thanks." The man shoved napkins into his jacket pocket. He accepted the papers and returned them to the folder. "Yeah, it's at the top of the hill here."

"In its own building? Can people just go there?"

"Yeah, you can visit it. It's past the wine shop. After the big intersection."

Tamsin tried to recall a big intersection in Rockport. Perhaps he meant the three-way intersection. That's about as big as it got. She wanted to clarify, but the man was already out the door.

"Thanks," she yelled after him. "And sorry, again." He waved an arm behind his back, in a hurry to get back to life. He mistook her for someone else. Someone who lived here.

Tamsin took a pinch of napkins from the dispenser and followed in his wake, stepping through the door. She skipped sideways to avoid colliding with a flannel shirt and a messenger bag, losing her balance. Her foot landed in a puddle, soaking her right shoe.

The man was her age. Maybe a little younger. He shook dark curls from his eyes. Eyes so green that moss could grow envious. How could so much fire come from such green eyes?

"I'm so sorry. It's the second time I've done that this morning." She stumbled through the apology.

"It's cool. My hands were empty. Looks like your shoe took the brunt of it."

Her light blue sneaker darkened with dirty water. Her sock was soaked, and her foot was wet. "I guess I started this day on the wrong foot."

"Punny. I like it." Green eyes. They seemed to take in more of her than most. "There's a shoe shop up the street. Across from the fudge shop. They have running shoes too."

Tamsin sipped her coffee and looked up the street, avoiding eye contact. Delivery trucks arrived with the day's side dishes, competing for curb space. "What makes you think I need running shoes?"

"I saw you trying to run up the road here this morning. It looked like you knew what you were trying to do, but your shoes were holding you back. At first I thought—"

"You thought I was someone else?"

"No, I thought you were you. Well, I don't know you so, not *you* you. But I didn't think you were anyone other than whoever you are. Certainly not someone I already know." He clutched the strap of his messenger bag. It looked heavy. Books. At this hour, it was usually fishermen, artists, and photographers. "You're not from here, anyway."

She almost offered her hand to introduce herself, but stuck it in her pocket instead, reaching for Owen, for comfort and direction, feeling for the pin. "Obvious, huh?"

He tilted his head to the side. She felt like a statue in a museum, the way he considered her. "Let's see. The only reason someone from here would go running up the street at that hour is to catch a boat. You were running to catch a sunrise. Without a sweatshirt. Probably because you either forgot to pack one, or you've run out of laundry. If someone in this town were having enough fun to miss out on that much laundry, the whole town would know about it. Nothing interesting has happened since a feral cat had kittens, and Sunny wrangled the whole town to trap them so she could take them into Gloucester to have them neutered and spayed. I'm pretty sure that you're not from here."

"Good detective work. I'm not from here. I visited a lot when I was a kid. My grandparents owned a house. But now I'm just—" Just what? She wasn't just a tourist. She wasn't a visitor. She was looking for blood here, and it was personal. The corners of his eyes lifted, and she felt less like a carved block of stone and more like a bottle of wine he could consume.

"Which one?" he asked.

"What?"

"Which house? Your grandparents owned which house?"

"It was a little place down on North Road. About halfway down on the left. It was green. I can't remember the house number, but it had marigolds and lupine in the summer."

"It's still there. Still green. Not the marigolds but there's still lupine in the summer. It's everywhere around here."

"Do you know who lives there?"

"Older couple. Quiet. They only use it in the summer. They're gone, now, for the year. Back to wherever they're from."

"Does it still look the same?" Stupid question. How would he know? He didn't have her childhood to compare it to.

"You could walk down there and see it for yourself. On your way to buy some running shoes."

She sipped her coffee. It would be nice to see the cottage, but she wasn't ready to face the changes yet. She preferred the way it looked in her memory with their bikes in the bushes and the lupine and marigolds. Plus, she'd stick out like a sore thumb in a town emptied of tourists, staring at other people's houses. She'd go soon, but not yet.

"Oh, and there's a laundromat on Main, heading out to Loop Pond."

She lowered her coffee and made accidental eye contact. She stepped back into the puddle again, putting distance between her and those green eyes. "Shit." Her shoes and socks were soaked. Her feet were cold. "Thanks. I'll need it."

When she looked up, the café door was closing, and he was gone.

* * *

One of her father's paintings hung on the wall of the shoe store. She tightened the laces of a pair of new running shoes and walked to it. A misty marsh of plants dotted with pools of water. Clumps of trees pointing to the heavens. His tight, loopy signature in the bottom right. A path of water cut through the marsh, and clumps of wild grasses reflected in its sheen. It wasn't a scene from town, but something from his imagination. Most of his landscapes were from his imagination. But was that true? Was there a family somewhere with a marshy backyard?

Behind the counter, a curtain slid on its metal rail, and a man emerged with boxes of shoes. He wore spandex and had the calf muscles of a cyclist. "I love that one." He left the boxes on the bench.

"It's nice. I like the lupine."

"An old resident painted it. His work is all over town."

"Do you know anything about it? Or the artist?" Tamsin had no detective skills, certainly none of Owen's interview skills, but she could play curious tourist.

"Before my time. Artists come here, they stay for a while. They donate work to silent auctions and whatnot. Sometimes they don't want to pack up a car load of canvases when they move, so they donate their work to friends. Stuff ends up in restaurants and shops all over town. The artist must have known whoever ran this place before me. I liked it, so I left it."

She slipped out of the running shoes, stuffed formed wads of paper back into the toes, and tried on another pair, pulling the laces tight and wiggling her toes. "This wasn't always a shoe shop, was it? I can't remember what was here before."

"General art. Pottery. Some supplies."

"That's right. I remember. She sold blocks of clay. There were brushes on a pegboard on that back wall."

"So you came here a long time ago?"

"Many years ago." Tamsin walked to the painting and back to the bench. "I'll take this pair. Can I wear them out?"

"Sure thing. I'll ring you up and put your old shoes in the box."

"Thanks. Poor wet shoes."

"Stick some newspaper in them and let them dry. They should be good as new in no time."

Tamsin propped her purse on the counter and dug through her wallet for her bank card. "Hey, if someone wanted to do some research on artists from Rockport, where would they go? Is there an association or a club?"

The man ripped the receipt from the register, shoved it in the paper bag, and held it out by the twine handle. "I'm not much of an artist, so I'm not sure. There's an Arts Alliance, but I'm not familiar with it. I've only lived here for about a year. It's an odd little town, if you ask me."

"What's odd about it?"

"Defensive, I guess. Old school. A little set in its ways. I shouldn't say bad things about Rockport. I love it here. It can just be a little difficult to get it to change with the times. Like this shop. To do what I want, I needed a zoning thing, and it would cost a lot. Just bringing it up in conversation with people put me on their bad side. There are a lot of obstacles because this place is so protective of its character. It takes care of its own, if you know what I mean. We've barely let go of Prohibition."

Tamsin commiserated, thanked the man, and stepped onto the sidewalk. She knew exactly what he meant. Rockport was a small town, protective of its past and its people. Small towns could be very protective of their secrets too. It would be a terrible idea to wander around, asking if anyone knew a woman named Ida before thinking it through. Ida could have moved away years before. May never have lived here at all.

She shivered at the cool air that pushed in off the ocean, opened the door of a tourist shop full of T-shirts and trinkets, and stepped into the putrid air conditioning. She needed something more fitting, less anxiety inducing, than her father's jacket. From her mother's closet to the airplane's overhead storage, the coat had felt like her own. A rightful claim she staked as her father's favorite. But the drawing in the chest pocket of her father's coat was a crayon-colored reminder that nothing was what it seemed. She may not have even been his first born. Her whole life, she idolized her father. A man of moral integrity who could do no wrong, who loved their mother and showered her with gifts, who carried Margaret on his shoulders when she was too small to see the world. He taught Tamsin how to see the color in the world. What if he wasn't who she thought he was?

Margaret had sensed a distance in their father and read into it a mystery. She blamed Tamsin for being unable to see it, calling her blind. What if her perfect childhood wasn't real? If it was a defense mechanism she built to see the good in things because she couldn't handle harsher truths? Did she do the same with Owen? Painting the past with such perfection that she couldn't let go of it or leave it behind?

The woman behind the counter looked up from her book and offered assistance, but Tamsin was good. Just a sweatshirt. Nothing fancy. She pushed the plastic hangers aside, looking at tags for one her size. Decades later and the tourist trade hadn't changed. Every hoodie had a screen-printed starfish or smiling whale, the town's name in a varsity font, just like the one Margaret had as a child. Light blue. She was three or four years old. She had it draped over her shoulder when she crouched in the water watching the barnacles gasp. It fell into the ocean. Covered in algae and soaking wet, it lay draped over the shower rod, forgotten when they went home the next day. Margaret cried until they stopped for ice cream. They never saw it again. Her grandparents didn't scoop it up and send it back, and it was gone the next summer. Was it outgrown and discarded, or did her father pass it off to Ida, a cast-off hand-me-down?

Tamsin laid the purple version of the sweatshirt on the counter next to the register and dug into her purse for her wallet.

"Funny, when you first walked in here, I thought you were someone else." The woman behind the counter shook her head. "I wondered why she'd be in here buying a sweatshirt. No offense. Locals don't tend to shop here."

"None taken. And, no offense, I'm only here because it's chilly in the morning. You're the second person to say I look familiar. Who did you think I look like?" *Please tell me that you know someone named Ida, and I look just like her.*

"Oh goodness. I have no idea. Just a familiar face, I guess."

"I must have a twin running around I don't know about, huh?"

"I bet we all do." *Of course it couldn't be that easy.*

Tamsin took her change, thanked the woman, declined the bag, and ripped the tag from her sweatshirt. She tugged it on over her head and turned right. Toward the church, toward the wine shop, and hopefully toward some answers at the Historical Society.

Ida had to be connected to Rockport. If she didn't live there, she had to be there often enough for the similarities in their looks to make Tamsin a familiar face around town. Finding Ida might be easier than she thought, but that meant Tamsin would have to think fast. She would have to figure out how to tell Margaret. Tamsin felt for the pin in the front pocket of her jeans, seeking guidance from the part of the universe that still connected her to Owen, to a time when everything just worked out.

Just have faith.

She adjusted her purse on her shoulder, shoved her hands into the fleece-lined pockets of her new purple sweatshirt and kept going.

Rockport had long been a destination for artists. Hornby. Buckley. Hibbard. Galleries lined the street. Even the shops that sold food or shirts or fancy kitchen tools were dripping with New England art. There was more to the town than the red fishing shack, and her father, and his father before him, had been two of many to paint the surrounding land. Much of it blurred together in her mind, but she would know her father's art anywhere, and there it was. On an easel in the window of a wine shop. Her grandfather's house. Lupine and marigolds. Purples and yellows against the little green house.

She'd seen a photograph of the painting. Her mother had an album of them. Margaret probably had it now. He gave many of his works away during his life. A few were sold, but many more were given to friends. Tamsin tugged on the door to the wine shop before she realized it was locked. The lights off.

"A little early, isn't it? It's not even breakfast for most people."

Tamsin spun and faced the green-eyed man. "I was just looking at this painting. Wondering if they knew anything about the artist." Behind him the sky was dark. A storm approached.

"This is the house, isn't it? The one you told me about. On North

Street? Marigolds and lupine."

"Yeah. I mean, I think so. It would be a big coincidence if it wasn't. A green house with marigolds and lupine." Tamsin turned her back to the man and faced the painting. He didn't need to know more than that.

"I imagine every house here has been painted two billion times by one billion artists."

"Probably. I wonder if the people who run the wine shop know anything about it."

"Ask Connor about it. He's a really nice guy. I bet he would sell it to you."

Tamsin turned to look at the green-eyed man but he was already five steps away, on his way up the hill. A flash of light streaked the sky. She called up to him. "Who's Connor?"

He paused, looked back at her. "He owns the wine shop. One of the nicest people you'll ever meet."

Tamsin turned back to the painting. There were no truths in it. Nothing in the brush strokes or clumps and daubs of paint told her anything she didn't already know. Tamsin stood outside the wine shop window, looking at the perfection of the art. Every drop of color a deliberate shade, shape, form. She wanted to stake claim on its excellence. Not to own it, but to declare it to be a part of herself and to mark her place in its existence like a leaf in a family tree. But betrayal ran through every brush stroke, tarnishing the image.

How could her father be that imperfect and create anything so beautiful? How could he so boldly have two different lives and live out one of them in the town where he brought his children? How many paintings had he poured his soul into that never appeared in the photo album because they were part of someone else's world? The closer she got, the less perfect the painting appeared. If he could be so desecrated, what did that say for her? What kind of karmic genetic material laced into her double helix?

Tamsin felt for the pin in her pocket, her study of the painting interrupted by a tapping at the window. She almost didn't hear it over the distant thunder. The face of an angry man mouthed words at her, flipped the Closed sign to Open, and waved his hand at her, shooing her away.

A bell rang out when he opened the door. "If you're not coming into my shop to buy something, move on. Move on. No loitering. The sidewalk's too narrow for standing around."

His anger was infectious. "Why do you have a painting in your window if you don't want anyone to stop and look at it?"

"It's not there for you. It's there for me."

"But it faces the street."

"So what? So what if it faces the street? It's my window. I can put anything in there I want."

"Not anything."

The bell chimed as he pulled the door shut. Tamsin pushed it open again and followed him inside.

"Get out of my store if you're not here to buy something."

"Is it for sale?"

"The painting? No."

"Everything's for sale. Everything has a price tag."

"Not in my store, it doesn't. What do you want with it, anyway?"

"I don't know. But my looking at it seemed to offend you, so I thought I'd buy it so I can look at it whenever I want."

He slipped behind the counter like he was taking cover.

"Are you Connor?"

"Why do you want to know?"

"Because that guy outside said you were the nicest guy in town, and if this is the scale they measure nice on around here, a lot has changed since I was a kid."

The man slammed his palms down on the counter. Bottles of wine clinked together somewhere below, out of sight. He leaned forward, but Tamsin stood her ground. "A lot *has* changed around here since you were a kid. You and your family aren't welcome here anymore and that's all there is to it." His voice was nearly a whisper.

"What do you know about my family? You don't know me. You don't know why I'm here."

"I know everything I need to know. So do you. Go home."

Tamsin's mouth went dry, and the rain came fast, pounding the sidewalk. How could he know? How could he possibly know? "Do you know someone named Ida?"

"Go home."

A kid, barely out of his teenage years, stepped behind the counter, arms folded, wearing a scowl like a bouncer at a seedy bar. "He said move on."

"I don't want to go home." She spun and picked up a bottle of merlot. She'd hoped for white. "I want to know how I can find Ida, and I want to buy this."

"No." Connor addressed the young man, but his grimace stayed on Tamsin. "Get back to work, kid. This ain't any business of yours."

Tamsin tapped the bottle on the counter. "You're telling me I'm not allowed to buy this bottle of wine?"

"I'm telling you no. Because you don't like that wine. I can tell. I know who you are, and I don't want you here. I'm not telling you anything about anybody in this town."

"But you're telling me she lives here?"

"I didn't say that. I'm not telling you anything about anybody anywhere. Satisfied with that? Go back to wherever you came from and leave this town be."

The town, saturated with her father's paintings, didn't seem to be on the same page. Maybe Connor knew things. Maybe he was just a crazy old man who hated strangers, but she doubted it. "How do you know who I am?"

He leaned across the counter. "I may not know your name, but I know everything I need to know about you. Half of this town knows who you are. And you're not welcome here. Period."

His folded arms and puffed up chest, the set of his jaw and the ire in his eyes, told her he would charge a lot for the education. If she was going to pay a high price for the schooling, she at least wanted a stronger grasp of the cost.

Tamsin pulled a twenty-dollar bill from her wallet and laid it on the counter. "I love red wine. Keep the tip. I'm not here for you. I'm here for me. Don't get in my way, and I won't get in yours."

The door slammed behind her, and she stepped into the thundering rain. She expected the man to follow, to throw the money back at her, to grab the wine and run. She sought shelter in the recessed entry of the store next door. The lights were out, and a For Rent sign was taped to the window. The torn corners of posters and electrical wiring hinting at its past as a record shop. She'd have to come back, to pry from his hands the things he knew, or thought he knew, about her family. About Ida. Once the storm had passed.

Storms were common at the end of summer. The rain blew sideways and reminded Tamsin of saying goodbye. Making one last crawl along the rocky beaches. One last ice cream cone. One last bit of fudge before going home to buy school supplies. To put brown paper bags on her textbooks and fill a plastic pencil case with standard number twos. The feel of the saturated air pushing into her hoodie made her want to go home. To run from this uncomfortable storm where she couldn't hear Owen and back home to where he was in everything. Owen would know what to do, how to find Ida. What to do when she found her and how to handle this angry man who wanted her gone.

She jumped at a bolt of thunder, the lightning shining a light on her loneliness. Storms always made her feel alone. Everything once meant for two had been divided the day he was rolled out of their house on a stretcher. Single dinners. Eating out for one. Sitting with strangers on the train. With Owen, she'd have scampered through the rain and found shelter in some little shop. He'd have loved Rockport. Probably would have rented a boat. They'd have made the most of it, laughing at the detritus floating down the river that threatened to take over the street. He'd have tugged her in to a hug and told her it would all be okay. But none of that that was true. Owen would have loved Rockport, but if he were still alive, they never would have come. He would have found the envelope, shielded her from the emotional fallout, stacked the possibilities like Tetris pieces until they formed a perfect package. He'd have listened. Without Owen, no one listened. No one answered. She didn't even know what questions to ask.

A little black cat rounded the corner and took shelter where the dry sidewalk met the rain. It swished its tail.

"Hey, kitty."

Swish.

"I bet you know everything about this town. I have a conundrum, and I could use some help. See, I don't know what the hell I'm doing. I thought if I just showed up that this would be easy, and the universe would tell me what I need to know, but I guess it's not gonna work out that way. I need help. I need to know who to ask so I don't ruffle feathers. I don't even know what the rules are, but I deserve to know the truth about my family, and I think this town has the answers. Do you know where the answers are?"

Tamsin crouched down and reached out a hand. The cat extended its nose but rejected the greeting. He bolted into the rain, across the street, and up the stairs of the Rockport Historical Society.

CHAPTER SEVEN

The welcome mat wasn't welcoming, its letters faded and its corners torn by snow shovels and shoes. The Historical Society didn't look historical either, carved from a house that looked more Gothic than New England. Tall, narrow third-story windows peered down in judgment from above as Tamsin faced the windowless door, painted gloss black. Only a small metal plaque affixed at eye level welcomed her to push to enter. She turned the knob and shoved with her hip, expecting a bell or a buzzer, but was greeted only by silence. She stepped into a long, dark hallway that would have been uninviting if not for the papers and business cards tacked to a bulletin board inside the door announcing art shows and babysitting services. The place smelled faintly of lemon-scented cleaner. Tamsin brushed the rain off her head and scowled when her hand came away wet. She dried it on her jeans, her hand running over the outline of the pin in her pocket.

"Hello?" She started down the hallway. If it weren't for the sign outside, she'd have thought she was in the wrong place.

"Down here. End of the hall."

She followed a familiar voice and paused in the doorway. Green Eyes faced her from the other side of the counter. They were separated by a plexiglass partition.

"Excuse the security features." He tapped the thick slab of plastic. "Used to be a doctor's office."

"You're everywhere," she said.

"Not really. I'm on this street a lot. But I'm not everywhere."

Green Eyes took in all of her with one look. He had no right to assess her, to size her up. The fire behind those green eyes burned her cheeks, but she couldn't recoil. He had control of the Historical Society and being defensive wouldn't put her on his good side.

"And you're very literal."

"Very literal. Is literal a scale? I guess it could be." He slid a pencil under the clasp of a clipboard and pushed it through a slot in the plexiglass like a nurse asking for her medical history. If she was honest with herself, she found his playful air refreshing, though it verged on flirtatious. "Doing some research on that green house?"

Tamsin accepted the clipboard, filled her lungs with the scent of old paper and lemon cleaner, and stepped into the room. "Yeah. I wanna learn more of its history. If there are any papers here about it or anything about other owners."

"We have some old deeds. The very old ones. Old newspapers. Some family histories. Everything we have is in the card catalog. Files are sorted by address and name. When you find something you want to see, write the number down on that sheet then bring it back to me. I'll dig it out of the archives for you."

"Thanks." The form asked for her name and phone number. No way.

She moved around the counter, into the research area. A row of solid wood tables bordered by mismatched dining room chairs sat in the center of the open room, surrounded by card catalogs. She dropped her purse into a chair and sat with her back to the counter and the man with the green eyes.

"What are you hoping to find?" He stepped from behind the counter and followed her to the table. Too close.

Connor said half the town knew who she was. Said she wasn't welcome in Rockport. She couldn't trust Green Eyes until she knew which half the town he belonged to. "What do I hope to find? You mean literally or figuratively?"

"I know what you're looking for, figuratively. Same thing everyone's looking for when they come in here. I meant literally. What information you want to see."

"I am literally hoping to find information about my grandparents' house."

"Okay, then what's your interpretation of what you're hoping to find? Figuratively." Green Eyes landed in the chair across from her purse. She stood her ground and folded her arms, clutching the clipboard to her chest as if it were bulletproof. She'd always had a thing for green eyes.

"Same thing everybody else hopes to find. Like you said."

"Touché." He draped his arm over the back of the chair and looked up at her, the corners of his eyes giving away the smile that hadn't spread across his face. He was handsome. Maybe five years younger than her. Out of reach, where he should stay. She tightened her grip on the clipboard but gave him no expression at all. "Half of our visitors are history students. Journalists. Storytellers. They're connecting with the past for fun and fulfillment. A quarter of them are retired. They're nostalgic, marking time. Another quarter don't say why. I don't think most of them know. Every single person who comes in here is connecting with themself. The research varies, but the search is the same. There's a mystery inside them that they can't solve. It comes down to untangling the great mystery of why we are the way we are." Green Eyes nodded toward the rows of card catalogs. Tiny drawers like the ones at the library she visited as a child. She never browsed them, preferring to wander the stacks, reading back-cover blurbs and running her fingers along their spines.

Tamsin pulled her eyes from his and walked along the rows of drawers, unwilling to admit she had no idea how the system worked. Each drawer of the card catalog had a yellowed slip of paper in the front with typed letters, faded by the passage of time. There were last names, company names, street names. She found the drawer for the block of North Road where her grandparents had lived, and inside, a dividing tab with the house number. She extracted the drawer and dropped it on the table next to her purse, across from Green Eyes who studied her the way an anthropologist watches a newly discovered species. Afraid he might see her hands shake under his scrutiny, she shuffled the cards and wrote down file numbers, however irrelevant they might be.

"Do you watch everyone while they work?"

"No. Some people already know how to find what they're looking for. I can't guarantee that everyone will be happy with what they find, but I can at least help them find it."

"You don't think I'll be happy with what I find?" She pushed the clipboard across the table, and he pushed it back.

"I don't think you're looking for what you really want to find."

Tamsin's ears grew red. She wasn't there for opinions and had no intention of hearing them. "Thanks for the judgement, but I'll take the files whenever you have a chance."

"That's not what I mean. I mean you're looking in the wrong place. Literally. Look up the people. Not the house."

"I'll start here, thanks."

"Suit yourself. I have all day." Green Eyes glanced down at the clipboard and back. "I do need you to fill out the top. It's policy. In case someone walks away with something. Nothing personal."

"I can't stay anonymous?"

"Not in the eyes of the Historical Society."

"Christ." She pulled the clipboard back, and it scraped across the table.

Her pencil had barely touched the paper when he called her bluff. "Your real name would be good. But I can understand if you don't want me to know. I'd be sad, but I'd understand. The only thing is, knowing me, if I know that you wrote down a fake name, I'd be inclined to find the truth, so I'd just walk down to the motel and ask Jim and Mandy."

"Are you serious?" Would he really follow up to make sure she used her real name on a stupid piece of paper at the Historical Society? Tamsin dropped the pencil. Maybe there was another path that didn't involve Green Eyes.

"I'm a curious person. I love a good mystery." He rested his elbows on the table and his chin on his hands, his eyebrows raised like he was expecting a retort. Fine. Information would only flow if it went both ways. Tamsin took a leap of faith, scrawling her name and number at the top of the page.

"Thanks," he said. "Know how the universe has a really strange way of giving you what you ask for? Even if it's not always in the way you expect? I've learned that details are the same way. The more open you are to receiving them, the more easily they come your way."

Green Eyes stepped behind the counter, into his warehouse of historical papers. Tamsin tapped her foot on the floor and the Historical Society shook with her. The little box of golf pencils shimmied on the table. If Connor was the most untrustworthy person in town, Green Eyes had just secured a position as second on the list. Now he knew who her family was, where they'd lived, and he knew her name and number. It was only a matter of time before the wildfire spread, and the whole town knew what she was there to find. The suspicious look of the motel attendant. Side-eye from people in town who said she looked familiar. Connor's angry words. This close and she wasn't even sure she was ready to find Ida. How would this woman change her life? That answer wasn't in a folder.

Green Eyes returned, slid into the seat across from her, the wooden chair scraping across the floor. Why wouldn't he leave her alone? He reached across the table and placed a stack of manila folders before her.

"Remember, no pens. Only pencils. There are more blank forms on top of the card catalog if you want to see something else." He fanned out the folders and tapped the one at the bottom of the stack. "I'd suggest looking up the people when you're done with the house. I found a folder for an Eliot, Bradley. Thought you might want it. Good luck, Tamsin."

"Don't I get to know your name? Seems only fair."

"Ansel."

"Like Adams?"

"Like Ansel Millard. That's me. They call me Andy. You can, too."

"Okay. Thank you for the files." She would not call him Andy.

He started to push away from the table but paused, prying into her soul again with those eyes. His taupe skin and dark curls. His hands looked strong for someone who shuffled papers all day. Tamsin looked away and placed her hand on her jeans, feeling for the pin, her ground wire to Owen.

"I hope whatever you find makes you happy, Tamsin. But it usually takes more than a few folders."

"As long as it takes."

He left her alone at the table to peel back the cover of the manila folder at the top of the stack. She spent the next few hours learning about the house on North Road. Her great-grandfather, Bradley Eliot, built a house on that spot that was destroyed by the Long Island Express hurricane in 1938, along with everything else. The original plans were lost, although the house was mentioned in newspaper articles as having been typical for its time, whatever that meant. They rebuilt the house and passed it to her grandparents, who lived there until her grandfather died and her grandmother moved to Luxembourg. A few years after her grandfather passed away, the local newspaper published an announcement that the house had been sold for a dollar to an unnamed couple. Tamsin knew the house had been sold but never the price tag or the reason why. Is that when Ida was born?

"How's it going?"

She felt Ansel over her shoulder, warm at her back. He reached over her and pulled on the edge of a paper, a floor plan that lay unfolded before her. "Good, I guess. Just articles. Old pictures of the house. I found these plans from when they upgraded water and sewer. It's neat. Looks like the road used to be even more narrow than it is now."

"Did you look into the people at all?" He leaned down. Too close. She could feel his breath in her hair. Leather and wood. He inched closer to the site plan to read an inscription, and Tamsin capitalized on the opportunity to lean away.

"Not yet," she said.

"You could always look up the company who drew these plans to see if they did more. Sometimes you can find things that archivists missed that way. I'm supposed to close in a few minutes, though. I don't have to if you want to keep going."

She took the folded site plan from Ansel and returned it to the folder. She'd been careful to keep things in order to avoid falling on his bad side. "Don't stay open for me. I have enough to chew on. You're open tomorrow?"

Ansel nodded. "Only closed on Sundays and Mondays."

"What time do you open?"

"About fifteen minutes after you get your morning coffee."

Tamsin stood and pushed her chair back under the table. She slung her purse over her shoulder. "Do you want me to leave these here?" she asked, glancing at the folders.

"Yeah. I'll take care of them."

"Thanks for your help."

"You're welcome. Your federal grants at work. Do you want me to do any follow-up research for you? It gets a little boring in here sometimes. I'd be happy to help."

"No. Thank you." Tamsin paused at the hallway door. She didn't even know what the finished puzzle looked like yet. She couldn't let Ansel put the pieces together before she did. "It's kinda fun to watch the stories unfold, you know?"

"I know what you mean."

Tamsin rushed down the hall, holding her breath until she reached the concrete porch. Fresh air was such a relief.

* * *

Air swept across the Atlantic, rushed into the Gulf of Maine, and found its way between the threads of Tamsin's purple sweatshirt. She fought the wind back to the motel, collected her father's coat from her room, and trudged back to the grill. The shoulder seams of the waxed oilcloth coat hung low on her deltoids, and the hem grazed her thigh, like a child playing dress up.

Her table by the window was empty. Not a surprise, given the drop in temperature and dearth of tourists. The end of summer pushed the people west, to orchards and colorful leaves. Tamsin ordered oysters and wine as lights reflected in the bay, pushed and pulled by ripples in the water. Tamsin's Rockport was a world of opposites. An artsy town clinging to a conservative past. A safe and blissful childhood playground falling to ruin around her. She harbored so many happy memories—wandering the narrow streets, eating junk food, and skipping stones at the rock-strewn span of beach—all clouding over, becoming an ominous place where no one could be trusted.

Her sense of self had always been tied to her sense of place. She defined herself by her hometown, by the quiet life she lived, by the places she frequented. She was from a small Pennsylvania town as if she'd been dug from the silt of its creeks and streams. Tamsin was the smell of the sea and the calls of the birds on a summer morning as mist rose off the water and baptized the land. The secrets and darkness descended on her like a lid on a lobster steamer pot, suffocating. But any blame she assigned to Rockport in light of her father's transgression was misplaced. His choices were his own, not the town's.

Light reflected; it rippled and waved in the water outside the window, and she envied it, separate but a discernible part of its creation. She'd been torn so far from her roots that she didn't recognize or resemble her own creator.

A distant buzzing brought her back from the water to the restaurant. A text from Marlow.

Hey. U never texted back. Guess u took the week off anyway?

Tamsin dug an oyster from its shell and chewed it once before swallowing. *Sorry. Yep. Got sidetracked. All good at work?*

He's being secretive. More than usual. Will text when I know more.

"I've had the strangest day, and I could use some company. If there's room at your table for one more." Ansel clutched the back of the seat across from her, messenger bag hanging from his shoulder, lighter than it was in the morning but it still looked like a heavy load to bear.

She leaned back and offered the closest thing to a smile that she could muster. Saying no wouldn't win her any favors. "Sure. Of course."

He dropped his bag to the floor and took a seat. "I love this place in the off-season. You can sit here as long as you want, and you don't feel like you're taking up table space."

"What's your poison?" She didn't really want to know, but it was the best small talk she could think of.

"Whiskey. The cheaper the better. Around here, it's all beer and wine though. Big history of teetotalling."

"I noticed that. I'm okay with it. I'd rather have wine than beer."

"There are a few places off the beaten path that make some decent drinks, if cocktails are your thing."

His eyes burned through the layers of her. Studying her. Drinks sounded a lot like an invitation, a tempting one that she had no intention of accepting. She held in a breath and gave herself to a count of ten, riding out the storm. Hoping he'd see the point in her silence and pedal back. When he didn't speak, she did. "Maybe you can make a list for me."

"Maybe I can show you."

"We'll see." She took a sip of her wine, letting the dry, sour smell of chardonnay overpower his leather and wood. She needed to get the upper hand with Ansel. She enjoyed the banter, especially with someone who didn't see her as a grieving widow or an unmarried woman who lost a boyfriend and was undeserving of the widow badge, but she was here for Ida. It should have been easy, but so many emotions were tied up in the search, and her judgment was clouded by her encounter with Connor. The man didn't come across to her as a curmudgeon. It was clear to her that he wanted to be seen as a threat. And the more she saw of Ansel, the less she trusted him. She offered a weak grin. She couldn't risk offending him or leading him on, but she really wanted to know if his constant presence was a coincidence.

"Why is it that I keep running into you everywhere?"

"That's a bigger question than I can answer. I don't have that kind of insight into the universe."

"Did you know I was here?"

"Am I following you? I'm hurt that you would think so. No. Given the size of the town, maybe this is a question of probability and statistics. I would ask if you're following me, but you seem to already be at the places I need to go. The café is the only spot for coffee before eight, the wine shop is between work and the post office, and I eat here all the time. I've known Deb since I was four."

Tamsin poked the lemon wedge in her glass of water with her straw, eyeing her dinner companion. Owen had been an excellent judge of character. He could have been a detective. She gave her trust away for free to friends and coworkers and spent her early thirties crushed each time it was broken. By the time she was thirty-eight, when Owen died, she'd stopped trusting almost everyone but him. Owen would have leaned across the table, leveled with Ansel, asked him if he could be trusted, and something in those green eyes that Tamsin couldn't see would have told Owen everything he needed to know. In the absence of his special powers, she'd have to be blunt about it.

"Can I trust you?" She gave it a playful spin.

"Like '*Can I trust you to watch this for me while I go to the bathroom?*' Or '*I'm an international spy with a secret mission, and I need help unraveling it?*' Those are two different forms of trust."

"No, they're not. You could blab a secret all over town and ruin someone's reputation or steal their credit card and take their money. Damage is damage. Someone is either trustworthy or they're not."

"I don't know if I agree with that. I think some damage is worse than others. But the answer is yes—to both. I can be trusted. And I do like to know what I'm getting myself in to. Something tells me you're not running off to the bathroom and this is more international spy, though. In that case, maybe I should ask if I can trust *you*."

"I'm not an international spy. I'm not any kind of spy. And I didn't invite you along for the journey. I was only asking if you were trustworthy."

"But you *are* looking for something."

Secrets. Her parents. This town. They'd all hid secrets from her. Now they were hers to find, to reveal. But uncovering a secret isn't the same as finding the truth, and that's what Tamsin really wanted. Not just the facts, but to know why. All these lies.

If she hadn't been searching those green pools for his truth, she would have ended the staring contest and handed the trophy to Ansel, but Deb saved her the trouble.

"Looked like you were running dry, so I brought you a second glass of wine." Deb set a glass on the table. The yellow liquid rocked from side to side. "How did you two meet?"

"I've been doing some research about the town." Tamsin knocked back the dredges of her first glass and pulled the second closer. A chess piece between them. "Ended up at the Historical Society."

"Tamsin, here, has been picking my brain."

"Well, it's quite the landscape in there. I hope you can make heads or tails of it." Deb returned his sarcastic sneer and took her tablet and pen from her apron. "What'll you have?"

"I'll have what she's having."

"Sitting here, I assume?" Deb gave Tamsin a wink.

"As long as Tamsin will have me."

Tamsin considered him, eyes narrowed just enough to let him know he staked no claims. "Please. Join me."

Deb nodded, her attention on the order pad. "Oysters and white wine it is."

"Make it red? Pinot Noir."

"You got it." Deb scribbled and turned to Tamsin. "Looks like you're still picking. I'll bring more bread to soak that up with."

Ansel leaned back in Deb's wake. "You want to know if I can keep a secret. Small towns have lots of secrets. Quarters are so close you can't live an anonymous life. Secrets become currency. You have to know when to keep them, when to let it be known that you have them. But everybody knows more than you think."

That's exactly what Tamsin was afraid of. "There's a secret here. Something's been kept from me, and I want to know what it is without anyone knowing I'm looking for it." Tamsin filled her mouth with wine to keep herself from saying more.

"Except me?"

"I haven't decided that yet."

"You found more in those folders than you let on."

"I'm not saying that. I'm asking you if you can be trusted."

Deb dropped oysters and wine in front of Ansel. He took a sip from his glass, and when he set it down, it was checkmate. His red to her white. He folded his hands and looked down at the placemat, soft curls tumbling down, obscuring his face. "This is fun, this thing with you. So you're looking for a truth that's being kept from you because of a secret. Whether you need my help unlocking it or you just need someone to talk to, I can't help you decide. You ask me if I'm trustworthy? If I tell you I am, I could be lying. There's nothing I can do to convince you to talk to me. You have to convince yourself whether you want the help bad enough to take the risk. As for the secret, facts are facts. There's a chance you'll find them, but what people do with facts is subjective. That's their truth. There are as many truths as there are people in the world, so there's no telling how many are tangled up in this secret of yours."

Tamsin sat back. Lights danced like fireflies on the water. He could string words together in such a beautiful way. They made no sense at all and spoke volumes at the same time. He was intriguing, but that didn't mean he could be trusted to help her find Ida, to uncover the truth of her father's lost time. He was right, though. The truth of what happened was more than the facts. It was more than the date and time of the transgressions, the lies that were told. It was more than the existence of Ida. The real truth was how those lies would impact what's left of her family. Her memories. A beloved father who may not have been what he seemed. Her mother. Had she known the truth? And the sister she'd been avoiding. The sister she hadn't told. It was too much to process. Too many questions and no way to prepare for the answers. She stabbed at the lemon in her water, and it went cloudy, seeds swirling with the melting ice. She changed the topic. "What made you want to work at a historical society?"

"I like solitude. Books. And history. Libraries were my aspiration because that's where history tends to end up. I stumbled into preserving archives after that, and historical societies are the temple mount if history is your thing. All those first-person stories. Primary source materials. I get to take care of them. Transcribe them. Make sure those voices survive."

"Truths. A building full of truths."

"And probably some secrets. Like yours. Your grandfather's?"

He had no right to make assumptions. Nothing about her world was any of his business. "No."

"Some family thing, though, right? A murder? A disappearance?"

"It's none of your business."

The look she gave him should have shut him down, but it failed. He leaned across the table with a mischievous smile that brought lines to the corners of those green eyes, and all she could feel was the pin in her pocket, the bent post poking into her leg. She couldn't hear Owen's voice when she tried to call upon the part of him that she kept with her always. When she tried to ask Owen what he would do, what he would say, she heard nothing at all. Why was he so distant here? Because they never came here together? Because this place was hers before him?

"You're right. It's none of my business." Ansel leaned back in his chair, taking his pinot noir with him. He swirled it in the glass, a narrow stem between his fingers. "Would it be fair to say, though, that what you'll find at the end, what comes wrapped up in that truth, is really a part of yourself?"

Tamsin dunked the corner of toasted bread into her bowl and let garlic butter wick into it. She had no intention of answering him.

"That's what I hope to find, digging around in the Historical Society. More of myself in the stories I read. There's comfort in knowing that no matter how much the world changes, people tend to stay the same. We all want the same things."

"What things?" Her eyes were drawn to him, but she fought the pull, sifting through toasted rounds of bread, sorting them. Saving the best for last.

"Love. Security. To be understood."

"That's a lot to ask from some old papers."

"Not if you know how to listen."

"Do you get a lot of visitors?"

"No. Twenty or so a month. Journalists. Email requests for information. More in the summer, when people come by to do genealogy. But the incoming papers outweigh the visitors. People die. They donate stuff."

Tamsin wondered if any of the papers her mother had destroyed could have found a home there. Maybe Margaret would have some. She'd have to ask one day. The thought of sorting through papers seemed miserable. "I'm not that good at sitting in silence. It makes me restless."

"The voices in those folders can be pretty loud if you know how to speak their language." Andy pushed his bowl aside, watery garlic butter pooling in empty oyster shells. His attention was solely on Tamsin, and it heightened her senses, making her aware of every movement she made, of every blink, and questioning how it could be interpreted. She kept her eyes averted, focused on a distant table cloth, as he continued. "What about you? What motivates you? Other than trying to uncover this secret and find the truth. What drives you?"

"You're not going to ask me what I do for a living? That's usually what people want to know."

"What you do for a living is how you make money. That's not what drives you. That's not what makes you interesting. Or maybe they are the same thing. What do you do for a living, Tamsin Eliot?"

"I'm in marketing. But I'm not passionate about it." Tamsin couldn't think of a single thing she was passionate about. Travel had been Owen's thing. That old truck in the barn had been his dream. Together they'd saved and scraped pennies to buy the farmhouse, but that was hardly a passion. It was a stupid question, and she'd never be able to answer to his satisfaction anyway. She shuffled in her seat, leaning back, and her knee brushed his.

"Sorry."

"It's okay."

Owen. Bile rose from the knot in her stomach, sour in her throat like acid reflux with oysters and wine. She reached behind her for her purse and pulled it onto her lap. Pushing aside the scraps of receipts, she grabbed her wallet, unzipped it, and laid a fifty on the table.

"Wait. Did I say something? Don't go."

"No, not at all." She pulled on her father's coat, but it was trapped under the leg of her chair. She fumbled her purse onto her shoulder, and it swung without grace as she stood. "I'm sorry. I...I realize that I have to get an early start tomorrow because I—" Because what? Because she had nothing to do with her day? She rescued the coat from beneath the chair, and shrugged into it, pulling it into shape by tugging it over her hips. The envelope in the chest pocket crinkled, reminding her of the colorful leaves and pine bark paint brushes of her dream. "I have an early morning. I have to get to Acadia."

"Acadia? The national park? You have an appointment in a national park?"

"No, I just...I want to spend as much of the day there as I can."

"That's an early start then. Acadia's about five hours from here."

Five hours. That was a long drive. "It's been years since I've been there, and I really want to see it. Tomorrow seemed like the best day."

"You'll have perfect weather for it. Fifty dollars is a bit much for dinner, though. Want your change?"

"No, that's fine. Deb's great. She deserves the tip. I need to get going anyway." Tamsin inched past Ansel, toward the exit.

He turned in his seat as she passed. "Okay, then. It was nice having dinner with you."

"You, too. Thanks for the company."

"Do you want me to look into the house some more? See if I can find anything else?"

"No. Please." Being rude wouldn't keep her on his good side, and she still needed the resources of the Historical Society. "Please don't. I may not even follow up on this. Such a silly thing. I may just spend some time drawing."

"Have fun in Acadia then. Good luck."

Tamsin would need it.

CHAPTER EIGHT

The weathered planks of the storefronts washed out beneath the streetlights, and Tamsin walked in a black-and-white landscape back to the motel. Her steps echoed off buildings and brick, and for all the wine, she let herself thirst for Owen, for his hand to hold. Light reflected in fragments from the pavement outside the motel. She didn't notice it was glass until it was under her feet. And she didn't realize it was from Owen's Cherokee until she noticed the windows were missing. Shards of glass were scattered on the faux leather seats and on the all-weather floor mats like ice that would never melt. She circled the car. The passenger and driver's side windows were gone. The rear window glass was a spider web but still intact. More than she could say for her heart. Owen's car. Smurf. The windows she peered through to watch the world pass by while Owen drove them to places she never dreamed she'd see. Stepping back, she saw the car was sitting lower than usual. All four tires had been slashed, lowering the SUV to its rims.

The glovebox was still closed. The half empty bottle of water from her drive still in the cup holder. Her hands shook too much to grasp the room key. She fumbled it from her pocket, and it fell onto the ground with the glass and cigarette butts and parking lot pebbles. Connor. It had to be.

She guided the key into the lock, holding the doorknob steady with one hand. The entire world was shaking, and Tamsin was but a rag doll to circumstance. She sat on the edge of the bed, the snow globe pin poking her through the pocket of her jeans, and thumbed through the binder of useful local information, looking for the nonemergency number for the Rockport Police Department. It was late, half past eight in the evening, but the phone rang and rang while Tamsin stumbled through the rehearsal of her greeting. What was she supposed to say when they asked why she was in Rockport? That she was sneaking around town and stalking someone who may be a resident? She had almost convinced herself to hang up when an officer answered and asked for her name.

Vandalism, he said. Insurance would cover it. If nothing was missing, there'd be no prints worth looking for. He made a note of the damage and gave her a police report number. She could share it with insurance, but they probably wouldn't ask for it. They'd just load it onto a tow truck and send it out for a repair.

Tamsin asked for a recommendation, and the officer suggested a body shop on Main Street, on the way out of town, toward the highway. He wished her luck and told her to enjoy the rest of her stay in a half-hearted way. He didn't seem at all concerned that someone was running around Rockport with blunt objects bashing in car windows and sharp objects, slashing tires. When Connor said half the town wanted her gone, did that include the police?

She closed the binder and let her racing heart settle. The more she thought about it, the sillier it seemed that someone who wanted her to leave would flatten the tires she would need to get away. She called her insurance company, listened to the prompts, and started a claim. Having a plan to fix the damage made her feel a little better, and the reassuring voice of the woman on the other end of the phone made her feel at ease and less alone.

Following the insurance woman's advice, she returned to the car and took photos of the damage. The rear window and the flattened tires, fragments of security glass scattered on the seats and floor. In the morning she would call for a tow truck to take the SUV into town.

The light was on inside the motel lobby. A woman with a trash bag flung over her shoulder stocked coffee pods, sliding them into the wire rack that let customers choose their own flavor. Tamsin pushed the door open and poked her head inside.

"I hate to bother you, but do you have security cameras on your parking lot, by any chance?"

The woman glanced at Tamsin but didn't divert her attention from cleaning the lobby. "No, ma'am. We don't really need that kind of thing around here."

"Seems you do. Someone broke my car windows and slashed all my tires. Nobody here saw or heard anything?"

"The office isn't staffed unless someone has a reservation. There's a bell here, and a phone number there on the wall, in case somebody comes by, but it's off-season. Not much happens around here. I just come in here and clean up."

"You didn't see all this glass when you arrived?"

"I came in the back. I never even saw the parking lot." The woman leaned, craned her neck to peer around Tamsin. "That's a hell of a mess. Did you call the police?"

"I did, but they didn't seem to care. They gave me a police report number and asked some questions, but they didn't send anybody down here or anything."

Tamsin followed the woman into the lobby. A radio chirped and warbled from a back room, half the notes lost on their way down the hall. Tamsin picked at a fingernail, unsure what she was waiting for, whether the woman who ducked down the hall was returning at all. Tamsin said the only thing that came to mind.

"I'd be happy to sweep up the broken glass if you have something I can use."

The woman returned with a dustpan and broom. If her jaw were clenched any tighter, she'd break her teeth. She mumbled something that sounded like, "I'll get it."

Tamsin stepped out of her way. "Do you have any trash bags and tape I could borrow? I'd happily pay you for them—"

"What do you need that for?"

"To cover the holes in my car."

"It's not supposed to rain."

"Has it never rained unexpectedly here? I seem to recall that happening all the time when I was a kid. That rain the other night wasn't in the forecast. Plus, all the bugs?"

"It's almost autumn." The woman gave in, waving her hand in a visual display of irritation. "Take what you need. They're in the cabinet under the sink there. There should be a roll of masking tape in one of the desk drawers. Help yourself."

Tamsin's blood boiled at the dismissal, but she kept her comments to herself, uttering a polite thanks for the help. The anger was misplaced, anyway. It wasn't the woman's fault that her parking lot was covered in broken glass and her night worsened by the inconvenience of having to clean it all up.

The masking tape did a poor job of holding the black plastic trash bag to the car, but it was better than nothing. She worked on one side of the car while the motel employee scraped clinking glass shards into the plastic dust collector on the other. She wanted to ask the woman about Connor, if he had a known mean streak, a history of vandalism, if he was part of an organized crime ring that filtered money through a chain of auto body repair shops. It was easy to put the blame on him, but it was far too obvious. He may have been gruff, but he didn't seem stupid. Maybe he was right, and half the town did want her gone.

Tamsin returned the roll of masking tape to the office and thanked the woman who ignored her but waved an acknowledgement. She closed the lobby door gently behind her and made her way back to her motel room, her pace slowed by her shallow breaths, her shaking hand fumbling the key. So much had changed in so few hours. Without that coat, without the drawing, she would be at home where nothing unexpected happened, where everything was clean and tidy and under control. She'd be locked in with Owen and real life and radio commercials from the local pharmacy and convenience stores.

Leaving her shoes at the end of the bed, Tamsin traded her clothes for pajamas and rescued the pin when it fell out of her jeans and onto the floor. She placed it on the nightstand next to her phone, a reminder of a time when the universe played in her favor. A reminder that things had a way of working themselves out and that no adventure would be complete without the fortuitous kind of chaos.

She rested her head on the pillow and flung out an arm into the vastness beside her. The truth was hers to find, not theirs to keep from her, and every fragment of glass on the ground strengthened her resolve to get what she came for and stretched the lengths to which she'd go to get it. If Mags was right, if there was some dark secret in her family's past and if Ida were a part of it, she would hunt that woman to the end of the earth.

CHAPTER NINE

Acadia would have to wait. So would Tamsin's call to the tow truck company. The sun was barely up, the repair shop wouldn't open for two more hours, and she had no interest in sitting in their parking lot, waiting for access to the traditional coffee slurry.

In the bottom of her purse, she found the nub of a pencil she used to check items off her grocery lists. She took it and the motel's complimentary notepad up the hill and across the street, toward the water, where she sat on an overturned milkcrate and sketched a view of Motif Number 1. It wasn't the most common view of a wall draped with buoys, the ancient sea stretching beyond. It was a hint she could see between buildings as she hovered close to the motel. The angle of the sun threw dramatic shadows across the water, but Tamsin neither saw nor sketched them. She focused on the corners of things. Where the peak of the roof met the sky. The contrast of wall and window. Her drawing was terrible. Dark lines on cheap paper.

As a teenager, Tamsin had coveted her father's artistic ability. She'd sit to sketch a neighborhood cat or a scene from her memory only to find that it lacked depth and perspective. Everything appeared too colorful, too much of something and not enough of something else. Not motivated to improve, she walked away from the attempt one day and never returned. More than twenty years later, she wondered what her eyes would be trained to see if she hadn't given up.

Behind her, a shuffling on the pavement, the scuff of pebbles and sand, told her that she wasn't alone. The scent of leather and wood. It was Ansel.

"What happened to your poor car?"

"I wish I knew." She spun to face him. "It was like that when I got back to the motel last night."

"That's horrible. Did you call somebody?"

"Yeah. I'm just waiting for the shop to open. Didn't want to call a tow truck and then sit there for hours, you know."

"Boring. Come by the Historical Society. You could always finish up your research and catch an Uber to pick it up later."

"I think I'll go with it. As cars go, it's not much, but it's a sentimental thing."

"Fair enough."

"Hey, I know you said he's a nice guy, but you don't think Connor could do something like that, do you?"

"Over a spat about a painting? Nah. I can't see him doing that kind of damage to your car because you loitered on the sidewalk and stared at a painting."

"How did you know he yelled at me about the painting? You weren't there. You were gone."

"I know because Dylan was stocking shelves in the wine shop, and he saw the whole thing. Told me about it last night at the grill after you left. He gave me a bunch of shit for eating dinner with the woman who riled Connor up so bad that he grumbled to himself all day over a painting."

Either Ansel was lying, or he didn't know what Connor had against her. Even if Connor didn't really know, if he was addled or wrong, or even if he was just a curmudgeon around strangers, he scared the crap out of her. But he was her shortest possible path to Ida and the only person in town she could trust to be exactly who he claimed to be. She couldn't tell Ansel any of that because she still needed his help, and she still didn't know which half of Connor's town he stood with.

"What a stupid thing to get so pissed about," she said. "Why put a painting in the window of your store if you don't want people to look at it."

Ansel just shrugged, squinting against the rising sun. "You want me to keep going? I can look up more info on the house. See if there are more plans hiding back there? There may be pictures of the place hiding in other folders. I could look around for you and show you tomorrow."

Tamsin couldn't accept his assistance. She wiped a sweaty palm on her knee, rubbing out the stain of suspicion. None of this was helping, the constant questioning and looking over her shoulder. Ansel liked his job. It was as simple as that. The same old trust issues always got in the way with other people, between her and what she wanted, and Connor's barbarism only made it worse. Nothing would change unless she made an effort. A cautious effort. "That would be neat. If there were pictures of the house from way back." It wasn't what she really wanted to find, but it was a step in the right direction. "It's nice of you to offer. I'm not very good at accepting help."

"Don't worry about it. It'll be fun. Like I said, I get bored in there sometimes." Ansel lifted his coffee cup in a departing gesture. "See you tomorrow then."

"Yeah. Thanks."

Ansel walked away. She checked the time on her phone, called for a tow, and sketched while she waited, one ear poised for the tow truck, the other to the water licking at the docks. Trusting Ansel to look for old pictures of the house, something barely relevant to her search for Ida, shouldn't have been hard, but trust had never been her strong suit. She couldn't even trust herself to make accurate memories.

Margaret said Tamsin's childhood was less than realistic. That their mother had been miserable, and there had been long stretches with no sight of their father. Unexplained absences that went on for days. Piles of excuses that Mom couldn't keep straight. Even Rockport wasn't perfect cotton candy colors and summer sunshine. The reality was weathered wood and scavenging shore birds.

The tow truck bumped and banged down the narrow street toward the motel. Tamsin dropped her pencil into her purse and followed on foot. When the car was fixed, she would have to search harder, before what she was looking for found her first.

CHAPTER TEN

The lobby of the repair shop offered few comforts. Just old issues of *Popular Mechanics* and some *Car and Driver* magazines with torn covers. Tamsin relaxed at the sight of a fancy coffee maker, the kind with plastic pouches of flavored something that turned into caffeine at a few presses of a button. Ten ounces. Strong.

Three hours and three cups later, she'd accepted her fate as a resident of Jack's Auto Repair, but she was still making sense of the decor. Two walls were papered with massive sepia-toned prints of town from the early days of cars and into the seventies. She took them in from different angles. A few stores on the Neck looked familiar but mostly it was just small-town New England. No hint of the season or weather, just a simpler time and place. She dug her ringing cell from her jeans and swiped at the green answer button as she saw Margaret's name flash across the screen, cursing to herself for not screening her calls better and cursing Mags for making her screen them.

"Tamsin? I know you're in Rockport." Margaret issued a shrill accusation.

"Margaret. Why would I care that you know that?" But she did care. She hadn't wanted her sister to know what she was looking for or why she wanted to find it. She didn't want Margaret to think she'd been right, because that would mean Tamsin's view of her whole life had been wrong. "Also, how do you know that? Are you stalking me?"

"I shipped everything to your office like you asked me to, but you never called to tell me if it got there okay. I called you at work and some woman named Marley said you were still out of the office. You made me panic. I thought something happened to you, and I was all alone in the world."

"Marlow. She's my office neighbor." Tamsin held the phone away so her sister couldn't hear the sigh. Controlling and dramatic were two badges Margaret wore like permanent tattoos. "You got married and created your own humans. Even if something happened to me, you wouldn't be alone in the world."

"When do you plan to go back to work?"

"Whenever I want to."

"You'd better not lose your job. There's no safety net. I hope you have enough savings."

"Whoa. Mags. Last I checked, I was the older one. I'm the one holding down an actual job in the real world, not sitting at home feeding kids."

"And yet you're also the one who is selfish and has no sense of responsibility to your family."

"Selfish?"

"You know, maybe I won't ship Dad's old paintings to you after all, since they weren't important enough to stick around and help pack up."

"You didn't even tell me about them—"

"And they don't seem to be important enough to stick around to receive, either. Where do you even get off? You told me you had to get back to work. Rushed me out of the house before dawn to get you to the airport and now you're in Rockport?"

"I was going to call an Uber, and you hoisted yourself on me. If we hadn't ridden together, you'd still be pissed about the last thing you were pissed about that I had to smooth over in the airport parking garage by pretending you aren't always so judgmental. Half the reason we get along is because I don't hold you accountable for the way you talk to me."

"This whole thing is just another selfish Tamsin moment. I can't talk to you when you're like this."

"Funny. I wasn't like this until you called."

"Jesus, Tamsin." Her name came out of her sister in the same sing-song, hands-on-hips tone she'd used since they were kids. A sarcastic scolding from someone who always knew better.

Tamsin sat, and the post of the pin jabbed her again. She leaned back and clasped it between two fingers, sticking it in her back pocket instead. She made a mental note to find some pliers. "I didn't plan this, it just came up. You're just jealous that you can't pick up and do things because you made different life choices."

"I like my life choices. You don't have any life at all. And you should be here helping your family, not on some holiday chasing your childhood."

"Did you want something specific or did you just call to piss me off?"

"I called to let you know that the stuff you wanted from Mom's house was shipped, and you can pick it up when you decide to go back to work."

The line went dead, and Tamsin was left to explain her sister to the only work friend she had. She opened her texting app and found her last texts from Marlow.

Got a call from my sister. Sorry. She can be a bear.

Marlow replied. *No worries. She was nice. Sounded worried. Told her u were in Rockport. Didn't know it was a big deal.*

It's all good. Work piling up? Should I come back?

Yes but no. Stay and enjoy. The shit will hit the fan in a few weeks. He's being tight lipped.

Tamsin felt her blood pressure go up. She held her phone with both hands and sat on the closest red plastic lawn chair. *News?*

Nothing yet. Just rumors. Bad ones, but rumors.

Tell!

Just rumors. No facts.

K. Text me w/ news. See you next week.

Great. Her job was her safety net. It was the reason she left the house every day. Looking back, Tamsin knew that having somewhere to go was the only thing that kept her rooted to reality in the weeks and months after Owen died. It was the only thing that kept her rooted still. One week off work and look what she'd become.

The clock was ticking on finding out who Ida was and what the drawing meant to her own past and future. The best bet would be to beg Connor, that angry man, to help unravel it, but the thought of walking into his store and asking for help making sense of her family made her want to quit drinking wine.

She examined the aerial photo of town that covered one wall of the repair shop. The tiny cottages and stores of the Neck and the houses on the mainland. They hadn't spent much time on the mainland when she was a child. Little was familiar. She knew the roads that led to the Neck, the small grocery store, and the art shop. Her father used to take her there for paints and brushes. He would end up in conversations, and she would wander the rows of shelves, looking at colorful tubes and jars of paints. She was never bored with him like she was when she went with their mother to the market or the fabric store. She found the art shop on a map. The parking lot wrapped around the building. The sign on a pole by the street, the way she remembered it.

"Your car's ready."

Four hours. "That was fast."

"We didn't have four of your tires, so we had to send out for one. Took a while to deal with the rear wiper, too. Anyway, you're all set. You have a $250 deductible for the damage and insurance will take care of the rest."

"Towing?"

"They took care of that, too." The man pushed a stack of papers across the desk, technical details about tires that she didn't care about. "You might get a call with an automated survey. If you don't mind letting us know how we did, it would be great."

"Sure." Tamsin dug in her purse for her wallet. "Hey, do you know if that old art store is still around here?"

"Art store?"

"Yeah, it had a sign that looked like a painter's palette. That wooden thing with the hole for their thumb, you know?"

"It's still there. Down on Broadway."

"Left out of here?"

"Yeah. You go left out of here and down a bit. There's a Dollar Store and then, like you said. You can't miss the sign."

If the universe had taught her anything, it was that everything was important. And right then, connecting with a happy memory felt very important.

CHAPTER ELEVEN

The sign hadn't changed. A weathered artist's palette with rainbow splotches of color. It mirrored her memory of it. Windows down in their old Chevette, the backs of her legs sticking to the seats. The way the whole town smelled of hot pavement. Her father always parked on the side, and a bell above the door would ring when he held it open for her.

Inside, the place was dark and verging on damp. Summer humidity seeped through the windows and soaked up varnish and paint thinner, filling the air with the scent of works in progress. Old paper, sketch pads, and canvases lined the walls in racks on shelves. Tamsin used to walk among them, run her fingers along the textures. While her father shopped and talked, she would squeeze the metal tubes of paint, smoothing their ripples and returning them to the racks.

The store hadn't changed much either. Small orange price tags were wrapped around brushes and barely clung to frames. The place still smelled of paint thinner and old wood, the vaulted ceiling and exposed beams lit only by what little sunlight streamed through the large stained-glass windows at the gables. The sun was high, limning the old wood floor like a sloppy watercolor painting. Reds and yellows and blues in temporary hues that would creep up her legs if she stayed long enough.

The bell quieted behind Tamsin. A woman approached the register, unloading items from her cart to the counter, and a man out of view called out. He'd be out in just a second. Tamsin took a basket and walked the aisles. Charcoals. Sketch pad. Colored pencils. A basic set of acrylic paints. The price of good brushes drove her to the discount bin, to plastic handles and synthetic bristles. She left the basket on the counter, by the unmanned register, and studied the bulletin board by the door. There were business cards for galleries and artists. Someone lost a cat. And there were photos stuck to the corkboard with push pins and stick pins and old rusted thumbtacks. Ladies in fancy hats outside drinking what might be tea. The rest of the wall was covered in paintings.

What a horrible place for those beautiful paintings, she thought. *Overlooked when you walk in the door, and the last thing an amateur like me sees before we set off to create our own misshapen views of the world.*

She stepped back, and a field of irises came into view.

Sometimes, standing too close to something makes it impossible to see. Like the way her eyes wouldn't focus on drops of water on the wall of her shower, or how it was easier to find a four-leaf clover if she looked at the wider field. If she hadn't stepped back, she wouldn't have seen the giant painting, some eight feet long and five feet high, secured above the door. *Field of Irises.* It was one of her father's favorite paintings. He made it in the dining room of her grandmother's cottage on North Road, and until today, she had no idea where it had gone. Could it be another sign? Everything was a sign. Everything was important. Her father taught her that. Every dark iris had a highlight. The truth casting a shadow on her father didn't diminish his light. The good in him was still there, looking down upon her from the wall of an art supply store.

"You find everything okay?"

Tamsin stepped to the counter and reached into the basket, moving art supplies onto the counter. "I did. Thank you."

"Saw you admiring that big painting up there."

"How did you even get it up there?"

"Two big ladders and two strong men. Neither one of them were me."

The man was weathered. Strong for his years. Like a hiker or a gardener, not someone who worked in an art shop. She tried guess his age, whether he was old enough to have worked there when her father was a customer. She handed him cash and took her change as the opportunities dwindled. He turned from the register, toward a back room.

"Wait," she called out to him. "I have a question. Do you know who painted it?"

He waved a hand, dismissing her request. "Some artist who lived around here years ago. He's gone now. Like the rest of them. They come, they paint. They go on to other things. No one paints forever, you know."

Her father would have. Her father did. Until the end. "Did you know him?"

"I did. That's him on the board, there. Top row, on the left. Second or third one? I can't recall. Let me see." He walked around the counter and slid his glasses down his nose.

Tamsin spotted her father before the man pushed a finger at the photograph, its matte finish yellowed by the years.

"There. That's him," the man said. His voice carried a hint of something. Remorse or condescension. "That's all there is to him."

"Who is the woman with him?" Long dark hair like her mother's. Those 1980s shoulder pads that made her look like a woman on a mission, like the ones her mother had worn and had come sewn into her Sunday dresses. The woman's arm was draped around her father. The way two people pose for a photo when they're familiar. That woman was not her mother.

"Who is the lady? Do you know?"

"That's my sister. Carol." The man was already behind the counter, on his way to the back room. She couldn't let him leave without an explanation.

"Did they know each other? Wait."

"Of course they did. The Arts Alliance met every week. They were all friends with each other. Most of them still are. But that man doesn't live here anymore, and my sister's in Maine."

"Wait." She had to keep him talking, from disappearing behind that wall. "Do you remember him? Anything about him? His family?"

"Why do you need to know? Why not any of those other paintings?" His demeanor went from friendly shop owner to pit bull with alarming speed. It was clear he wanted nothing to do with her or the conversation. Eyes narrowed, nostrils flared, he moved toward the door behind the counter, and Tamsin stepped back, putting space between herself and the unpredictable man.

Grasping her purse strap in one hand and the pin in the other to keep her hands steady, she set her jaw and held her ground. "Did they have more than a friendship? They did, didn't they?"

He stopped at the doorway. The weight of her purse tugged on her shoulder. She adjusted it and shoved her hand in the back pocket of her jeans, feeling for the snow globe pin.

"I don't know what you're after, but I don't have anything else to tell you about that artist or my sister."

"The man in that picture is my father. I believe he had another daughter named Ida, who was connected to Rockport. I met a man in town who said he knew who I was and why I was here. He was really angry about my being here, but I'm not leaving until I find Ida."

"Well, you're not gonna find her through me." The man slipped into the back room and closed the door with force. It wasn't a slam, but it was close.

Tamsin moved behind the counter, one hand squeezing her purse strap, the other clutching the pin. The bent post dug into her palm. She knocked on the door. "Please. I just want to meet her."

The man's response was muffled through the closed hollow-core door. "No. Why are you even here, making all this ruckus. She didn't think of that man as her father, and she isn't gonna want to hear from you. I don't either. If you bought what you came for, you can go."

Her skin flushed with the adrenalin rush of truth, hearing it out loud for the first time. Ida didn't think of that man as her father. But he was her father. "If we're related, I deserve to meet her. If my father cheated on my mother, and if I have a half-sister, I deserve to know who she is."

"No one in this life deserves anything, lady. You don't deserve a six-figure job or free healthcare or anything else, and that includes access to my niece. If she wanted to talk to you, she probably would have already."

"Does she know about me?"

"I don't know if she does or not, and if I did, I wouldn't be telling you. If your father felt you deserved to know, he woulda told you. So why didn't he?"

First, Tamsin swallowed back the bitter truth, put in such blunt terms by a stranger. Then, she swallowed the temptation to bite back. "I can't answer that question. He's gone. So is my mother."

"Then maybe you're not supposed to know. If he didn't think it was any of your business, what makes you think it's mine?"

"It's blood. My blood. I get to decide if I want to get to know her or not."

The man's laugh was dry and raspy. The kind of laugh that can't be helped, even though it should. "No, you get to *ask*. There are two people in that conversation you want to have. You can't force her to talk to you. You can't force her to wanna be your friend. What do you want from her, anyway? Do you even know?"

How dare he make that demand of her. It was none of his business what questions she had for Ida. But this guy had answers. He had access. And she wanted both, so she had to play along.

She didn't know what to say to Ida when she found her, what questions to ask, but since when did not knowing the answers mean she should stop looking for them? She wanted to account for her father's time, to reconcile the man she knew with the man he was. To account for her mother's knowledge, what she knew and when. But most of all, she wanted to look Ida in the eye, to come face to face with the person she could have been if the tables had turned.

"If you want to know, can you open the door? Please? How do you know I'm not raiding your register out here."

"Because I can see you on the camera." The door knob turned, and the door inched open of its own accord. Tamsin pushed it open and stood at the threshold. It was a bold move, but she couldn't let one closed door stand between her and family.

"My father was gone a lot. My mother made excuses. Said he was at art shows or away for work. Whether she knew or not, I'll never know. It haunts my sister Margaret more than it haunts me, because she hung from my mother's apron strings. I was Daddy's little girl. I don't need to be Ida's best friend. I don't need to forge a life-long friendship and take Caribbean cruises together. But it would be nice to fill in that missing time. I know this isn't Ida's fault, and I'm not here to blame her. I'm not here to blame anybody, but I am here to find out whether or not my father, who I adored more than anything, who lied to my family, had any love for the child he hid from us, because that's the difference between his destruction and redemption, as far as I see it."

The man sat on a wooden chair, facing a desk covered in jars of liquid.

Brushes soaked in them. An ancient laptop sat open, fingerprints of paint on its case and keys. The side of his face was lit by the eerie blue glow of the screen, the shadows deepening the lines of his jowls and his forehead.

"You can't make her responsible for all that," he said. "You can't put responsibility on her or anybody else for the way you react to things. If you don't like the things you've learned, you have to learn to live with them. Keep scrolling, as they say on the internet." He turned back to his laptop, the screen reflected in his glasses.

"Twitter? Seriously? I'm begging you for help, and you're looking at Twitter?"

"It's more interesting to me than helping you. Why should I help you? What's in this for me, other than disrupting the life of someone I care about to satisfy someone who doesn't have Ida's best interest at heart?"

"Look, it took a lot for me to get this far. I don't travel. I'm afraid of travel. I lost my father, and four months later, I lost my soulmate. I locked myself in my house for half a decade. I cherish everything my partner breathed on, because it's all I have left in this world. Leaving the house to do anything more than the routine means leaving behind everything I need to survive, and I'm just trying to find my half-sister so I can ask her some questions. It would mean a lot to me if I could find a silver lining here. I don't want to disrupt Ida's life or cause anybody any pain, but if she would just be willing to talk to me, to tell me what she knows and remembers about my...our father, it would mean the world to me. It would mean the difference between knowing the truth, whatever that is, whatever it becomes, and spending the rest of my life coming to terms with losing every man who was ever important to me."

"That's got nothing to do with her."

"But that's what it means to me. Doesn't she deserve a chance to find out what the truth would mean to her?"

"Maybe. But she's not here."

"Did she move? Where did she move to?"

"She lives here. But she's away. Helping her dying mother."

"In Maine." Tamsin hadn't considered Ida's mother, the other woman. No wonder the people who knew Ida were protective of her. Her mother was dying, and the history of the father who abandoned her was being dredged up and trampled all over town. "I'm sorry."

"It's not yours to be sorry about."

"About the timing."

"You didn't know. Leave me your cell number, and I'll text or call you when Ida gets back."

"Really? You would do that? Are you going to call her and tell her about me? What will you say?" Tamsin hoisted her purse into her arms and dug into it, looking for a scrap of paper. A pen. Some way to pass her number on.

"Slow down. She's supposed to be back in a few days. By the weekend. I'm not going to worry her with this while she's up there. When she gets back, I'll go see her and tell her that someone is here who knew her father and wants to meet her. I'm not doing your work for you. And I'm not promising that she'll want to talk to you, either."

Tamsin took a pen from her purse and clicked it open. She wrote her number on the back of her receipt.

"Here." She held it out to him, and he took it between two fingers like a nurse accepting a germy tissue. She didn't trust him any more than he trusted her, but she had no choice. "Did she know him? Does she ever talk about him?"

"I'm not talking to you about any of this. I'm not getting in the middle. Her life is her business." He turned away from her and swirled a brush in a jar, kicking up a glittery whirlpool. "You lay low. Don't cause a stir in this town. If you start digging up old hurt, you won't get what you came for."

"Yes, sir. Trust me, I won't." She had plenty of reasons of her own to stay in the shadows. "I suppose I don't need to ask you to keep this confidential? Who I am and why I'm here?"

"You don't run the only art store in a town like this by breaking promises and telling other people's secrets." He waved the end of a paint brush, thinner dripping onto his desk. "If we're done here, I have a store to run."

"Of course. Thank you. I'm grateful."

Tamsin moved as silently as she could until she reached the door, and the bell announced her exit. The sun was beginning its slide to the west, casting shadows. She squinted at her watch. One thirty. She let her eyes adjust while she loaded art supplies into Owen's Cherokee before heading back to the motel.

There was no way to deny what was right in front of her. Ida was real. Not a stick figure artist from a distant town. Not a two-dimensional figment from the past. She was flesh and blood, and if Tamsin played by the rules, she would meet her.

CHAPTER TWELVE

The first time the phone rang, Tamsin assumed it was the auto repair shop, calling with a survey. She sent it to voicemail. Driving and talking on the phone was probably a punishable fine, and her luck hadn't been very good in Rockport. There was no sense flirting with the law. The second time the phone rang, she saw *Renee* flash across the screen just as she rejected the call.

Tamsin hadn't talked to Renee in years. Renee would wave out her car window when she passed Tamsin running on the street. Tamsin sent Christmas cards before she lost touch, like she had with everyone. One moment, their porch was full of friends. Coolers with beers and wine sat under the trees, and dozens of people ate at folding tables in the yard. Owen grilled steaks and chicken, and Tamsin made corn on the cob. The next moment, people knocked gently on the door and brought her casseroles and frozen trays with heating instructions on little notecards as if she could turn on an oven with any guarantee that in an hour, she'd be able to get up off the floor and turn it off. People came. They sat. They left. Eventually they stopped coming. Stopped emailing her with invitations that she had to decline with excuses.

Renee wasn't calling for a girls' night out. She wasn't calling because she had tickets to a football game. Something was definitely wrong.

Tamsin pulled up to the motel, cut the engine of Owen's SUV, and tugged the key from the ignition. Her phone dinged with a new voicemail just as the screen lit up with another call from Renee.

"Renee? Is everything okay? What's wrong?"

"Don't panic. You're not at home, right? Are you away?"

"I'm in Rockport. On vacation. What's going on?"

"Good for you! I mean, I hope it's fun. Anyway, I'm calling because the cops came by our house to see if we were okay, and they asked if we knew where you were."

"Why are the cops at your house? Why do they want to find me?"

"No, no. You're not in trouble." Renee paused. After a sigh, she fumbled with words, starting and stopping sentences. "I don't have all the information. It's pieces of things. They caught some guy breaking into houses on our road, and he squealed. Said your place was one of the ones he broke into. I guess the cops came to see if you were okay, but you weren't home, so one of them came next door to our place, because neighbors know sometimes, you know? I freaked out and rushed over here and tried to call you. It went to voicemail, so I was like, is she dead in the bathtub? The cops said the house was empty, and I called again, and here we are. I figured maybe you were at your sister's or something. I don't know."

"Are you at my house now?"

"I'm on your front porch with a cop. Two more are still inside. Your window next to the door is broken, and there's glass on the porch. The cop said the door was wide open when he got here."

"I'm four hours away in Rockport. I'll come home right now. Did they take everything? Is it a mess?" Everything she owned was sentimental. The dishes it took them forever to find. The silverware they bought on a spontaneous Target run. The alarm clock radios scattered throughout the house that she purchased from thrift stores after Owen died because she couldn't stand hearing his voice in her head but not in the hall.

"I haven't gone inside yet, but the cops are coming out now. You can talk to them if you want. It looks like your television might be gone. That corner table is empty."

"Okay. I can replace that. That's easy. I'll come home." But she needed to find Ida. Why couldn't this have happened a few days later? Or not at all?

"Tam, if you're on vacation, you should stay. What will you do about this now that can't be done in a few days? Look, I can totally take care of this. We've got tons of plywood in the shed. Mike and I can come over here and board it up. Do you have your homeowners insurance info? You can call them and schedule a window guy for when you get back."

"I'd rather use that place on Route 73. With the yellow sign?"

"Witton's?"

"That's it."

"Mike works with them sometimes. Why don't you let Mike and me board up this window and have someone from Witton's meet you here one night next week after work. I'll text you when I have a time. You just call insurance and get a claim number. Okay?"

"Are you sure? This is a huge imposition." It was more than Tamsin deserved after walking away from their friendship.

"It's not, though. You're my neighbor. And my friend. I'll go inside and clean up for you, so you don't have to come home to broken glass if you want."

"No!" An old friend wandering through her house, through her time capsule, judging her for what was missing and what remained was too much. "No. I'll clean it all up. But boarding up the window. That would be a huge help."

"Of course. I'll text you. And I'll see you when you get back. Come over and we'll have a cocktail or something. I miss hanging out with you."

"Same here."

The muffled voices of officers echoed on her porch and through the phone. "I'm gonna hand you off to an officer right quick, okay? Hold on. And I'll text you with more. You stay in Rockport and have a good time. Try to relax, and if you worry, don't hesitate to call."

"Okay. I—"

"Ms. Eliot?"

A man she didn't know had been in her house. Two cops had been in her house.

"Ms. Eliot?"

"Yes. Sorry."

"Officer Muir. M-U-I-R. I left a business card for you on the counter in the kitchen. Renee here said that she's going to board up the window for you and secure the house. She has a key?"

"Yes sir."

"That's a good neighbor to have. When you get home, go through the house and make a list of everything that's missing. Then give me a call. We've recovered many items from this guy already, and we'll do our best to reunite you with your stuff."

"How bad is it? Is there a lot of damage?" Tamsin fiddled with the brass-colored key to their house. The first thing they did after buying it was change the locks. Her chest clenched, and she rested her forehead on the steering wheel. They would have to be changed again. She wouldn't be able to use Owen's key to unlock the door anymore. "Is my Mini still there?"

"It is. The house looks okay. There are no holes in the walls or anything. A pillowcase is missing, so that's an indication that he took something. Looks like your tv is gone. A few items are tossed around, and he looked through your drawers."

Her underwear. The invasion of her personal privacy was nothing compared to knowing someone had been in her house, among Owen's things, breathing the air that she dare not disturb. Images flashed through her mind. His beer in the fridge, long expired but still more valuable to Tamsin than gold. The snow globes on her desk. His wallet still on his nightstand and her father above the fireplace. Tamsin switched hands so she wouldn't drop her phone, wiping her sweaty palm on her jeans.

"Is there a brass urn on the mantel?"

There were footsteps and a pause. "Yup."

"Oh thank God."

"Let me ask you. Did you have any weapons in the house?"

"Weapons?"

"Guns. Knives. In a drawer, maybe, or in a locked box?"

"No. We've never had guns or anything like that."

"That's good. Just call me or email me when you have a list. My card is on your kitchen counter. We'll keep you in the loop on the court case, if they want you to provide a statement. That kind of thing."

A statement. She couldn't let herself fall down a spiral of what-ifs and why-nots. If she did, she would end up in the car, back at home. She could miss her chance to meet Ida forever, and everything at home would still be a mess. She pulled her purse across the seat and onto her shoulder, put her feet on the ground and slammed the car door on her way back to her room.

She sat on the bed, the snow globe pin in her hand, running her finger over the smiling lobster. Owen would let Mike take care of it. He would have put on his running shoes, gone up the street, and eaten a lobster. Tamsin wanted comfort from someone, anyone, but all she had was a snow globe pin and an old green coat that belonged to someone she thought she knew. Mags would only tell her that it was all her fault for leaving in the first place. She would tell her that all these signs, the damaged car, the break-in, were the universe trying to tell her that she should go home and stop being…whatever Margaret would say. But what was waiting for her there? The home she shared with Owen had been shattered. Someone else had been in their world, gone through their stuff. Touched things for the first time since Owen died, and she couldn't even let herself mentally walk through the rooms because the thought of what could be missing was too much to bear.

Hungry, tired, with nothing to do but wait for a text from a man who ran the art store, she splashed water on her face. She sat on the closed lid of the toilet and sobbed into a washcloth for all that she'd lost. Things she could never replace and a sanctuary she could never restore. Renee would help, like she tried so hard to do in the days after Owen died, but no amount of trust in an old friend and neighbor could mend the guilt of not being home, near Owen's memory. But she'd come so far. She was so close. If she went home now, she wouldn't return. She would shut herself up in the farmhouse, closing herself off from the world, losing herself in the effort of reclaiming what was left, mending the wounded places. She needed some way to occupy her time until she could meet Ida. Just a few days.

Tamsin dropped the washcloth on the edge of the tub and washed her hands, splashed water on her face again. Her shaky breathing steadied. Housekeeping had tidied her nightstand and arranged the travel brochures on the shelf under the window. A map of Acadia National Park sat on the top of the stack.

Acadia. She had happy memories there, painting on rocky ledges by the water's edge. She could never relive them but she could revisit.

She shoved the map in her purse, threw her pajamas and underwear into the bag from the shoe store, grabbed her father's coat, and did the only thing she knew how to do when a situation was out of her control.

CHAPTER THIRTEEN

Daylight offered Tamsin only half an hour more as she pulled into a parking area on the south side of Acadia's Jordan Pond. It reminded her of walking with Owen in the woods behind the farmhouse and the candle that sat on her desk. He gave it to her for Christmas their first year in the house. Such a silly thing, but the smell of the pines reminded her of those early months of unpacking boxes and settling in. She hoped it was still there on her desk. It probably was. Who would steal a candle?

She grabbed her purse and sketch pad and crossed the street, stepping onto the boulders that looked out over the pond. The sun was low, almost below the trees. Crawling down the rocks, she found a flat spot by the water and dug into her purse for the plastic case of charcoals. It seemed a lifetime had passed since she bought them and cornered the owner of the art store in his office, demanding he introduce her to Ida.

Charcoals made easier work of shadows than the stub of a number two pencil. She struggled with perspective, with the scale of forest and the curved slopes of the distant hills, but she smudged the lines with the tip of her finger and contours took shape. With no napkin or tissue to clean her hand, she collected a leaf from the water pooled around the rocks. She thought of the painted leaves from her dream, and the past and present swirled together.

When Tamsin was little, she would paint alongside her father. Him in his green coat, her with her little watercolor books. The kind with the paint already on the pages. She would dip her brush into the ocean and paint characters from Saturday morning cartoons while her father painted landscapes and seascapes and little coastal buildings. She would grow frustrated that her cheap watercolors looked nothing like his oil paintings. He would tell her to be patient. Someday, she could paint with oil.

When she was older, she cast off cartoon watercolors and took on crossword puzzles in their wake. Sitting by the water with a cheap plastic neon push-point pencil, learning the inner workings of Will Shortz's mind and watching her father paint. It looked like nothing for days. Blobs of color with no definition. She asked how he knew what colors to put where. He said that trees and fishing shacks and fields of flowers revealed themselves as layers of color were added. It wasn't obvious to him at first where they needed to go. He just followed where the painting took him. But how he went from blank canvas to colors that stirred emotion was a different question.

He told her that art takes two people. The artist puts it on the canvas, but the viewer gives it meaning. Meaning comes from outside a work, not from within. But if he ever saw a tube of paint that said *Meaning Inside!* he would buy it in a heartbeat.

Charcoal may have made her work better, but a viewer would still find it meaningless. With the sun setting to her left, she packed her charcoals into their case and walked through the trees, back to Owen's car.

With half a tank of gas, she could get pretty far before she needed to refuel, but a ten hour round trip to make one blotchy sketch of a pond seemed stupid. Two days seemed more reasonable, even if paying for two hotel rooms didn't. In Rockport, she would only sit and watch the water and place a grievance value on everything she owned that could be missing or violated. She decided to try again the next day. On her way back to Route 1, she found a hotel next to a gas station with a rusted awning and flickering lights. It reminded her of an old video game, where zombies lurked in the shadows. She checked into a room and walked next door, light pulsing through three glass walls, making the inside look like a stormy fishbowl, and found two triangular sandwich halves in a plastic pyramid peel pack, some iced tea, and a bag of chips—a decent enough dinner to feed a traveler's spirit. Not willing to acclimate herself to the stuffy room, she ate on a bench next to a trash can outside the hotel entrance. A text came through from Renee, sent while she was out of range in the park. The window was boarded. The porch swept. Tamsin returned her text with a thanks.

She finished her chips and searched Owen's Cherokee for a napkin. He'd always kept napkins in the car to combat Tamsin's proclivity for spilling. She cleaned the grease from her hands on a thin brown towelette and something about the night, the earthy smell of a parking lot mixed with the carbon and exhaust fumes from passing cars reminded her of a trip with Owen. Eating at a diner with a giant smiley face on the sign. It was an old, renovated Waffle House. They were lost, it was raining, and she could have been miserable. She wanted to stay in the room, but Owen wanted to see the town, so they walked through the rain to the closest bar, and he cheered her up. Like he always did.

Tamsin closed the glove box, slammed the passenger door, and walked across the street to Helen's Tavern in search of a napkin and a drink. It was the kind of place Owen would have loved.

Helen's had a small lobby. It was more like a mudroom with light summer jackets hanging from plastic clothes hooks that were barely screwed into the cheap wood paneling. A thick cobweb fluttered above a cigarette machine, its chrome tarnished, and its plastic windows yellowed with time. It was a dark room. Dusty. And inside, the bar wasn't much brighter. Patrons sat in ones and twos, mostly on their own, sipping bottles and glasses. No radio, just the sound of passing cars, filtered by the windows. A ceiling fan tapped at the air, and every once in a while, someone would clear their throat or set a glass down a little too hard.

Tamsin took a cocktail napkin from the bar and put two empty seats between her and a man who cleaned his nails with a pocket knife. The woman behind the bar didn't appear to be in any hurry. She would get there in her own time. Tamsin took the snow globe pin from her back pocket and pushed at the post with her thumb. Someday she would break it free.

The bartender was at least ten years younger than Tamsin. She had one of those noses that seemed genetically predisposed for the nose ring at which she picked. She had a sleeve of tattoos up one arm, colorful and bunched together on her slender real estate. They were hard to discern. Tamsin would have asked, for the comfort of conversation, but the woman seemed to be somewhere else. She seemed to belong somewhere else. Somewhere other than behind a bar.

"'Cha havin'?"

Tamsin tried to catch her eye, but the woman wasn't interested. Instead, she eyed the bottles on a rack below the bar as if noticing them for the first time.

"Surprise me."

Tamsin got a cold stare and a lukewarm bottle of Corona with the cap still on. The guy two seats down reached over and snapped the cap off the beer.

"The bartender ain't much of a bartender here," he said. "She's more like an angry stepmom who can't cook and don't care 'cause she's got one foot out the door. Only thing is, this one ain't leaving any time soon."

"Well, that's okay. I didn't come here looking for Mary Poppins, so I'm good if she keeps the beer coming. Cold would be good. Maybe a lime. Do they do Coronas with lime in Maine?"

He shrugged. "Insider tip. The takeout cooler is colder than the broken cooler behind the bar. Buy a six pack to go and keep it down here by your feet." He tapped a bag with the toe of his boot. "My last beer will still be colder than your first."

"Wise advice. Thanks."

The man looked gruff. Thick arms growing like trunks from his sleeveless shirt. A stained hat. Harmless local enjoying a drink after a day of hard work. She wasn't there for conversation, so she turned her attention to the pin. The post moved in millimeters. Might have been her imagination.

"Whatcha got there?" Sweat ran down the bottle when the man let it fall to the bar. "It broken?"

"Yeah, I guess. Well, no. I found this pin, and it reminded me of something. Anyway, the post is bent, and I keep fiddling with it, trying to break it off. I probably shouldn't though. My luck it wouldn't break off clean, and I'd just make it worse."

The man reached down the bar and laid out his open palm. "Drop it here."

She closed it in her fist and shoved it back in her pocket, protective of the comfort it gave her and unwilling to let it go. "No, thanks. It's cool."

His hand still outstretched, he wiggled his fingers. "I got a Leatherman and strong hands. I'll get it off for ya. Got a file in the truck. If it leaves a hangnail, I can smooth it off when I'm done."

She waved him off. "I don't know. It's stupid." But it wasn't stupid. A snow globe showed up on the first real trip she'd taken without Owen. It was a sign. He was with her even if she couldn't hear him, and the post was destroying the pocket of her jeans. Maybe this stranger was Owen's way of polishing off a rough edge.

"Your call." He pulled his hand back and settled it on his beer.

She *could* trust him. What was the worst that could happen? Tamsin dug the pin from her pocket again and laid it on the bar between them. "Okay. Can you do it without breaking the enamel? I know it's dumb, but I really like it."

"Got yourself a lucky charm, here, huh?"

"Something like that."

He unclipped the tool from his belt and popped the post off with the pliers. "This do it?"

It was perfect. Nothing remained but a little gold-toned spot of solder on the back where the post once clung. He slid the pin down the bar, and she stopped it with her hand. "Thank you. Really. Can I buy you a drink?"

"Nah. I got cold ones down here." The paper bag crinkled with the tap of his boot. "Easiest thing I did all day."

"I bet."

The man's focus returned to his beer, and Tamsin accepted the solitude. She slipped the enameled snow globe with its smiling lobster in her back pocket, took her phone from her purse and checked her email. Twelve new. Most were spam and sales from retailers, but a few were from actual people. Mags said she was sorry for being angry on the phone. She's trying to be less judgmental, and she'd send all of Dad's paintings next week.

An email from Human Resources, forwarded by Marlow because she knew Tamsin didn't sync work email to her phone. Her presence was required at a mandatory company-wide meeting the next week. Marlow's note said, "It will be raining pink slips. You should be safe. Definitely come back in time for the meeting, though."

She thanked her coworker and tried to catch the bartender's eye. The woman was immersed in her own phone, her back to the bar and its patrons.

"Excuse me." When the woman looked up, Tamsin lifted her chin. "Can I get a six pack of Yeungling to go?"

It took a while for the request to register, for the bartender to budge and six bottles to find their way from the cooler to a carton and into a bag. No one seemed to care about the pace. They all slumped like travelers passing through, waiting for a train. At home, there would have been outrage, but here, at least inside this bar, they accepted what came, whatever the timetable. There were no hands on the bar, reaching in want. Just hard-working people in a good enough place.

She paid in cash, left a decent tip, and smiled her thanks to the man with the handy pocket tools. Back through the entry room with the bubbled-up carpet and ragged floor mat, and onto the curb. A few cars sped past, and she crossed the street to the hotel.

Some white plastic lawn chairs, scratched and mildewed, sat along the wall of the lobby. She dragged one to the window outside her hotel room, dropped the beer by her chair, and twisted the cap off the first one her fingers grasped. The days of reaching out to take Owen's beer cap were gone. The days of delaying the first sip for ritual cheers were in the past. She'd never felt so alone.

Owen's voice was faint and intermittent. He seemed a million miles away. Five hundred miles away, to be more exact, where he rested under an oak tree in a cemetery she chose on a whim because it was close to home and had a plot under a tree. What rested under that tree wasn't even Owen anymore. It hadn't been since the moment he died and something severed the bond between his spirit and his body. Since whatever invisible essence made him walk and snore and love and laugh rose up and dissipated into the air. She felt him there, in their home, all around her. He was in the steam coming off her coffee cup, floating in the sunlight that bled around the curtains, in the gaps between the floor boards, and in every breath she took.

Down the wall, at the other end of the hotel, car doors slammed. A couple jingled keys, fumbled with a door. A woman placed a hand on her girlfriend's back, and they giggled. Life and love go on. Her grandmother gave it all away. Packed what she could and sold what she couldn't. She boarded a plane for Luxembourg and lived out her days in Europe, seeing things she only dreamed of when her husband was alive. Her mother did much of the same. Tamsin hadn't waited to live, and now she couldn't let Owen die. She had no dream to chase as a last resort. She'd traveled to places she never even aspired to see. But looking into the paper bag at her feet, at the five unopened green glass bottles, she knew there were roads she still hadn't traveled, even if she'd been down all the ones that had been on her map.

Tamsin chugged her beer and opened a second. Third. Perhaps she was a beer girl now. Swigging from bottles in dark bars where it didn't matter how long it took the bartender to serve her. Giving local tips to strangers who pass through town when they slinked up to the bar and squinted through the dust with their tired traveler eyes. It's the kind of life Owen would have loved. What if she didn't go back to work? What if she just stayed in the cheap hotel forever? She could call that girl from high school. Eva? Evie? The one who was always posting about real estate on Facebook. She could put the house up for sale and live a simple life with truckers and travelers and families just passing through. She could totally change her past. Make up a whole new story. What if it really was that easy?

With the toss of a coin, she could have been Ida, growing up in Rockport. She could have been a man of few words at a bar in Maine who owned a multi-tool and fixed things for the sense of gratification. She could have been a passionless bartender who took the easy way out. But she was

Tamsin, for whom a perfect childhood became a perfect adulthood before it all fell apart. The constant effort to keep up the façade made her miss out on the simple joys of things just being good enough. That's what it would be like if Owen were in a chair next to her. All of this would be good enough, and that's what would have made it perfect.

Unearthing her father's flaws hadn't changed her view of her childhood. She had been happy then, and there was no reason to let those memories sour. There had been flaws with Owen, too. He had a habit of leaving the barn door open and raccoons got in. He saved way too many spiders for her sense of security. And he left too soon. But if she had known about the raccoons and spiders and that it would end in such devastating loss, she still would have plowed ahead. So why couldn't she live life now? Why couldn't she find joy? She'd been living on the inside of the painting, among the paint daubs and brush strokes, for so long that she forgot to step outside, to take a look at her life, and see the meaning in it. To see that it really was beautiful, but it wasn't finished yet. She'd shut herself inside for the comfort, to freeze time, but the world kept going without her.

With eighteen percent of the battery life left in her cell, she made a note in her calendar for the following weekend. To text Renee. To make a plan and get together. Then she replied to Mags. She knew she should tell Mags the truth about Rockport, about the drawing and Ida, but she still had more to learn. Besides, the small screen and autocorrect made long emails a challenge. She told Mags not to worry about it. Everything was forgiven. She would fly to Minnesota at Thanksgiving, and they could go through the paintings together. She proposed a cruise next summer to someplace tropical. Maybe Tamsin was a cruise girl now. Flip-flops and Coronas by the pool. It didn't sound so bad.

CHAPTER FOURTEEN

Charcoal wasn't Tamsin's medium. Shading and smudging and dirty fingers weren't her favorite artistic expression. She gave up on Jordan Pond and drove back to Rockport to an '80s soundtrack, where she unloaded the Cherokee at the motel and took colored pencils and the sketchpad to sit at the spot where she did Rainbow Brite watercolors as a kid. She found a place to sit among the empty lobster traps and hoped today was the day that Ida would return. If it wasn't, at least she could improve upon her mediocre drawing skills.

Her half-hearted sketches began as a displacement activity, a way to expend the energy and connect with her father. But now, working in layers, creating a framework of outlines and filling in with shading, giving careful attention to the depths of the shadows and gradients of color, she was doing it for herself and enjoying the art of improving. Holding it at arm's length, she could see Motif Number 1 taking shape, the wrong shade of red but the right perspective, perched on the dock across the water.

The wind picked up the scent of leather and wood. Ansel was behind her. She turned and held up her sketch.

"What do you think? Not bad, huh?"

"Not bad at all. I like the choice of green for the water."

"It's not done yet. I still have to shade it and—"

"No, I know. I wasn't being critical. I like it. The water does look green like that. The roof of the building reflected in the water. I like that you worked on the highlights, leaving that negative space. It's cool."

"I'm no expert. This is probably the eighth thing I've drawn since I was a kid." Tamsin dropped her sketch pad and stood, dusting off her jeans.

"I saw you down here and thought I'd bring you these." He swung his messenger bag around to the front and pulled out a manila folder. "I didn't see you yesterday, so I carried them around with me."

He didn't ask where she was, so she didn't offer. She didn't want to tell him about the break-in at home, and it would open floodgates she'd managed to keep closed. But she didn't want to lie, either, because she needed the good karma. She took the folder.

"What are these?"

"Those are copies of old deeds to the property on North Road."

Within the folder were color copies of typed documents and yellowed records, some handwritten in old fountain pen. "Oh my gosh! These are amazing." She closed the folder on her lap. "I have to pay you for these."

"Don't worry about it. Consider it a gift."

"But the form I signed said copies cost ten cents each."

"I took care of it." He turned his messenger bag around. "Nice sketchpad. Did you stop by the art store on Broadway? The guy who runs the place is really nice."

"He is. Yeah." She'd promised to lay low, not to raise a fuss. Creating a direct link between her and the art shop probably wasn't the smoothest way to divert attention from her search for Ida. She opted for a change of topic. "Are you open today? Can I come by and do some research?"

"Sure. I'm heading back from lunch now. It would be great to have you there." The corners of his eyes lifted when he smiled. The sun picked up the green in his eyes, and her stomach twisted into a knot. She grounded herself and shoved her hands in her back pockets, feeling for the pin.

"I can head up in a few. I'll put this stuff in my room and grab something to eat."

* * *

"It's just me! Tamsin." She emerged from the hallway into the Historical Society and moved around the counter, dropping her purse in the empty seat at the head of the table before heading to the card catalog.

Ansel called from the back. "Anything specific you want to look up?"

Tamsin was already thumbing through the yellowed cards, looking for her father, last name first. "I thought I'd look up my dad. He painted so much around here. Maybe there's some information on him and his art. Old art shows. That kind of thing."

"You could always check with the Arts Alliance, too."

A horrible idea. Knowing that her father met Ida's mother through the Arts Alliance made it feel less like a place for historic research and more like a battleground. But she couldn't tell Ansel that. "I could, I guess. Maybe when I've exhausted this place."

"You could never exhaust this place." Ansel was beside her, that look in his eyes, like he could see things ordinary people couldn't. She let her smile stay, but she couldn't bear the weight of his eyes, keeping hers fixed on the card catalog.

"You want to write the list for me as I go?"

He took a form from the stack and wrote down the file numbers as she called them out. When the form was full, he brought the folders, and she spread them out on the tables, looking through them, one by one. There were articles about his paintings in the local newspaper, artist profiles that filled in space between the community calendar and movie showtimes in Gloucester. His photograph appeared in a series from gallery showings in

1984. A black-and-white photo of women in boxy dresses and men in sweaters and jackets eating food from small plates. They all wore that smile, as if they were grateful for free crudités but desperate to get on with the wine. She barely recognized her father, he looked so stiff. He was wearing his green coat with its brown corduroy collar.

There were opinion pieces he'd written about the quality of the roads and photographs from a community garden of her father planting vegetables with other people from town. Her father sitting at an easel at the end of T-Wharf. He was teaching an art class, and the students faced Motif Number 1 like seagulls in a fast food parking lot, bracing against the wind and waiting for french fries.

Tamsin sorted the newspaper clippings and spread a dozen on the table. Ten grainy, black-and-white pictures of her father with people from town. The tall brunette she knew to be Ida's mother was in every one. In the background at the gallery, Ida's mother stood, her eyes fixed on Tamsin's father. Next to him at the community garden, their spades poised in ceremony above dry earth. He leaned over her shoulder on the Tuna Wharf, pointing out the flaws in her work. This woman was the flaw in Tamsin's childhood. She was the flaw that Margaret knew about all along. That Tamsin had denied. The woman who brought her mother anguish. The woman who lay dying in Maine, the mother of her half-sister.

"How's it going?"

Ansel stood over her shoulder, examining the newspaper clippings and pouring that scent over her. "Good, I guess. Just articles. Pictures."

"This is your father?"

"Mm-hmm." She stacked the newspaper clippings and returned them to their folder. Ansel slid one to the side and leaned close. Close enough for her to feel his breath in her hair. When he lifted the grainy photo from the art gallery and took a closer look, Tamsin leaned away.

"Who's this woman?"

"I don't know. There are no captions." She tugged the scrap of newspaper from his hand and returned it to the folder with the rest.

"She was in a few of those."

"Some local artist, I'm sure. It was all art shows and community stuff. Small network, I suppose."

"I could look these other people up for you, if you want. Maybe they live here and have memories of your father? You could go out for coffee and visit with a few of them before you leave town."

Tamsin stacked the papers. "Nah. I don't think I'll be here long enough to meet with anybody. That's a great idea for next time, though." She said it, though she knew there wouldn't be a next time.

Ansel took the folders, held them in his arms. He leaned back against the table and looked down at her. This time, she had no excuse. No card catalog to turn to. She let his eyes find hers.

"So, I'm about ready to lock up. Done here for the day. You want dinner? There's a fish and chips place down at Tuna Wharf. I could go for something greasy. Plus, the weather's starting to turn, and it'd be nice to get some fries with malt vinegar before it stops feeling like summer. You want in?" He nudged her knee with his and an electric shock made its way to her ears. She tugged at a warming ear lobe. Going along was impulsive, she knew, but she shot out of her chair and slung her purse over her shoulder.

"Absolutely. You lead the way."

CHAPTER FIFTEEN

Tuna Wharf was a short, narrow street that ended at a concrete pier. It was lined with shops huddled against each other, sharing weathered buildings. Tamsin walked beside Ansel, who matched her pace. She kept her fisted hand in her pocket, the pin against her knuckle. It felt as awkward as it probably looked, but she liked the feeling of her nails digging into her palm. It kept her grounded. She hadn't walked next to a man since Owen. Since the last time they walked from the grocery store to their car, arms loaded with grocery bags for a week of meals Tamsin wouldn't make. She smiled at the memory of it, a little surprised that the recollection didn't hurt, and stopped when Ansel motioned to a window next to a painted plywood fish. A woman inside nodded, and he nodded back. A casual acknowledgement of familiarity that reminded Tamsin of her outsider status.

"Two please," he said at the closed plexiglass window. She nodded again and turned away. A seagull picked french fried carbs from the sidewalk and stayed close. There would always be more.

Ansel turned to her, and she felt her stomach clench, a spasmed response to a question he hadn't asked yet, and she hadn't prepared for.

He shoved his hands into his back pockets. "Have you been past the house yet?"

"No. I haven't. Crazy, I know. It's right over there. I just haven't been by."

"Here's an idea—and you can say no—let's walk past the house and take this back to my place. I have a view of Back Harbor that should cost way more than it does."

She shouldn't go back to his place. The whole evening would be full of awkward near touches and attempts to make distance without seeming cold. The pin pressed into her knuckle, urging her to say no, to make an excuse about an early morning or a late night. But she enjoyed talking to Ansel. She even enjoyed silence with him. Despite those probing green eyes, he never gave off an air of expectation, like he was waiting for her to reveal more of herself than she wanted to give. And he knew nothing of Owen or her losses. He didn't offer her sympathy or coat his words with pity. He knew nothing about the layer of grief she wore like a second skin. Talking to him was a distraction from living with so much pain, and in a moment of personal honesty in her quest for truth she knew that she wanted, she needed that distraction. "Sounds great. You think Connor would sell me some wine if we stop by?"

"Well, good news. You won't have to find out. There's plenty at my place."

The plexiglass slid open, and an arm presented two white paper bags. Grease already bled through one corner. Ansel paid with cash and dismissed his change with a wave.

"You don't have to buy mine. Let me pay you back." Tamsin shoved a hand in her purse, her hand on her wallet. She'd been racking up emotional debt with Ansel, finding comfort in little kindnesses she didn't know how to repay, but he'd already started to make his way back to the main road.

"It's my treat."

The streets were empty. No cars. The distant jingle of a dog's tags came from a woman and her pet a block away. She followed him across the street and onto North Road, a little L-shaped lane lined with two-story cottages and haunted by a past Tamsin wasn't prepared to face. The house on the corner with the poodle that barked and nipped at their heels and a little wooden fence where she leaned her bike while tending to Margaret's skinned knee. Leaning against the wood-plank siding, drinking colored sugar water that feigned to be juice from little plastic barrels. Her father had to shove the straw through the thick foil cap. Walking to Dock Square at dusk to watch the fireworks on the Fourth of July, squeezing her father's hand with each big boom while her heart skipped a beat. It all seemed so carefree. And oblivious.

Ansel tucked their fish and chips in his messenger bag. "Has it changed since you were a kid?"

"In some ways. Everything's taller. I remember some parts of Rockport more than others. There used to be an ice cream place at the end of the street. Everybody sells that soft serve yogurt now. They had those cake cones with the normal hard ice cream you had to scoop with a heated spoon."

"That's the best ice cream."

"I know, right? Vanilla with fudge ripple."

"Strawberry."

"And there were a few other stores that are gone now or moved. There was a fudge place down here. You could smell it some mornings."

"You only came here for the summers?"

"Yeah. We lived in Pennsylvania. I still do. But my sister and I spent our summers here, usually with my parents, but sometimes it was just us and our grandparents. Rockport was different then, but I guess the whole world has changed. Back then, we left the house after breakfast and ran all over the town, up around the bend to Rock Beach. That's what we called it. You can't let kids run free like that now. There's too much evil in the world. Anyway, we'd go home for the school year. I haven't been here for...maybe twenty-five years or so."

"What about the town? Does it still feel the same?"

"No. Maybe it was a little truer to itself then. I feel like it's made an industry of being a small town. It had an organic feel back then that they've had to work to hold onto. That's not a bad thing, to hold onto your roots. Maybe it just felt that way because I was younger. The paint fade was legitimate paint fade because these were summer homes and people had less money."

"You know the story of Motif, right? The color red?"

"That they had to find a company to custom make that shade of red after they rebuilt it? Yeah. But would you have it any other way? I wouldn't. That's what it should look like. It feels right."

"It does. It feels like home to me."

They turned the corner, and there it was. Ahead, on the right. The house wasn't as large as she remembered. Narrow. Two stories, like the rest. Still green but weathered in all the right ways. Everything in Rockport looked older than its years, battered by time, by wind and water, even in the places where it was manufactured. Its patchwork slate roof had been replaced. The mailbox was new, and the lupine was gone, replaced by golden coneflowers.

There were no street lights, and the setting sun threw deep shadows on the street. Ansel stepped into them, out of her view.

"It's not much different than I remember." She looked back at him and reached into her purse for a folded paper, a copy of an old photograph from the late sixties. Folding back the white border on one edge and holding it up, she closed one eye, lining the edges of her grandparents' world with a new reality. The windows had changed. The door was the same, but the trim had been replaced. The wood-framed screen door was gone. Her heart sank; she could still hear the slap of the door when it closed.

She folded the picture and put it back into her purse before she got carried away with emotion. "We should go. Before dinner gets cold."

"Was it like you remembered?"

She shrugged. "I know it's because I was so much smaller. Perspective and all. But sometimes I think it's because I build these places up in my mind."

"People, too. Time is like looking through binoculars sometimes."

Tamsin buried the past, covered it with a deep breath of sweet air. "I forgot to ask. Cod or haddock?"

"Cod."

"Which is your favorite?"

"Cod. Definitely cod."

"I've always thought haddock, but they're both delicious."

Ansel's apartment was at the top of a flight of stairs, the unfinished wood a reminder of brutal weather that beat them down so fast and so often that they weren't worth painting. He lived behind a gray metal door with the letter C on it that opened on the short end of a living room and dining room. Immaculate and monochrome. A sofa faced a small television and a wall of bookshelves wrapped around his bedroom door. Across from his bedroom sat the kitchen, no bigger than a closet. Behind his modest dining room table was a sliding glass door that opened to a balcony overlooking the harbor.

There, surrounded by his books and art, Tamsin lost track of the risk. She forgot about the sleepless night she sought to avoid, the obligation to Owen's memory she carried within her like a stone. The sound of the ocean breaking against the boulders came through the open sliding glass door, and

Tamsin let go of it all, lost in Ansel's retellings of Rockport's histories and tales of winters that encased the town in ice.

Fish and chips and a bottle of wine later, Ansel scraped the crumbs into the trash. Plates and glasses clinked together when he closed the dishwasher. Tamsin was at the back door, lost on the sea among the buoys and street lights that bobbed on the water. A cold October breeze pushed through the screen.

"What's to the right? Those little lights."

Ansel filled the space next to her with leather and wood and hand soap. "There are piers over there. Rocks."

"It must be nice to fall asleep to the sound of this."

"You tune it out. Unless the weather's bad, I don't even hear it anymore. But the beauty of it just becomes a part of your life after a while. I can't imagine living anywhere else."

"When I was here as a kid, I knew when the tide came and went. When there'd be more or less beach and more exposed rocks. You just got used to the coming and going of the water. It's funny to think that's just been happening day after day since then, and that this is the same water and those are the same rocks. Maybe a little more weathered, but they're still the same."

"I think about that sometimes. How every wave takes something away from the rocks and carries it out to the ocean."

The tide had worn away parts of Tamsin, taking away rough, sharp edges. Breaking off pieces—the hurt from Owen and the tension of work and the anxiety of finding Ida—and carrying them out to sea until they were specks on the horizon, indiscernible from passing ships. And at her feet, with each lap at the land, the tide deposited its weathered pebbles, the smoothed-over shrapnel from a billion years of bedrock and rubble. The tide pushed and pulled on her perspective. So many people before her had loved and lost, had dug through boulder and fought through lava to find relief and accept the pleasures of living. Why couldn't she roll with the tides like them? Tamsin filled her lungs with cool air and accepted what the tide offered. She turned her back to the ocean, slid between Ansel and the door, and reached for his hand.

"I didn't ask you here for this," he said.

"I want it anyway."

"Are you sure?"

"Stop talking."

Ansel stepped into the space between them, making an offering of his own. His hands on her back, pulling her in.

"Ansel." His name escaped with her breath.

Tamsin clawed away the layers, let herself be tumbled ashore on his waves. She was the storm eroding the rocks, dragging sand from the shore. She took, and he gave.

When nothing was left but the sound of the water against the rocks outside, she let the tide recede. There was terror in the quiet. An urgency to run from the shame of what she had done, using Ansel to fill a need.

CHAPTER SIXTEEN

Owen slept facing the door. Always. Each morning, Tamsin woke with the alarm and reached out a hand to touch his back, and he would stir. They'd pad down the stairs for coffee. But one morning she reached out a hand and touched his back, and he didn't wake, and it was nothing like the movies. The sound didn't drop out of the scene. No one screamed. Birds chirped outside the window and a distant truck bumped through a pothole.

There was something about the way his body rested that seemed lifeless. His back didn't rise and fall with his breath. His shirt was cool. The warmth from his body didn't seep through to her hand.

That's when her ears started to ring. She'd never seen a lifeless body before. Not one that wasn't in a coffin at a funeral, posed in an unnatural dissolution. It didn't dawn on her to get out of bed, to call someone. She lay there, studying the hair on the back of his head, the way it fell on his pillow. The seam of his shirt sleeve rounding his shoulder. It was a shirt he bought at a national park. She forgot which one. It was his favorite sleep shirt. She touched the bottom of his foot with the top of hers, tucked her knees behind his, curled up against his back. The tears began when the space between them didn't grow warm from her embrace.

There would be so much to do. People to call. Things to plan.

Paperwork. Everything involved paperwork. But as long as she lay in bed, her cheek against his sleep shirt, all of that would be delayed, and she could pretend he was still asleep, and he would wake like he always did, and they would have coffee and get ready for their day, and he would help her find her keys, because she could never find her keys. There were eight cups of coffee in the coffee pot downstairs, and she couldn't drink them alone. Owen. She choked out his name, and he didn't say hers.

Tamsin turned and faced her side of the bed. She sat up just in time to grab the trashcan and spill the contents of her stomach. They'd had shrimp the night before. Everything had been so normal. Dinner. Drinks on the porch. She'd never eat shrimp again.

One ray of light shot around the edge of the blinds and bits of lint from the blanket swirled in it. What if bits of Owen's spirit, the essence that animated the muscles and made him laugh, was swirling in the air with it. Could she gather it up in a net? Grab it in her fist? Shove it back into him? Maybe that's really how CPR worked. Bits of escaped life pushed back in.

Stumbling around the bed, wobbling on knees that weren't a part of her, she got a good look at his face. No. CPR wouldn't help. The taught muscles that made up his smiles and frowns had slackened. His lips were bluish.

Back around the bed for her cell phone. She dialed 911.

"It's not an emergency so much as I need the coroner, I guess. My boyfriend died in the night. No, I don't think CPR will help. Or an ambulance, unless that's what you send for things like this. It's a long driveway off Route 73. House number 4508. I'll unlock the doors. What? No, he didn't overdose. He barely even drank. He was healthy. He was fine yesterday. One glass of wine. Maybe two. No, there's no one I can call. No one can come and wait with me. You don't have to stay on the phone with me. You can go. I'll wait for them to get here. Thanks."

Two men came. A woman followed. Tamsin waited in the hallway, obsessing over the walls in a disembodied sort of way. She could never live with a ding in the wall if the gurney did any damage as they took Owen from their house. She'd look at it all the time and be stuck somewhere between wanting it gone but cherishing it as the last mark he left on earth. On their house. On her. It would be horrible, tacky to ask them to be careful, so she stood in the middle of the kitchen and listened for the front door to close. The doors of their van to slide shut. The engine to start. Taking Owen on his first car ride toward nothing. Away.

The woman talked to her and gave her papers. Asked questions about a funeral home. Owen had no plans. None Tamsin knew of. But she'd look in the filing cabinet. The funeral home between their house and the closest town, North Wales, would be good enough. Owen's parents were gone, and he was an only child, so it was only the two of them and some friends. And his work. The woman suggested she call his work and her family. She put off calling her mother and sister. She didn't need their brand of condolences.

Owen had password locked his phone, and it took forever to unlock it. It was the year they bought the house. All she had to do was touch the little circle icon in his contacts and call his work, but she had no idea who would answer or what she was supposed to say. Kyle answered. Owen mentioned Kyle often, but she'd never met him, until that day. Weeks later, Tamsin wouldn't be able to recall her own words, what she spit out, if it even made sense. But she would never forget how angry she was at the questions he fumbled through, as if he had any right to make her answer questions. Once the world knew Owen was gone, it would be real. The grief would be unavoidable. Irreversible. Kyle said he would bring Owen's things from work to the house, Human Resources had the address. He would leave them on the porch unless she welcomed company. He sounded shocked. Saddened. In need of comfort. It was the first of many angry moments, being called upon to soothe the recipient of the news. As if telling the woman who checked them out at the grocery store that Owen wasn't sick but dead was more of a strain on her than it was for Tamsin. He was so young.

Yes, she knew.

Or the guy they always saw gardening when they went out for a run. Such a shame.

Yes, she knew.

Managing their reactions would become a burden.

Kyle came over and placed some calls. His wife had died years before. He brought bagels and told Tamsin to eat. He told her stories about the help he needed when his wife passed, and she'd always be grateful Kyle was there, an impartial figure. Opposite poles to Owen's life, the home, the work. Kyle found important things in the filing cabinet and set them aside. He sat with her while she posted things on Owen's social media accounts, asking the internet for time and space. She scrolled through Owen's texts and sent a few replies to his banter. *This is Tamsin, please give me a call.* Five calls in, she had the script down. Kyle made a list of accounts to close. The bank. The car loan. And all the while, Tamsin's father looked down from the brass urn on the mantel where he'd been for four months. She had no regrets, except that she hadn't married Owen. She hadn't given him the one thing he asked for, as simple as it was, because she'd been too afraid to break a relationship that wasn't broken. Together, they'd achieved everything they set out to do. Their house, their lifestyle. But in the end, she was even lonelier than her grandmother and her mother because she had no dreams to keep her warm.

There were calls and visits for a while. Old friends brought casseroles, and their children teetered on the area rugs Tamsin and Owen had bought at a nameless store in the mall. People came by, and she'd sit with them on the porch, keeping them at arm's length. Tea and lemonade. Renee walked over and asked Tamsin if she'd like help cleaning out the closets. Tamsin declined. That was the last time they spoke in person.

There were invitations by phone. By email. Come for dinner this weekend. Stop on your way home from work on Thursdays for a walk through the park. Tamsin declined for a while. Then she ignored the voicemails and emails and texts. Eventually, the invitations stopped coming. That's when she bought the alarm clock radios with their faux wood cases and their large red digits. She found the first one at a thrift shop, and it reminded her of college. She put it in the dining room so there'd be a sound in the house to drown out the pops and creaks that told her she was alone in an old house. She bought another for the bathroom, the basement, the living room. She bought seven of them one weekend and set them all to oldies stations and AM radio. Songs out of tune and from another time.

She never spent another night in that bedroom, sleeping in the guest room from then on. She rarely stepped foot in the room at all. Owen's pillow still had the depression where his head had been. All of his shirts just as they were. His dirty laundry still in the basket where he had left it. Throughout the house, his presence was just as it had always been. His toothbrush and razor. His soap in the dish and his shampoo in the shower. Boots by the door.

CHAPTER SEVENTEEN

Ansel leaned off the edge of the bed, reaching for the top sheet. Tamsin touched the curve of his shoulder, the round of his back. His skin was warm, and her mouth watered and soured, a warning that her stomach contents were next. It wasn't bad dinner or too much wine. It was a million sorrows swarming like bees and seeking release.

"I should go," she said.

"No. Don't." He rolled back to her with the sheet, pulled her close and buried his face in her hair. "You smell wonderful."

Tamsin pulled away and reached down for her jeans. "This isn't fair, what I did to you."

"What you did to me? What did you do?"

"I took. I was in this for me, and I shouldn't have used you like this." One leg of her jeans was turned inside out. She shook it free.

"It felt pretty mutual to me. If it felt a little more one sided to you, then I was happy to give. And I'd do it again."

"It isn't supposed to be this way. It should be—" She climbed out of bed and found her bra and T-shirt in a puddle in the doorway.

"Loud? Rough? What should it be that it wasn't?"

"I should be able to look at you, and I can't. It should be emotional and deep or something. And I shouldn't be somewhere else. I shouldn't be thinking about Owen."

Ansel rolled onto his side and propped his head in his hand. "Who's Owen?"

Her socks were impossible to find. She gave up and sat on the edge of the bed, her back to Ansel, willing her stomach to settle. Unwilling to face him or what she had done. "Please don't say his name."

"Is he your husband? Your boyfriend? He was in the room, right? In your mind. So why can't we talk about him?" He reached out to touch her, and she twisted away, looking beneath the bed for her socks. "You're married, aren't you?"

"We were never married. And he's gone. He died. He's not here anymore."

"Christ. Tamsin. I'm so sorry. You really should have told me that."

She wiped her sweaty palms on her knees. "Why? Why is he any of your business? Why can't I have one thing that doesn't involve being a grieving—" She stood and spun. Those damn socks. "I'm not even a widow. There isn't even a name for what I am."

"How long ago did you lose him?"

"Five years. Is there anything else you need to know, or do I still get to have some privacy?"

Ansel piled the pillows behind his back and sat up. "I'm sorry. You're right. You have the right to keep private anything you want. It's not like we have a commitment here. There are no terms. I just wish I knew. I wish I had the chance to be more sensitive, maybe. I could have done things differently."

"How? By treating me like I'm damaged?"

"No, by being with you, wherever you were in your head. I had no idea that I was stepping up to his vacancy sign."

"Vacancy? I didn't go looking for you. For this. There's no vacancy." Tamsin's face was hot. She tried to cool down with a slow exhale. "This is exactly what I mean. It's not possible to talk about this with you, and I just don't want to get into it." Owen never put up a vacancy sign. He didn't choose to leave, and she hadn't let him go. She swallowed back the anger at herself for losing touch with him, for caving to a carnal need in search of comfort. She would have told Ansel he was wrong, but she knew he was right. He had deserved to know. She put her hands in her back pockets and fixed her eyes across the bed, on the frayed strands of tan carpet where the wall met the floor. "This is a huge mistake."

"Okay. I'm sorry. That's a horrible analogy. Not vacancy." Ansel reached for his pants. "Band-Aid. I didn't know I was ripping off a Band-Aid. I'm sorry. I should have felt that something was raw with you. I'm doing a terrible job of communicating right now. I'm not wearing any clothes, and you're calling me a mistake, so I feel a little vulnerable."

She scanned the room and her memory, desperately hoping for her socks. She needed to leave before she made things worse. "You're not a mistake. This was a mistake. I'm embarrassed and stressed out right now, and I feel like I used you."

"You didn't. You didn't manipulate me. I was here with you. Look, I'm just trying to get back to the playful Tamsin from earlier. I'd love to lie here with you and talk about this."

"I can't. I wish I could. I wish I was that person but I'm not. I can't. I shouldn't."

"Can't and shouldn't aren't the same thing."

"I know. But they both apply." Tamsin threw her hand up in surrender. "Do you see my socks anywhere?"

"No, I don't. And no, they don't both apply. Maybe you can't stay. That's one thing. But there's no reason we shouldn't have been together.

JENNIFER M. LANE

There's nothing to be ashamed of. It's been years, right? You're allowed to have this. You're allowed to feel something with me, even if it's only physical. The only thing you owe me or yourself is honesty. Sometimes it's like that, one person takes a little more than the other, but wouldn't you rather look me in the eye and know I give willingly? Know that you're safe. Know that you're cared for?"

"I can't. That sounds great, like some Netflix show where it all works out, but I can't. And it isn't fair. To you or me. To the truth I need to find. To the person I'm on my way to being."

"I understand."

Through the open bedroom door, across the living room, Tamsin saw a sock beyond the coffee table, lying on the sofa where she'd first taken him captive. Maybe she wasn't a flip-flops and Corona girl after all. "Thank you for understanding. I don't want to hurt you. I wish that I could relax with you and enjoy this moment as much as I enjoyed the last hour. It's just not that easy."

"I know. I wish things were different for you. I hope I get another chance."

She swore he wouldn't.

CHAPTER EIGHTEEN

The shower in Tamsin's motel room was tiled with tan, speckled squares. The same eighties tile that was in the first apartment she rented with Owen. The grout had been brown with mildew, so she'd dug it out with a spackle knife, and Owen regrouted it while she was at a hair appointment. The motel shower, however, had perfect, clean, white lines of grout. Shampoo swirled down the drain, bubbles clinging to the gritty lines of nonslip tread, before they vanished behind a wall of tears, and she went to her knees, letting it all go.

The first few days after Owen died, she'd sat on the sofa, listening to the sounds of the house. The pops and creaks of hardwood floors and the click of the thermostat on the air conditioner that Owen had placed in the window of the upstairs office. The motor would start, and the fan would whir. Little bird feet would click on the window sills, and Tamsin sat. Listening for all the sounds she'd never hear again. His slippers coming down the stairs. The sound of water in the shower and the opening and closing of the medicine cabinet door before he shaved.

The gritty lines of nonskid tape dug into her knees as she scrubbed at every inch of her skin, scraping at the guilt and shame. She knew guilt and shame well, old friends who'd arrive when she lost Owen in the rush of life with their heavy baggage. Tamsin deserved everything they brought with them. She deserved the break-in for being so blind, for hiding the truth from everyone. From her sister, herself. The universe gave her enough of the perfect life only to take it away because it found her undeserving. Had she seen it all along, her father's infidelity? Did she sense it deep down and whitewash it with lies? She deserved the broken glass, the shattered windows, the stolen pieces. Nothing that thief could do would even begin to make her pay for hiding from reality, from lying to herself and everyone around her so she didn't have to face the truth. She'd betrayed Owen's memory, pushed everyone away, lived in isolation under the blanket of lies she justified as self-protection. Mags was right. She was selfish. And she would have given anything to hear Owen tell her she was loved.

Looking for comfort with Ansel wasn't fair to him, or to herself. No amount of soap and hot water could wash away the shame of pushing Owen away and clinging to Ansel. She should have anticipated the pain it would bring to both of them. And he was right. He did deserve to know about the third person in the room. She'd deceived him, and he didn't deserve that. He deserved the affection of someone who was free to live, and Tamsin had lost her freedom to live along with Owen.

Why was it so hard to move on? Lots of people heal, incorporate the past into their lives and move on with a new partner. Tamsin couldn't even bring herself to reorganize the kitchen. She always thought a day would come when everything would be okay. She would wake up and be one of those people who'd loved, lost, and lived. But the thought of it brought back the familiar guilt and shame, reminding her that she'd have to let go of the perfect life they shared and that nothing the future could bring would be half as good as where she'd been. Letting go of Owen wasn't an option. There had to be another way.

Searching for comfort in the past had only shown her how blind she was, how desperately she'd clung to perfection, even when it wasn't there. Rockport had been a shrine to her childhood, but returning to it, all she saw were the lies. Lies her family told her. Lies she chose not to believe. Lies she'd told herself. Lies Margaret had seen all along. If she really wanted to live, she would have to stop pretending that everything had been so perfect. All those lies were keeping her from finding comfort. She would have to stop holding onto a perfect past that didn't exist. She would have to accept the truth alongside the lies, that her family wasn't what she thought and that Owen wasn't here to live life alongside her. Then, maybe, the universe would give her something new to hope for.

Something to hope for.

The tiny bar of soap was gone. Dissolved. Flaked into tiny chips and washed down the drain. She turned off the water and grabbed a towel from the rack above the toilet. She dried off her reddened skin and pulled on her pajamas before seeking physical comfort in the soft bed with fresh sheets. What the room lacked in space it more than made up for with a plush mattress.

With her phone plugged in next to the bed, Tamsin opened the photos folder in cloud storage. A few weeks after Owen died, during a lull at work, she'd made an album and named it *Owen*. She put every photo of them into it, pictures of their adventures and the places they'd seen. She hadn't opened that album since the day she made it. Scrolling through photos, she found plenty of imperfections. The times they missed their destination because Owen hated maps and relied on his sense of direction, which was often misguided. They always got by and made do, which was half of the fun, letting go of their loose plans to make room for the bumps in the road. Maybe it wouldn't be so bad to take a detour, to let the road unfold ahead of her and lead her somewhere new.

There had been plenty of blemishes, all of them beautiful. And there'd been plenty of letting go before Owen died. She closed out of the apps and placed the phone back on the nightstand, knowing that if the roles had been reversed, if she were the one who had died, Owen would have let go. She would have wanted him to.

CHAPTER NINETEEN

Tamsin woke next to her phone with another splitting headache. She downed two Advil with the dredges of a bottle of water and straightened her room while they took effect, packing her dirty laundry into her suitcase. Cleaning the room did nothing for her throbbing head, though it helped a little with the tangled threads of her unfurling tapestry. Sitting on the edge of the bed with her bags at her feet, she tidied the nightstand, placing the envelope with Ida's drawing into her purse. But the pin she couldn't let go of. Running her thumb over the enamel, feeling the raised metal lines that separated the lobster from the snow, she couldn't help but wonder if this was the last snow globe she had left.

At home, on her desk, sat two of her favorites, gifts from Owen. Were they gone now? Smashed or stolen? She zipped the pin in her wallet, where it rested with her change, and let go of the urge to rush home, to assess the damage and fall back into comforting isolation. Going home wouldn't change the outcome. It would only drive her further from the truth, and the truth was too important to leave behind.

In her father's coat, with her painting supplies, two canvases, and a cup of weak coffee from the motel lobby, Tamsin walked to Tuna Wharf. A mist rose off the bay and across the Neck, obscuring the back side of the red fishing shack. She found a lawn chair on the dock, where she got comfortable enough to outline in pencil her view of Motif and the boats next to it, her canvas propped on empty lobster traps. Content with perspective and scale, she mixed paints with a palette knife and began to work, cleaning her brush in a plastic cup from the convenience store that she filled with water from the Gulf of Maine.

Rockport had only begun to stir. Around her, seagulls fought for airspace, crying out and staking claim to rocks and fish. Shop owners unlocked doors, and delivery trucks inched down the narrow street. She welcomed the arrival of life. The calls of impatient birds and the lapping of the sea against the rocks hadn't been distraction enough to keep her emotions buried. Anger with Ansel for thinking Owen had left a vacancy that anyone could fill and at herself for not letting go. Wishing she could confront her own isolation, rail against it. The night before had been a cry for help, a passionate attempt at sweet release, but in the end, she was left with regret for leaving, for not having the difficult conversation that she owed to Ansel and herself.

Using a knife to drag brick-red paint down the canvas, creating the vertical lines of the weathered wood siding, her hand was steady, the lines unwavering.

"Some storms take prisoners when they do battle with the coast."

Tamsin didn't turn to face Ansel. She dragged paint down the canvas, stopping where the wood planks met the foundation.

"The land is the first hostage," he continued. "All these shore lines get eaten away by the water. Sometimes I look at the rocks and wonder what they looked like five hundred years ago. How much more shore there was then."

Tamsin cleaned her brush in the cup of gulf water. She took another, smaller brush and coated it with dark gray, painting a rectangle window.

"Then it's the boats. Buildings. Fishermen. A lot of wicked storms have come through here. Cold weather can be just as harsh. It was snow that destroyed the original fishing shack back in the seventies."

Her brush slipped. Gray paint bled beyond its border. She already knew the story. "The town wasn't willing to face life without even a replica, so they replaced it." She dropped her brush in the cup. Better to let the paint dry and cover over the mistake. She had been focused on the buildings and missed the sky's slow fade from pink to blue. What was the saying? Something about red sky in the morning, sailors take warning? She faced Ansel, who held out a cup of coffee.

He extended his arm again in a second offer. "I saw you down here on my way to the café, and I thought I'd bring you a cup. It's an excuse to see you."

"I need to apologize for last night."

"Please don't. You may wish you could take it all back, but I would do it all over again, so an apology would only hurt."

He looked smaller than he had before. Timid. He held out the coffee again, and she took it and let it warm her hands. When her eyes met his, she knew she was no longer under examination. He didn't study her or take her in this time. He gave instead. It was empathy. Compassion devoid of pity. He wasn't someone trying to fit into Owen's space. He only wanted to connect with her. She couldn't break him.

"Then I won't apologize."

"On a scale of one to ten, what are the chances I get to spend more time with you before you find the truth you're looking for and leave?"

An alert went off on Tamsin's phone, and she silenced it. The grill was open for breakfast, which meant Ansel was late for work. The incoming tide slapped at the underside of the dock, and Tamsin stood, wiped her hands on her jeans, and faced him, shoving her hands in her pockets of her father's coat.

"I'm not who you think I am," she said.

"Who are you, then?"

She shrugged. "I'm whoever you'll make me out to be. However you remember me. I'm the girl you slept with when she came here on vacation. I'm the girl who wanted answers but wouldn't ask any questions."

"Is that who you want to be?"

"No. I just want to be Tamsin. I'm just me. Trying to figure this out without hurting you in the process."

"Why let me choose? Why be whatever label I apply to you? If you care what I think, why not show me who you are?"

"Because it doesn't matter who I really am. To anyone. No one cares. In the end, I'm going to be whoever people think I am when I'm not there to change their minds. When I'm long gone from Rockport, your opinion of me will change a thousand times. There was a time in my life when I would have tried to influence that, but there really isn't any point, is there?"

"That's depressing. It sounds like giving up. Like you don't care what I think."

"Nothing I can say or do is going to change how anybody thinks of me. Selfish. Irresponsible. Grieving girlfriend who can't get over it. Whatever."

"How about hurt?"

"I have no desire for your pity or anybody else's. It's not my job to manage how other people see the world. Most days, I'm barely hanging on, myself."

"So you don't care if I remember you as anything more than a woman who came here on vacation and slept with me? You're okay with being nothing more than that? I don't think that's true."

Fishing boats bobbed in the rising tide, and Tamsin wished she could climb in one and be carried into the Atlantic. "No, I'm really not okay with that. But I can't change your mind, so I'll accept the roll of the dice."

"Well, I'm the one who gets to roll my dice. And I want you to show me the Tamsin you want me to remember. Come over for dinner tonight. Seven o'clock. If you don't show, I'll know you want nothing to do with me."

Tamsin wiped paint from her knife as Ansel made his way along the narrow wharf road.

* * *

A breeze pushed off the water and across the neck of land. Tamsin wore her father's coat as a shield and trudged up the hill. The wounds were raw and torn open again. She felt the loss of everyone, moving slow and heavy as she had in the weeks after Owen died. Her mother had told her that she carried Owen with her in her heart. Did heartache weigh as much as a departed soul? Is that why her legs had to work so hard to hold her? Because they carried the weight of two?

She pushed on the door of the grill. Deb was behind the counter, wrapping silverware in napkins, one eye on the television screen across the room where the national news ran down the list of ways the world was doomed.

"Table for one this morning?"

Did Deb know about Ansel? Did the whole town know? "Yes, please."

Tamsin followed her to the back, to a seat by the window. She was grateful for the water view. "Thanks."

"No Andy this morning, huh?"

Why would she ask that? "I suspect he's working." Tamsin kept her eyes fixed to her menu, so she wouldn't have to hide her red cheeks.

"I saw him with you down at the dock while I set up the tables. Saw the two of you walking through town last night, too. You've been spending a lot of time together, haven't you?" Deb reached into her apron for a straw.

161

She dropped it on the table, but she didn't leave.

"Yeah. He's been helping me with some research. He's a nice guy."

"I used to watch Andy when he was little. His dad worked second shift at the hardware store. His mom ran off when he was small. She came back eventually, but that's another story. Andy would stay with me after school until his dad got home at eight or nine at night. Every day after school, the boys in this town would take off on their bikes. There's more to the town than just this bit by the water. A little ways up the street here, the boys would meet up at the convenience store. They'd go down to the beach and throw rocks in the bay. Try to catch frogs up at Mill Pond. Not Andy. He'd be under a bridge somewhere, reading. He was reading Shakespeare and Nathaniel Hawthorne before he was ten. He had squirrels eating out of his hand at six. He's special. A lot smarter than the others. He doesn't trust many people, but he seems to trust you."

"I suppose he's just being nice to me. It's easy to see how much he loves history, and I guess he enjoys helping people with their research."

Deb slid into the seat across from her. "This town is small. Everybody here knows each other, and locals don't usually tangle with tourists. What I'm trying to say is that he doesn't make a habit of getting to know people, and if he's taken a liking to you, could you go easy on him?"

Tamsin aligned the scalloped edge of her paper placemat with the edge of the table. Sometimes the universe gave her what she needed, and it seemed the universe thought she could use a practice run at being open and honest. She was going to need all the practice she could get if she was going to tell Margaret about Ida. "Trust me. The last thing I want to do is hurt him."

"That's good to hear. I know that you have some stuff going on, just like we all do. Sometimes, when we're so focused on ourselves, it's easy to miss the impact we have on other people. I'm not trying to tell you what to do, and it's none of my business really. I'm just saying that I know he's an attractive man. He can be sensitive, that's all. I'm just looking out for him."

Tamsin picked at the frayed stitching that held the lamination to her menu. She had to let go of it all at some point, and set down the burden of her father, Owen, her sister, the drawing. And Ansel. She dropped the menu and laid it on Deb. "The potential for hurt is mutual."

"Is it, now?"

Tamsin shrugged, a nonchalant outward expression that diminished all of it. "He's different."

"He's introspective. He really likes to figure out how people tick. People are like books to him. He has to figure out what they're like. Happy? Sad? A mystery? Then he has to dig ten layers deep into everything. Most people don't like being pried open that way. They want to hide their wounds, and Andy likes to uncover them."

"I noticed that. I find his openness refreshing."

"And he's empathetic. If you hurt, he hurts along with you. He connects with people."

"I noticed that, too."

"He's a smart man. I'm sure he can take care of himself, but he's had a his heart ripped out, and I'm just letting you know, because you don't live here, and you wouldn't have seen the damage. You wouldn't know that he might still be a little raw."

"I'm kinda vulnerable myself."

"I know. And you're exactly his type."

"Because I'm a little raw myself?"

"Not just that. You talk the way he does, and you look like his type. I've seen you two together. You seem like a nice girl, and I wanted you to have all the information, so you could make the right decision."

"And what do you think the right decision is? Should I stop talking to him? If he feels something for me that I don't return, am I only going to hurt him when I leave?"

"You'll only hurt him if you're not honest with him."

Tamsin flipped over her empty coffee, ripped the top off a plastic tub of half-and-half, and dumped it into the cup. She couldn't wait to get home again. To real creamer, to isolation, and to not having to take responsibility for other people's emotions. "Is there such a thing as too honest?"

"Not when it comes to Andy. So what'll ya have?"

She had a mess. She had a man who terrified her, not because of who he was but because of who he made her forget. Being honest with him would mean showing up at seven to face him, to face herself, and to stare down the memory of Owen.

"Western omelet. Thanks."

"You got it." Deb patted the table when she stood.

Outside, water lapped at the rocks on its way to high tide. Someone turned on the background music, and a classical station announced upcoming concert performances. Tamsin checked her email to pass the time.

Marlow had information, finally. Her brother was selling the company. He had no control over who they would keep, and it didn't look good. Marlow was worried for her, living in an old farmhouse with a single income. Her brother hadn't named names and wouldn't say what he knew, but Marlow wanted to know—if Tamsin was among them, if she lost her job, would she be okay?

Tamsin sent a quick reply, setting Marlow at ease. Que será, será. But the news flipped the hourglass on finding Ida. She needed to get home, to get back to work, to keep the job that was her sanity, her only routine, and her only connection to the outside world. She tucked her phone into a pocket inside her purse, next to the envelope that held the stick figure drawing. Two more days. That's all she could spare.

After breakfast she returned to her room, collected her painting supplies and her last remaining blank canvas, and found a comfortable spot with a view of Motif Number 1 surrounded by Back Harbor with Rowe Point in the background. On this side of the Neck, there were no lobster traps. Birds bobbed in the water, ducking their bills beneath the surface, and the sweet smell of life by the sea filled the air. She painted the little green house on North Road from memory.

She could still hear her father's voice booming through the cottage, warning her and her sister to head home when the street lights came on. Their bikes clicked, and the pedals spun on their way out the back door and down the road. She painted the green cottage as it appeared in her happiest memories, soaked in peachy golden sunlight from the west, windows blazing. The roof in mottled shades of gray. The porch light hanging in its mason jar globe. A little white sign pronouncing it the home of The Eliots, surrounded by lupine and marigolds. It was a spiritual process, calling each detail to remembrance. Much more meaningful to Tamsin than accepting the blurry edges that spontaneous recollection offered.

She'd forgotten who that little girl was, the one who stood at the corner with an orange Creamsicle in one hand and the handlebar of her bike in the other. She'd forgotten how that little girl used to make faces in the bathroom mirror and wonder what she'd look like at twenty, forty, fifty years old. If only she could look back into her own eyes and wish herself to be happy. As Tamsin painted the second story window at the top of the stairs, next to that bathroom, she told that little girl the truth. Not all dreams involve ponies and castles, some dreams do come true, and sometimes dreams come undone. She willed that little girl to keep on living, and that little girl told her it was almost dinner time.

She checked her watch. She'd missed lunch. There was just enough time to add a little red Huffy bike to the painting before she cleaned up and walked up the hill for dinner.

She risked the wrath of Connor by stepping into his wine shop but was greeted, or rather wasn't greeted, by a woman tapping on her cell phone who rang up her wine and handed her a wad of change without making eye contact. The door chimed on her way out.

It was a three-minute walk from the wine shop to Ansel's, where she faced his gray door with the letter C on it, a very different person than the girl who once faced Owen's door.

Owen's ground floor apartment had been next to the communal laundry area. The hallway smelled like detergent, and she'd been hopeful and excited to see him. A weekend bag slung over her shoulder by a ragged strap. She had been twenty-two then.

Now, she faced Ansel's door as a widow, haunted by a loss she'd nearly forgotten in a moment of passion with a man she just met. She had no idea what to expect when she knocked on the door. Twenty-two-year-old Tamsin would have had the jitters. Forty-year-old Tamsin had shame, guilt, and too many apologies to make. Some to herself. She knocked. Ansel answered.

She held out the brown paper bag with two bottles of wine. "Did you think I wouldn't come?"

"I hoped you would." He held the door open, inviting her in. "I admit, I was watching the clock. I'm glad you're here."

"Connor wasn't working, so I brought wine." Tamsin passed the sofa, where she'd made a complete fool of herself the last time she was there. She set the paper bag on the table and draped her sweatshirt over the back of the chair. "Whatcha cookin'?"

"Chicken parm. It's easy, and the oven does the work."

"It smells great."

Ansel closed the door, his hand lingering on the doorknob. "Tamsin, I wish you'd—"

"I'm sorry. I want to start over, but I don't want to take back what happened. I know you think I'm probably here to tell you I never want to see you again, but it's not that. There's more to say."

He let go of the doorknob and shoved his hands in his pockets. "I was going to say that I wish you'd worn a coat. It's freezing outside."

"I left it back at the room. It's a short walk."

"You could always stay. But it might not be appropriate for me to suggest that right now."

Tamsin gave him half a smile and slipped the pinot grigio from the bag, which, wet with condensation, fell apart. She held up the bottle. "Before it gets warm? I have a lot of talking to do."

"You talk, I'll pour."

She trailed him to the kitchen. On the counter sat an electric wine opener, but Ansel used an old-fashioned corkscrew from the junk drawer. He dropped the cork on the counter and offered her a glass of golden wine. She wanted to tease him about choosing the harder path, but he beat her to it.

"I like the feel of a real bottle opener. Removing the cork. It's the beginning of the experience, right? I got that electric opener as a gift. It's convenient, but it's not the same thing."

"I can appreciate finding meaning in the experience. And the preference to go about something the hard way."

"Just because it's not the easy way, doesn't mean it's necessarily the hard way."

Another double meaning. The longer she waited to tell Ansel the truth, the harder it would be to start. But the hardest way would be never to tell him at all. She pointed at the timer on the stove. "Can I have those five minutes?"

"Sure. Shoot." Ansel returned the corkscrew to the drawer and leaned against the counter.

"To make a short story long, I'm a widow. I've never said that out loud before. I always say that Owen died. My partner is gone. But I never gave myself a label. We weren't married, and there isn't a word for what you become when you lose your unmarried partner. It's a disenfranchised type of grief. You know, I never went to a support group or read a book. I just cried my eyes out until I couldn't cry anymore. Then I put one foot in front of the other and figured it out. The house, the cars, the bills. Sudden, unexplained goodbyes cost a lot of money, you know? But it costs you a bit of yourself, too. There are all of these unexpected taxes you have to pay. About a year after he died, I was in the grocery store, near the tortilla chips. They were never my thing, but he loved them. I don't know why I went down that aisle, but there I was, staring at tortilla chips, feeling like a giant piece of me was missing. Part of me wanted them, just to remember what they tasted like when I'd steal one out of the bag. But then I couldn't. It was Owen's thing, and some part of me just said nope. You can't have that anymore. That's over. I'm not saying it's right or wrong. It was never a conscious decision, but I did the same thing with intimacy."

"That doesn't seem very fair. Your life's not over."

"There's nothing fair about any of it. Wasn't fair when I lost him. Wasn't fair when I put him in the ground because I couldn't bear to let his body go even though he once told me he'd rather be cremated. Wasn't fair when my brain decided that my stomach couldn't have another tortilla chip ever again. Isn't fair that I wince when I talk about him in the past tense, because I'll never stop wanting him to be here. It wasn't fair that my dad died a few months before him. Or that Mom died a few months ago leaving me alone in the world with a sister who makes me crazy because I pushed away everyone who ever showed me friendship. It was easier to grieve if no one judged me for doing it."

"You didn't have to push people away. Most of those people probably wanted to be there for you."

"No, I had to. Every time they looked at me, all I saw was pity from them. And that grief becomes such a huge part of who you are that it's impossible to make a new friendship without it coming up. I spent a lot of effort running away from connecting with other people because it was a reminder of what I'd lost. Then I came here. Maybe there's something about being around strangers that makes me let go a little, or maybe it's you, the way you talk. I really do feel a connection with you." The timer on the stove counted down the seconds. "And last night—"

"It doesn't have to be that way. You are allowed to move on."

"I know. Now, I know it was a choice, all that time in isolation. But that's not what upset me last night. It wasn't being close to you. It wasn't anything you did or didn't do. You asked about Owen, if he was in the room? What hurt the most was that he wasn't."

"You let go—"

"And it scared the shit out of me that he was gone. The memory of him. The way his hands felt. The way he used to touch me. The way he smelled. I was here with you and..." Tamsin took in half of her glass of wine. "It was just you and me. Until it was over and I realized what I had lost."

With a few second left, Ansel turned off the timer. The oven door creaked when it opened, and he pulled on a green mitt. He dropped the pan on the stovetop and refilled their wine. "I've never been in your situation. I don't really know for sure, but this sounds like normal stuff. Of course you're going to have feelings about it. You have to give yourself room to feel things. And time. It takes as long as it takes."

"I do owe you an apology though."

169

"No, you don't."

"I do. I should have had some foresight. It shouldn't be your responsibility to coach me through it or—"

"That's not how this works. This is that intimacy thing, isn't it? You think you don't deserve some kind of deep connection with another person? It's like you lost your teammate, and you think you're never allowed to join another team."

"I don't want to be on another team."

"You did the other night. And there was nothing wrong with that. There's nothing wrong with living life and wanting intimacy with another person or, gasp, a relationship."

"We didn't talk about what this was, but it's definitely not a relationship."

The corners of Ansel's eyes wrinkled with his smile. "I would have asked what this was, but you told me to shut up."

Tamsin aimed her smile at the floor and sipped her wine while Ansel placed chicken and melted cheese on plates.

"Look, interactions between consenting adults come in all flavors," he said. "For all I knew, I was your one-night stand while you were on vacation."

"Ouch."

"That's what it was, wasn't it? And that's okay. But I want you to know that it was something to me. It was a connection. I'm sorry that it was weird for you when it was over, but I'm a little happy to hear that when you were with me, you were with me."

"I was. I was with you."

"I know you're here looking for answers to some questions you're too afraid to ask. I know you don't want to tell me what that's all about. I'm okay with that. But if you want to tell me about anything in the middle or what comes after, I don't have to be just a one-night stand."

"I know. That's why I have to apologize. You told me not to, but you deserve better than that. I shouldn't have told you to shut up. I should have told you the truth all along, about why I'm really here."

She carried her plate and followed Ansel to his dining room table. It had a faux-marble top and a metal band around the side, the kind you would find in a diner, in some distant era where people wrote letters and had real conversations over dinner.

"After my mother died, my sister and I went through her house to divide up her things. I found my father's favorite coat in a closet, and inside a pocket, there was an envelope with a Rockport postmark. Inside that was a child's drawing addressed to Daddy. It wasn't mine. It wasn't my sister's. And I came here to find out what that means."

"Not just who the artist was, but for what it all means to you." Ansel peered across the table at her like a professor whose student finally caught on.

"Right. I thought I had this perfect childhood, and it turns out there was a dark side I chose not to see. My sister did though. She saw what it did to our mother, how our father's absence affected her, but I chose not to see it for some reason. Just like I chose not to see the little imperfections in all of my memories with Owen." Tamsin ran her finger along a scratch in the table's surface. A scar from a knife, perhaps. How many people sat at this table and looked past that scratch, choosing to ignore it while they paint perfect memories of holiday dinners? "Maybe on some level I'm here looking for the imperfections so I come to terms with them."

"That's a lot of pressure to put on one vacation."

Tamsin laughed through a long exhale. "When I left home and headed for Rockport, I had no idea what I was doing. This is major progress."

"So what happens if you don't get a lead on this other person before you have to go back home?"

"That's not an option."

"Answers first. Truth later."

"Something like that." Tamsin sipped her wine, trading one set of lies for another.

"What do you want from the experience?"

"What do you mean?"

"What are you going to say? What if they don't know about any of this?"

Tamsin swallowed hard. "I'm just going to take what comes."

* * *

Ansel was her ballast. She lost the night, tangled, then unraveled by the comfort, floating in the wake.

"I have to go to work tomorrow." Ansel played with a strand of her brown hair. "Wish I didn't have to."

"I may join you. I don't know how much more I'll find in your archives, but I should at least exhaust them before I exhaust myself."

"You're more than welcome to come with me." Ansel unwound her hair from his finger and collected another strand, making curls that wouldn't stay.

CHAPTER TWENTY

Ansel had apologized a dozen times for the tattered bath towel, but that was the least awkward stride of Tamsin's stroll down memory lane. The otherworldliness of fumbling through someone else's shower and finding a place for a second towel in a bathroom designed for one reminded her of those early days with Owen and getting ready for work on a Monday morning after a weekend of playing house.

She walked with Ansel to the Historical Society, following him down the hallway and into the study room. Sunlight streamed through the tall windows, fading the chairs and warming the long wood table. Ansel ducked out of sight, fumbling with his computer, checking voicemails, and starting his day. She took the drawer from the card catalog that held the index for the Eliot family and turned on a green banker's lamp. Her skim through the catalog produced no new leads, and she hadn't expected it to. Under the family name of a previous North Road resident, she found references to newspaper clippings, so she made a list and collected the files from Ansel, who continued his morning slog.

A long, yellowed newspaper page showed a picture of the street and its cottages, close to the road. The photo was from 1910. If there were cars on the Neck back then, there were no visible driveways. In another photo, a young girl with a sash, Miss Something-or-Other, posed with her parents outside the cottage. It brought back memories of rainy days, raiding their grandmother's closet, playing dress up with her Sunday hats and old tubes of lipstick that tasted like candle wax. Had Ida been born yet when Tamsin played dress up with Margaret? Was she living somewhere, down some other narrow street, just out of view?

The old, familiar heat of shame flared in the pit of Tamsin's stomach, a smoldering guilt for not telling Margaret the truth. About Ida. About herself. About how she lived as if life were over. A phone rang in the back room, and Ansel answered it, his voice coming across the counters in fragments of phrases. It hadn't been so hard to tell him the truth the night before. Not as hard as holding it in had been. But she barely knew Ansel. A conversation with Margaret came with its own history of anxieties. The nitpicking and judging, decades of conversations laced with assumptions and accusations. Ansel thanked someone and hung up the phone, the little beep when he ended the call on the ancient cordless phone told Tamsin he couldn't be standing far away.

He rounded the table and slid into a seat across from her, and she decided to come clean, all the way. Tell him the whole truth in practice for the harder conversation to follow. She was supposed to be lying low. Not telling anyone in the town that she was there in search of Ida.

If Ansel slipped and told anyone, especially Connor, it could anger the owner of the art store. She might miss her chance to meet Ida. Someone could destroy her car, keep her from getting home and back to work, putting her job at risk. Telling him meant betraying a secret that only her half-sister had the right to share. But it was also her secret, and the more she held it in, the more it ate at her like a cancer. She reached into her purse and pulled out the envelope with the Rockport postmark.

"I want to show you something." Tamsin unfolded the stick figure drawing and laid it on the table.

"This is the thing you told me about? That was in your father's coat?"

"Yeah."

Ida loves Dabby. The stick figure with the green coat. Standing on a gray rock. She smoothed out the creases and turned it around so Ansel could see it. Sharing it, showing it to someone else, someone who wasn't her sister, added value to the drawing and drew out its fragility. Like being the first to discover the Dead Sea Scrolls and casually handing them off to a stranger. "This is that drawing I found in my father's coat last week. It doesn't seem like that big of a deal except my name isn't Ida and neither is my sister's. There was no return address, and it was postmarked from Rockport. All smudged and I couldn't read the date."

Ansel pulled it closer, but Tamsin knew there were no clues hidden in the drawing. Nothing could be found in the fibers of the paper. She'd looked. "I know it's strange to hunt down a person when you know nothing but their name, especially when it could destroy your family, but right before I found this, on the plane, I had the strangest dream."

Tamsin wound the string from the neck of her hoodie around her finger. It seemed absurd to put so much weight on a dream. "I know it sounds silly. It was bits and pieces of reality, all woven together with bizarre psychobabble. You know, that stuff your brain dredges up when it has something to tell you. This isn't something random that he found on the street. It wasn't sent to our mailbox by mistake. This woman. Kid. Ida. She's my half-sister."

She stopped to catch her breath, to let her heart catch up to her words. "I know, deep down, that my father had this secret. Maybe he led a second life. Maybe I wasn't his favorite after all. You can say something profound to try to make me feel better, but I know that it's true. I know that meeting Ida will change everything."

The look Ansel gave her was somewhere between sympathy and kindness for a lunatic stranger. He folded the drawing and passed it back. "Have you thought this through? You only found this last week, right? Your other sister. Margaret? Does she know? What if you find Ida and she doesn't want anything to do with you? Or if the two of you become the best of friends, and your sister hates you forever for keeping this from her?"

"I gotta deal with other people's emotions when they come. I can't be responsible for the way other people react to this. Mags is gonna hate me no matter what, but she'll get over it."

"What about you? How is meeting Ida going to change how you view yourself?"

Tamsin looked down at the list of newspapers she wanted to see, times when her family home was ripped apart by storms, rebuilt by the community. She tapped the end of a golf pencil on the table, but the sound annoyed her, so she tossed it in the box and leaned her head back against the chair, staring at the drop ceiling. "I don't know. I was Daddy's little girl. I didn't know back then that this had happened. Margaret knew something wasn't right. My dad was gone for days at a time, and there was always a reason, conventions, art shows, retreats. Long sales trips for work."

"What about your mom?" Ansel's arms were crossed, his elbows on the table. He leaned forward, drawing meaning from the facts. "She never said anything?"

Tamsin shoved her fists in the pocket of her hoodie. "If my mom knew the truth, it died with her. But I had no idea. There was no room in my picture-perfect, white-picket-fence world for that kind of negativity. I don't know how I'm going to feel. Does Ida already know? What kind of childhood did she have? Will she hate me? And how do I walk up to a woman I've never met, hold out this piece of paper—this drawing she made for her father—and ask her if he's the same as mine? If we have DNA in common, along with all the lies? And when you realize that so much of your past *was* lies, how do you know what to trust in the future?" She kept her eyes wide, hoping the air would dry the tears before they fell.

Ansel's eyes were fixed on the folded drawing between them, his knuckles brushed against his lips. "Tamsin, I need to—"

A doorbell rang, a quick single chime from the back room, from somewhere behind the desk. Tamsin hadn't heard it before. It was attached to the entrance and nearly cloaked by the slamming of the door.

"Andy!" A voice called down the hall, urgent and angry. "Why are you prying in my shit?"

Ansel pushed away from the table, standing to face the rage. Tamsin winced, hunched over the folder and sifted through yellowed newspapers. Tucking her nose into history was her best shot at avoiding the woman's angry presence.

Heavy boots landed on the hardwood floor, and Tamsin kept her head lowered. She turned enough to catch a glimpse of the woman from the corner of her eye. Obscured by the partial wall, all Tamsin could see of her was a shoulder covered in long brown hair, a leather jacket, a militant black boot, and the aura of rage.

"I fucking hate the smell of this place." The woman's jaw was set. She looked like she was about to demand answers that had nothing to do with the town and everything to do with their history. Ansel was silent, standing helpless. "Gina from the Arts Alliance called me last night. Said you were prying into my shit. Everything I'm going through right now, and you're down here poking around in my business. What's wrong with you? Why can't you leave me alone?"

"I swear to God, I didn't know. I wasn't trying to pry. Can we talk about this outside?"

"Nothing is ever private with you. You just have to weasel your way into people's lives and pick them apart until they feel like shit. You're like a parasitic disease, infesting people until they're exhausted, then you lie dormant until they've healed just enough to be strong again, and you find some new soft spot to attack. Stop. Stop messing around in my life. Stop talking about me, asking questions about me. I'm done with you. Does this make sense? Do you want me to write it down, and shove it in an old book for you?"

He seemed to shrink before the woman's outrage. "I'm sorry. I am. I am so, so sorry. I didn't know. It was for a totally different reason than you think. I really wasn't trying to pry. I'm so sorry about your mother."

Tamsin was driftwood caught in their wake, picking up phrases and hints of the waves they rode. She sat frozen, hoping to melt into the scenery, pretending to read a newspaper article. But the woman turned on her anyway.

"You look just like his type. If I were you, I'd find some other place to do your research. Run. He's an asshole, and you'll learn all the wrong things."

The woman spun and left, a buckle on her leather jacket clicking with each step. The door slammed behind her.

Tamsin winced, trying to give Ansel some sympathy. "That was rough. Sorry. Was that the ex?"

His hands clenched in his lap. "It was. I'm sorry I didn't introduce you."

"Oh, don't worry about it, I—"

"No. Tamsin, please. I was trying to tell you before she came in. That was Ida."

CHAPTER TWENTY-ONE

"That was Ida? You dated Ida?" Tamsin pushed away from the table, her chair scraping against the floor. Her shaking hands fumbled as she gathered newspaper clippings, pushing them back into the folders. Her purse swung into the edge of the table when she grabbed it from the back of the chair. She threw it over her shoulder, keys and change clattering. "I can't believe this. I have to go after her."

"Wait. Let me tell you everything I know. Let me explain. You don't want to talk to her when she's pissed, and you should think through what you're going to say. Maybe I should try to calm her down first. Let me help you."

"No. No, I have to go." Tamsin ran a hand over her face. She still smelled like his soap. "I can't believe this. The answers were next to me all this time. How did this happen? I slept with my half-sister's ex-boyfriend before I even met her. This is not the way this was supposed to go. She's going to hate me forever. And what was that about? You were prying into her life? She was in Maine. Her mother is dying."

"How did you know that?"

"I met her uncle at the art shop."

"Of course. And you didn't want me to know who you were looking for because—"

"Because it's a small town, and her business is her business."

"But you were going to tell me anyway."

Tamsin threw her purse down on the table. Keys and change rattled. "Because I worked really hard to convince myself to trust you!"

"I wasn't hiding this from you. I didn't know. I swear. I was about to tell you when she walked in the door."

"Is she the ex you told me about?"

"Yes. We were very close. At one time." Ansel cracked his neck. "This is the part you're not going to like. Please listen to me before you get angry. You remember the photos from the newspaper? The woman in the pictures with your father?"

"Yes." It was more like an escape of air than a word. The pieces fit together, falling into place like a rickety game of Mouse Trap. He'd known all along. "That's Ida's mother. You knew all this time. You son of a bitch."

"Wait. No. I didn't know. Those grainy pictures—"

"That's bullshit. Connor knew. Right away. And he said half the town knew and didn't want me here. I don't know how he knew, if it's some family resemblance and we look alike or what, but he knew who I was."

"He's Ida's step-father. He's probably been waiting for someone to show up for years."

"Connor is Ida's step-father? No wonder he was such an ass. Shit this town is small. If he figured it out, how could you not know? Was this some kind of revenge?"

"No. There's nothing to get revenge over. I know it sounds like she hates me, but she was just mad, and I didn't—"

"She seemed more than angry to me." Tamsin threw her hands in the air while she caught her breath. "I can't believe you knew. You saw those pictures before we slept together. You knew, and you didn't say anything."

"I didn't know. I didn't. I'm trying to tell you that I didn't know. And you initiated it. In my apartment. I didn't start what happened between us."

"You found me at the restaurant. You followed me from the Historical Society, and you sat down, ate dinner with me, and tried to pry it out of me, why I'm here. You've been trying to get this out of me the whole time. And you knew."

"I kept seeing you all over town. Your shoes got wet, and it looked like you could use help. Then you came to my work with some big mystery you wanted to unravel. I was being nice when I sat with you at the grill. I was curious, and I thought I could help you."

"Instead of telling me that you already knew, you let it get back to her. I told you that it was private. If you cared about her at all, you wouldn't have let this get back to her. And if you thought you could help me, you certainly went about it the wrong way."

"It didn't happen like that."

"There were probably a dozen right ways to do this, you know. You could have gone straight to her and been sensitive about it. You could have told me. Tucked a note under my door. Slashed all my tires and shattered my car windows. I dunno. I still haven't figured that one out. Now it's even worse than if you'd just left it alone. When she finds out that she was in the same room with me, and you still didn't say anything, she's gonna be even more pissed. This whole town will want me dead by lunch time."

Ansel put up a hand. "Wait. Please. For both of us. Let me call her. I'll find a way to fix this, but it didn't happen like that. Right after you saw the pictures in the paper—"

"Stop making excuses." Tamsin shoved her chair under the table hard enough to shake the lamps. She felt bad for the table, bad for sending a look of alarm across Ansel's face, but the sound of those little pencils rattling in the box was gratifying. "Stay out of it. Please. For the love of

God, I am begging you to stay out of this. Say nothing to no one. Not Ida. Not Connor. No one at the post office or the coffee place or the grill. This isn't gossip. It's not small-town fodder or some kind of tool you can use to get revenge on her. These are people's lives. Families. This is our history, not yours, and I'm asking you to stay out of it."

"I won't say anything to anybody. I swear. I have nothing to gain. I wish you would let me explain though."

"I've heard enough." Tamsin threw her purse over her shoulder, left the newspaper clippings scattered on the table, and followed in Ida's footsteps.

Tamsin itched to run, but sprinting through town would only draw attention, so she slinked along the curb, unnoticed, back to her motel, kicking herself for not asking Ansel how to find Ida, where she lived, where she worked. She couldn't go back to him now and ask. The ball was in Ida's court. Her uncle would tell her, and she would figure it out. And then what? She would probably never see her half-sister again. And she would have to go to Margaret, tail between her legs, and explain that she had destroyed any chance of meeting their half-sister because she was selfish and reckless and slept with the woman's ex-boyfriend.

Every happy childhood memory of Rockport turned sour. Snippets of sunny summer days that used to bring her joy now had monsters lurking in the shadows. She stayed close to the buildings with her head down, avoiding contact with the few pedestrians and shop keepers. At the bottom of the hill, she turned toward her motel room.

The room smelled like laundry detergent. The bed had been made. Clean sheets. New towels in the bathroom. She pulled a bottle of water from the little refrigerator by the bed. It reminded her of college, trying to fit real world food in a fake world fridge. Ida was a few years younger. Younger than Margaret. Had she been to college? Did her father give Ida the same experiences?

Tamsin twisted the cap from the water and stepped from the room onto the deck, into the sun. She narrowed her eyes against the bright light and leaned against the metal rail that separated the deck from the rocks. The breeze pushed her hair into her face, and with it, the smell of Ansel's two-in-one shampoo. Hair that looked like Ida's.

All three of them looked like their father. Tamsin's eyes and cheekbones, her chin and her upturned nose. Everyone always said that Margaret looked just like her big sister. Tamsin saw those same things in Ida. The way she squinted one eye in anger. The sun went behind a cloud, and a chill kicked up off the bay. Tamsin kicked herself for trusting Ansel. She yearned for home. She could pick up the pieces, pack them into Smurf the Cherokee and head back to the farmhouse, where she'd be safe among the remnants of the perfect life they'd built, once she cleaned up the broken glass and fixed the broken window. Or she could run. Find Ida. Tell her the truth. Beg her to answer the few questions that bobbed on the surface of the murky water. There was still time. She decided to wait, to think, to be deliberate in approaching the woman who may not know that she had half-sisters. Tomorrow. She would find Ida tomorrow, and then she could go home.

She fumbled in the darkness of the motel room and found her sketchpad and a pen. She sat on a plastic lawn chair on the deck, looking out over the rocks, and broke down the challenge as she would any obstacle, listing the points of impact. A list of the wounds that the sisters would carry as scars. For Tamsin, there was growing distance between her memory of her father, of the man who trudged across the fields of their home in his green jacket and spoke so well of abstract things, and the real man with two families who walked the streets of Rockport. There was a chasm between the young Margaret, who couldn't accepted their mother's word and the woman she became, who struggled with the possibility of

183

their mother's lies. Tamsin hadn't seen the truth the way Margaret did because she wanted that perfection so badly. But why? What purpose did it serve if it wasn't real?

And Margaret. Standing in the airport parking garage, talking about all the missed chances to get at the truth. That was the first time they'd picked at the scar since Mags visited Tamsin in college and blubbered about it in a drunken oblivion. Did she know more than she let on? Had she known the truth all this time and hidden it from Tamsin because she knew it would break her? Either way, Margaret would be furious with her for sifting through their childhood memories, for dumping out the toy box and scattering the pieces, then breaking them all by sleeping with Ida's ex-boyfriend. When Tamsin handed their broken childhood back to Mags, she could lose her sister forever. Keeping it from her wasn't an option. Tamsin couldn't bear any more lies by omission.

But before she could get there, she had to get to Ida and face whatever anger resided there. She had to approach Ida with compassion. Tamsin had no way of knowing how she and Margaret would change Ida's life or what old wounds could open.

The little black cat that had greeted Tamsin at the record shop rounded the corner and sat at her feet, peering across the water at the horizon.

"What do you see out there, kitty?"

He flicked the end of his tail, his attention fixed on unseen prey.

"Everybody's supposed to be afraid of you. Some superstition that makes no sense. You don't even care, do you? You just do cat things, keeping people safe from mice. You've got a job to do, and all the hang-ups people have about black cats don't bother you one bit."

The cat slipped between the railings and slinked onto the rocks, moving closer to his quarry. Tamsin clicked the pen closed and tucked the notepad under the clip. She wished she could be more like the cat, stop worrying about what Mags thought or how Ida would be impacted by the truth. All she could do was make it known. Maybe she wasn't so selfish after all.

The sun emerged from behind the clouds, sweeping air across the water, rustling the notepad, and bringing a chill. She collected her charcoals and her father's coat and walked to the end of Old Harbor Road where she sat on the rock wall that separated the Neck from the bay. She covered her sketch paper with gentle smudges, drawing pristine water. The source of life. She added the boats, the shadows they cast. She didn't look over her shoulder as she'd done before. She wasn't aware of her surroundings. Just the breeze and the water lapping at the rocks, slapping the sides of the boats. One would rock and others would follow. With no tide, no wake, she wondered what force of nature moved the water. A giant whale, many miles away or the tiniest pebble tossed from a distant shore. Whatever the cause, they were the ripples of a greater plan.

CHAPTER TWENTY-TWO

The dorm-size refrigerator rattled when the motor stopped. Tamsin was already awake, watching the faintest hint of blue leak around the edges of the curtain to stain the ceiling. She thought about Ida. Wondered if she was somewhere watching the morning sneak its way into the corners of her life, not knowing that everything was about to change. Had her uncle told her yet that someone was looking for her? Had she put the pieces together? How similar they looked.

She showered, dressed, and sat on the edge of the bed while she slipped on her running shoes. The stick figure drawing was on the nightstand. She folded it and tucked it into the back pocket of her jeans, zipped herself into her father's jacket, and walked across the street for coffee.

Tamsin ordered a large cup and pointed to some kind of strudel, a chocolate-filled impulse buy to satisfy a growling stomach. She marched up the hill to the Historical Society with the cup warming her hand. The only regret she had was that she hadn't asked Ansel where Ida lived, and she had no intention of leaving Rockport with regrets.

She held in a deep breath of crisp, morning air and tugged open the door to the Historical Society, leaning against it and letting the release of it steady her nerves. Anger had no role to play. She pushed it away and plunged down the narrow hallway. The mechanical door chime had given her away. One hand in her coat pocket, the other gripping the white paper cup, she stepped through the doorway.

"Ansel." Her stomach fluttered, less like butterflies and more like a murder of angry crows that had settled then took off all at once. "Ansel!"

He emerged from the back room, books and papers in his arms. "I was hoping I would see you again before you left."

"I'm not here for you." She stood just inside the door. Not one step closer.

"I know you're not. I wish you would listen to me. Let me tell you how this happened."

"I know exactly how it happened, because it happened to me. But I'm not here to rehash this. I want you to tell me where Ida lives."

"Don't go there. Not like that. Let me find a place where you two—"

She rolled her eyes and resisted the urge to throw hot coffee across the counter. "Jesus, Ansel. Not everything is some giant ordeal. Just tell me where she lives."

"She lives above the wine shop."

"Okay. I can see how that might be less than ideal." Tamsin adjusted her grip on her coffee cup. "Where does she work?"

"She owns a bakery on the way out of town. From here, go across the triangle intersection at Dock Square. Then it's just a few doors down on the right." He dropped books and papers to the counter.

Tamsin held firm. "When does it open?"

"It opened half an hour ago. She makes cakes and cookies for kids' birthday parties. She always starts early on Wednesdays to get ready for the weekend."

"Thanks. I won't tell her you told me."

"I appreciate that."

Tamsin turned to leave, took a sip of her coffee, but stopped when Ansel cleared his throat. There was no way he was getting the last word. She didn't turn to face him, keeping her eyes fixed on the door at the end of the dark hall, straining to find light at the end of that tunnel.

"One thing," he said. "You want me out it. You want nothing to do with me, and that's fine. I wish you'd listen to me, but I understand in light of the situation." His ran a hand over a manila folder, lifted it and clutched it to his chest like a school boy carrying his books. "Be as pissed at me as you want to be. But for someone who never wanted me involved and wants me to stay out of it, it took balls for you to walk in here and drag me back in. Trust me, if you ambush her, she's gonna know the info came from me. By telling you where she lives and works, I'm opening myself to even more of her wrath. News spreads fast here."

"What are you saying?" Tamsin's patience was wearing thin.

"I put myself on the line for you, so maybe when you look back on this you can remember that, even if you can't remember me fondly."

"I'm pissed, but I'm not an unreasonable person." She looked back over her shoulder. "I won't leave without saying goodbye."

Down the hallway and onto the street, across the triangle with its three-way stop sign, and there it was. The bakery. Its sign was a little pink cupcake, smiling out at the traffic. It had a simple name. Cookies and Cakes. On the door was her name. Ida Wynne, baker. She used her mother's last name. Tamsin spent a moment being proud of her half-sister for owning her own store and living a brightly colored, vibrant life where leather jackets lived side by side with cupcakes. But Tamsin could stand outside forever and never be prepared for meeting her. Everything she came for was inside that door. The seed of her sister's discontent. The flaw in her family's work of art. The woman who, until this very moment, had existed only to change Tamsin's life forever, probably for the worse. Part of her wanted to walk in the door and stake claim on their father. Play gatekeeper to her family's acceptance of Ida, she knew she was opening the door to her own judgment. Ida would have to accept her too. She patted the drawing in her back pocket, felt the familiar wrinkle of paper.

She threw her empty coffee cup into a municipal trash can and stepped through the door, beneath a ringing bell, and into the smell of chocolate chip cookies.

If Tamsin had a superpower, it was her sensory memory. She could catch a smell of fast food from a passing car in the summertime and be transported back to her grandfather's pickup truck. Driving down Main Street and just out of town to get a burger from McDonald's, when one finally came to town. Standing just inside the door of Ida's bakery, she knew that, for the rest of her life, she'd associate the smell of chocolate chip cookies with the day she met her half-sister.

The store was empty. From the behind the counter, the hint of a radio station swept across the counter. Trays of cookies wrapped in plastic rested beneath a glass counter, next to boxes of fudge, some cupcakes arranged in the shape of a Muppet she didn't recognize, and rows of pastel macarons. There was a display of baking supplies for sale, pans and piping bags and tips. It seemed generous. Give a man a cake and he'll indulge for a day. Give a man a piping bag and he'll go into a diabetic coma. She tucked her hands in her pockets, and her stomach turned with regret. She should have left the coat at home. She shrugged it off, draped it over her arm, and smoothed its collar.

She would order macarons. A dozen. And then she would tell her. Tamsin approached the counter. An oven door closed, the industrial kind that creaked and slammed. A metal tray landed on a flat surface with a scrape and a clang. Then a voice. "That you, Lynda?"

Panic knocked Tamsin back like a tidal wave. This woman had work to do, a store to run. She was baking, and Tamsin intruded on her day to change her whole life. After begging Ansel not to be insensitive and blaming him for his poor judgment, she stood in the middle of the bakery thinking that maybe he wasn't the worst one in her story after all. She brushed aside the useless excuses. White lies wouldn't do. Make an appointment. She could make an appointment.

"I'll be out in a second. I think you'll love this. I made the butterfly wings pink."

"No," Tamsin called out, her voice cracking. She swallowed. "No, it's not Lynda."

Ida appeared in the doorway that led to the back of the store. Her hair was tied back. "It's you, from the Historical Society. Enjoyed getting to know Andy?"

"I've been doing some family research." Tamsin searched Ida's face for a hint of recognition. All she saw was her own nose and chin.

"The Historical Society is a good place to start. If you've finished over there, and you've come here to research Andy, I can tell you everything you need to know in one word. Run." Ida leaned behind the register and moved a stack of folded papers. Menus maybe. Order forms for birthday parties. She rested her forearms on the marble counter. Maybe it was granite. Tamsin never could tell. Ida stacked the papers into a neat pile, earning Tamsin's respect. A punk rock baker who kept her shop organized. "I don't mean that. He's not that bad. I'd forgiven him until he put his nose in my mom's business. I owe you an apology."

"No, you don't."

"I do. I was away for a few days because my mom is sick. She lives up in Maine. Anyway, I'm up there helping her, and I come back to a voicemail from one of these catty Arts Alliance women who hated my mother. Andy'd sent her some old newspaper pics of my mom, trying to identify her. Of course these women are like, 'We're so sorry, dear. What could your ex-boyfriend possibly want with these old pictures of your mother? We thought you'd want to know right away.' They're never up to any good. And they never buy their cupcakes here either. Anyway, I'm rambling. Sorry I yelled at him in front of you. If I'm honest, the poor guy probably just stepped in it with them. He means well." She waved a hand. "What can I get for you? Cookies? Box of fudge?"

"Macarons?" Tamsin pointed to the tray of pastel clouds, grateful Ida didn't press her about Ansel, that she didn't have to lie or hide the truth. "A dozen, please? They're my favorite. Do you make them here?"

"Yeah. Took me a while to get them right. The filling is easy, it's the shells that are delicate. Flavors?"

"Surprise me." *It won't be half the surprise I have for you.*

"You got it."

"Which is your favorite?" *As a kid, did you dig the chocolate out of the Halloween stash first, like me, or did you go for the Nerds and Bottle Caps and Sweet Tarts, like Margaret?*

"I make one that tastes like mimosas."

Are you a wine drinker, too? "I'll definitely take a few of those."

Ida wore clear plastic gloves, like the one Tamsin wore when she dyed her hair. A few glimmers of Ida's grays were picked up by the overhead lighting. Tamsin wondered if the DNA for gray hair was on her father's side. If Ida dyed her hair, too.

Ida slid the box of macarons into a white paper bag and punched numbers into the register.

Cold air washed over the back of Tamsin's head before she heard the ringing bell. Another customer. Lynda, come to collect some butterfly baked goods with little pink wings. Tamsin reached into her back pocket, where she knew she'd stashed a twenty, careful not to disturb the drawing.

There was no drink cooler, nothing to add to her order that would fix her dry mouth or unstick her throat, so she paid, accepted her change, and shoved it back in her pocket alongside the envelope. She stepped aside and offered the generic smile she reserved for networking events and interrupting waitresses, turning to leave like any ordinary customer. But she wasn't an ordinary customer, and she couldn't chicken out. She couldn't walk outside and go back to her motel, to her life in Pennsylvania where everything was buried beneath a layer of grief and drowned out by alarm clock radios. She had to say what she came to say, even if she didn't know what the words were or how to get them out.

Next to the door, a small table sat under a dainty white table cloth. She could picture a hundred wedding cake tastings happening there with a hundred happy couples, starting happy lives. Tamsin threw her father's coat in a chair, tossed her purse on top of it, and dug a macaron from the box. Ida was right. Mimosa was the way to go. She would have killed for the real thing.

Lynda made the expected fuss over the butterfly cake with the pink wings. Tamsin never would have gone for pink. Ida didn't look like a pink girl, either. Margaret, though. She would have. She'd always been a girl's girl. My Little Pony and Strawberry Shortcake. Tamsin spent more time in mud puddles. The most outdoorsy thing Mags liked was Barbie's pink RV.

As her punk rock half-sister rang up her customer, Tamsin realized that she didn't need answers from Ida after all. She didn't need information or family history or gaps of time filled in. She wasn't there to make up for lost time, to burden Ida by asking her to account for the past or accept a future. Instead, she had something to offer. The freedom of truth. Not hers or Margaret's. Ida deserved the freedom to find her own truth.

Tamsin took a thin blue napkin from the pile on the table, and with a pen from her purse, wrote down her name and number. She folded it and tucked it in her back pocket as Ida followed Lynda to the door. The two women said their goodbyes with a hug and a kiss on the cheek and best wishes for a lovely party.

"You good?" Ida wore Doc Martens. She collected a broom and dustpan from behind an empty coat rack.

"Yeah. I have to run." Tamsin took the stick figure drawing from her pocket. She put the thin blue napkin with her phone number on it inside the decades-old envelope with its Rockport postmark. She said a little goodbye to the drawing of her father—their father—and left it, and two dollars, in the tip jar at the counter.

Tamsin shrugged into her father's jacket, slung her purse over her shoulder, and turned to Ida. "You have a beautiful shop, and you make the most amazing macarons."

"Thanks. I got lucky. My mom sold our house when I turned eighteen, and she used the windfall to help me open this place. I get to bake all day and make people happy. Best job ever."

"I bet. I don't know how you stay so skinny."

"Five mile run every morning. It's the best I can do."

"I enjoy a good run, too." Tamsin held up the bag and turned the doorknob. "Thanks, again."

"Come on by any time you're here."

"I'm staying down the hill at that old motel. Leaving in the morning. First thing. But I'll never forget these macarons." Tamsin pushed through the door, the wood releasing from the jamb and layers of paint with a crack. It closed behind her, solid and final, and she stood on the sidewalk. No cars. No pedestrians. Tamsin was alone.

CHAPTER TWENTY-THREE

Tamsin had found what she'd come for. Not the facts of her father's betrayal and what her mother knew. Those were mere brass tacks. She'd found that none of it mattered, none of it deepened the wounds or healed them. The search, the act of seeking outside of herself instead of turning on a radio to drown out the noise was what she needed most. What it all meant, the truth of it, would have to make itself known, and that would take time.

With nothing left to search for, she decided to make the most of the time she had left in Rockport. She carried an armload of paintings and art supplies to the Cherokee on her way to apologize to Ansel, Connor, and to thank Deb. It was a cadence. A to-do list. A shopping list of relief to pick up on her way out of town.

Tamsin tucked her keys in her coat pocket and walked up the hill, past shops branded with her father's memory. The little store where he bought sunscreen and snacks on their way to the stretch of rocky beach. His painting in the shoe shop and in the window of the wine store. She may never know why Connor displayed one of her father's paintings in his window and screamed at people for looking at it.

Her stomach growled. She wondered if Deb was one of the people who knew who she was from the moment she arrived. Either way, she'd deserved a thanks for the moments of clarity. But first, Ansel. The church bells struck noon when she reached the steps of the Historical Society. She caught her breath and pushed the door open, hoping that Ansel hadn't run off for lunch yet.

She called out his name as she made her way down the hall, pausing in the doorway to catch her breath. Where was he? The bell must have rung when she opened the door. "Ansel. Are you here?"

"It's time for goodbye, huh?" He emerged from the room behind the counter and leaned in the doorway, his mop of hair falling over his green eyes. A pencil tucked behind one ear.

"I'm leaving in the morning. I found Ida. Thanks for the tip. I didn't tell her you were the one who told me, but she may have figured that out on her own." Tamsin stepped forward and leaned against the rounded edge of the wooden counter, still catching her breath. "She wasn't mad, though. It seems like she's over it."

"That's good. I'll apologize to her."

"She seemed mostly pissed that the women from the Arts Alliance were looped in on her mom's life. I guess there's some history there." Tamsin wondered if it had anything to do with her father. She had to get home. The clock was ticking, and she didn't have time to entertain the thought.

"Did you tell her we—"

"No. No, it didn't come up. She started to tell me I looked like your type, but then she launched into why she was mad."

"Listen, I had no idea that the woman in that picture was Ida's mother. I didn't know Ida when we were kids, and her mom moved before we started dating. I met her a few times, but she's changed a lot since the eighties, and if Ida looks like her at all, those grainy pictures sure don't look like my ex-girlfriend. How was I to know it had anything to do with your family? I scanned two pictures and sent them to Gina at the Arts Alliance, because I thought she might recognize the woman. Yesterday, when I got in, there was a voicemail from Gina. I called her back, and she said it was Ida's mom. I thought it was great news that I had a lead for you. But I promise you, I had absolutely no idea Ida is your half-sister. I only ever knew Connor to be Ida's step-dad. I didn't put these pieces together."

Tamsin ran a thumbnail along her lower lip. The details were clearer, but her emotions were still fuzzy. "I know this is going to sound hard to believe, but I'm not usually this chaotic. I can forgive people and misplaced anger isn't a thing I usually do, but everything's been so mixed up lately that I don't know which way is up. Margaret still doesn't know about any of this. I found that drawing and realized that my family wasn't what I thought it was. Being here brought back all these memories. Most of them happy, then all of them falling apart. I found Ida. I'm coming up blank when I try to string together the right words to apologize for not listening to you, for jumping to conclusions. I'm really sorry. You didn't deserve to be roped into my madness."

"It's okay. I get it. So you came to say goodbye?"

"I did."

"That's soon." Ansel's green eyes clouded over. Tamsin tried to capture the memory of them. "What about Ida? Have you talked to her about the whole family thing?"

"No. I left my number and the drawing in her tip jar. It's up to her what she wants to do about it."

"I'm sorry it ended that way, that you didn't get your answers."

"I got all the information I need. Anything else is icing on the cupcake." Tamsin raised a shoulder to keep her purse strap from slipping and stepped back toward the hall. Facing him for the apology had been easier than meeting his eye to say thanks. "Anyway. I wanted to thank you. For everything. I feel like there's still something unsaid between us, but I'll never forget you. Thanks for being that person. You know what I mean."

Ansel nodded. The hint of a forced smile crossed his face but didn't touch those green eyes. "I'm glad I got to be that person for you. Thanks for letting me be there."

He turned, stepped into the room behind the counter, and she heard his footsteps fade. Just like that. Back to his books, to his papers, and the past he loved so much. Perhaps he was right. Whatever solace she had found with Ansel was temporary, and it was time to let go. Tamsin took her last trip down the darkened hallway and into the sun, blinking against the momentary blindness while her eyes adjusted in the harsh sunlight.

She turned left and made her way to the sandy stretch of coastline that, as a child, she'd known as Rock Beach. In truth, it was more like a cove. Rocks jutted from the water. Timeless. Immovable.

Owen had been from the desert of America, where water came to the land by way of ancient streams and rivers. It dug deep trenches in the earth. It was separate. Just passing through. It gave the gift of plants and grasses and took with it bits of rock and earth when it left. He once told her that, as a child, he pictured the coasts as giant cliffs. Big walls that kept the water from the land. She took him to a sandy Delaware beach, and he stood for an hour where the ocean met the land, watching the sand bury his ankles. The constant, churning overlap of water and earth. That night, they ate Thrasher's french fries on the boardwalk, and he'd never looked more at peace. In all the chaos of screeching gulls, of kids and parents with their neon umbrellas and beach towels, and benches covered in sticky ice cream, Owen found a oneness about life, an interconnectedness, that he'd never found in the rocky soil of his home. The walls had tumbled down.

Tamsin closed her eyes, took a deep breath. For the briefest moment, she craved the smell of salty air. Of french fries and cotton candy. People laughing and seagulls begging for scraps. But the air was empty, and she was alone. Just water and rock and soil. There was no yearning in her for the time and place she shared with Owen or for the warm summer beach of her childhood. When she opened her eyes, she was content to have the memories.

"I hope you're satisfied."

Tamsin turned in the sand. Her feet were cold, her shoes dangling from her hand. Connor stood at the bottom of the steps that led from the street. He didn't look half as angry as he had when he caught her staring at her father's painting.

"I am. I still have questions, though." She walked toward him, ready to face the man who raised her sister. The man who may have slashed her tires and broken Smurf's windows.

"All this upheaval. For what?"

"Because the truth is important."

"What good is the truth if it destroys a person?"

The wind swept through the cove, and Tamsin folded her arms, trying not to shiver. She didn't want Connor to find a weakness. "Isn't truth for the sake of truth good enough? People can live through a lot, Connor. This hardly qualifies as the biggest tragedy. And it doesn't have to be a loss."

"Easy for you to say. You're the one who always had it all."

Tamsin laughed. "You know nothing about me."

"Really?" Connor stepped from the stairs onto the sand. He wore muck boots that covered his calves and squeaked when he walked. "I know far more about you than you think I do. And I knew your father very well."

"Why do you have his painting in your window if you dislike us so much?"

"Because that's where I like to keep it." He stepped past her and looked out toward the ocean. "You look at this whole thing and see the surface.

You see that rock over there poking out of the water, and you think there's probably more rocks in that water. You don't know shit about the shipwrecks down there. And the sharks that feed on the bones."

Tamsin set her shoes on the sand and shoved her hands in the pockets of her father's old green coat. "Then why don't you tell me? Tell me what I need to know."

"Because those skeletons don't belong to just you."

"Would Ida tell me?"

"She don't know either. But she's smart enough to know that she doesn't need to. She's happy being who she is." He looked Tamsin up and down. "Standing there in your father's coat and a sweatshirt you borrowed from some tourist town. She's whole. You're just sewn up pieces looking for more thread."

"How do you know this is my father's coat?"

"Because your father was scum, and I'll never get the vision of him walking around this town in that coat out of my head."

"He made mistakes. Broke promises. He wasn't honest. But I won't accept that he was scum."

"You're welcome to see it your way. He slithered around here like he owned this place. Whatever you and your family were to him, it wasn't enough. He made a second family here and expected all of us, and me—his best friend—to stay quiet while he treated the woman I loved like was bad leftovers. I bought her a ring. Got down on one knee, but she didn't love me. She picked him, and when he changed his mind and decided he belonged with you, he tried to buy her off with a house. She went without to raise that little girl. Shunned by this town, by her friends. And when she got tired of waiting and wanted something more for herself, she married me. I put off all my dreams for her, to raise her little girl. Several times. First when I proposed, then when she broke my heart, then when your father broke hers, and again when we got divorced. But every bit was worth it, because I raised that little girl as my own, and she still thinks of me as her father. I was the father yours never was. And you never had a clue. If you think he walked on water, that's just fine, but don't spread your bad religion here."

Tamsin held herself together and fought off the chill. "We knew something wasn't right. There were gaps. Times when he wasn't home. A vibe from my mother, like something was wrong. The stories she told us didn't sit right with her, and my sister could tell. My little sister still doesn't know about Ida. She suspects, but I haven't told her about any of this."

"I bet you think you'll have to now."

"I do have to. Truth is important."

"At what cost?"

"How do you calculate that? How do you know until you have the facts?"

"You don't. But you weigh your options and realize that there's unknown danger. Shipwrecks beneath the surface. Sharks. And you decide that the smart thing to do is to stay out of the damn water." Connor's boots kicked up sand and tumbled pebbles as he walked to the stairs.

She couldn't let him leave without asking. "What about the painting?"

"It's not for sale."

"I don't want it. I want to know why you keep it in the window."

"Ida loved it. Her father painted it. I keep it out there as a reminder that even beautiful stuff can come out of bullshit. Plus, it matches the decor. Now, you got what you came for. Get out of here and leave this town in peace."

"Did Ida tell you I stopped by? That I left something in her tip jar?"

"You're a special kind of stupid, aren't you?"

"Did she talk to you? Did she tell you?"

"No. She didn't have to. I saw you walk past my store and go into hers. You got what you came for. You have your facts. Now go home."

"Did you slash my car tires?"

Connor's mouth twisted, a weak attempt to conceal a smile. "Truth is, no."

"Do you know who did?"

"I have my suspicions. When your father and I were kids, acting out meant smoking cigarettes and listening to our music too loud. Kids these days have to work harder when they like a girl and someone comes to town, digging up a woman's dirt and making nice with her ex. My guess is, karma put you in the path of the kid who works at my store and has a crush on my daughter. I assure you it wasn't me. I don't fix my problems like that."

"You don't value accountability in your employees?"

Connor turned away. "I'm done answering your questions."

The *flop, flop, flop* of his muck boots faded into the sound of the bay. He was wrong. She had considered Ida's feelings. Maybe she hadn't gone about finding her the right way, maybe she missed a few key points when considering how the news would impact everyone, but she tried. And she couldn't take responsibility for the way Ida or Mags or Connor or anyone else reacted to the facts. All she knew was that withholding the truth was worse.

Tamsin sat on the stone wall beside the street and brushed the sand from between her toes. If she'd done real damage, she deserved the chance to make it right. She patted the hip pocket of her coat and found her cell phone, turned up the ringer just in case and tugged her socks and shoes onto her feet.

She couldn't help but feel some sympathy for Connor, a man who gave up everything for the woman he loved. To never get that fairy tale ending must have broken his heart. Tamsin knew the price of deferred dreams.

She'd found every bit of truth she'd come for, and Connor was right about one thing. It was time to go.

It was a short walk to the grill. Tamsin paused outside the door, at the spot where she found the pin of a lobster in a snow globe. It seemed a million years had passed. The front room of the grill was empty. No one was buying sandwiches from the counter or drinks from the cooler. Tamsin waited while Cyndi Lauper played "The Goonies 'R' Good Enough" on the radio and she smiled, remembering how much she loved that movie as a kid and the crush she'd had on Josh Brolin. Heartache had chipped away at Tamsin since those days. A life that once was perfect had become merely good enough. Her dream job had become good enough. Her house. Her relationship with Margaret had been good enough, even if she'd never been good enough for Mags. She would never live a life that was only good enough ever again.

"Hey, there." Deb poked her head around the corner, wiping her hands on a dish towel. "You here for lunch? Place is all yours. Sit anywhere you'd like." She pulled a menu from the top of a stack and passed it across the counter.

"Thanks. I'm here for one last lobster roll. And ice tea?"

Deb returned the menu to the pile. "I'll bring it right out."

"Unsweetened, please."

"You got it."

Tamsin slid into a seat at the table in the empty back room. The autumn sky had a golden tint to it that stained Motif Number 1 orange. This was Ida's view. Ansel's town. Knowing she would never see this view again, she took in every hint of light and stroke of shadow, painting them in her mind. Maybe she would replicate them on canvas one day.

Deb dropped a glass of tea and a straw on the table. "You're going to miss the Harvest Festival next weekend. There's food and pies. They serve beer in a tent down by the water."

"Maybe I'll come back for it next year." It seemed the thing to say, even though she knew she wouldn't.

"I hope it all works out and you do. Did you find what you were looking for? More important, did it come in a package you can live with?"

"I did. I got the facts, anyway. It took a while, but I realized that it doesn't really matter what package it comes in. I'm gonna live with it anyway. And it's funny, it came from the last person I thought would give it to me."

"Connor."

"How did you know?"

Deb looked past Tamsin, out toward the sea. "I didn't know at first. I don't even know Ida that well, to be honest. She used to come in here with Andy, but she keeps to herself mostly. I know her as Connor's step-daughter. I figured it out when the Arts Alliance girls were in here eating. I guess Ansel sent them an old picture, trying to identify a woman who turned out to be Ida's mom. One of them had seen the two of you walking through town and thought you were Ida. They were putting the pieces together. Talking about the past and whether or not it was the right thing for Gina to do, to have told Ida that Ansel was digging into her family history."

Tamsin sipped her tea to hide her disgust. Anything that required morality by committee in a public place equated to gossip, and she hated being on either end of it. "I'm sorry that it got out that way."

"It's just the other side of small-town life, that's all. I haven't said anything to anybody. If I couldn't keep a secret, I wouldn't have any customers."

"No, it's fine. I wanted to thank you for being kind to me. And thanks for your discretion with Ida. I had no idea how to go about finding her.

When I left home and came here, I had no idea what I was doing. I should've had a plan."

"Should is a horrible word. It's just an opinion about an obligation. It might help you learn from mistakes to ask yourself what you should have done, but you didn't do anything wrong by trying to find the truth. It's not like you were insensitive about it at all."

"It feels like harm has been done anyway, and Ida has no one to blame but me. Margaret, my other sister, is really gonna be pissed. If I had done this differently, I could have saved some people a lot of hurt. I was totally selfish about this."

"I don't know the full story, but if there's any truth to the gossip that the Arts Alliance girls were tossing around here, your father, bless his heart, is the one who's to blame. You may not have known how to unravel his mess, but you can't carry around the blame for the consequences of his actions."

Two lemon wedges floated in her tea. Tamsin poked at one with the straw and bits of seed escaped. "I still wish I could fix his reputation, so the truth of him lined up a little more with how I remember him. I never asked to carry around the weight of his bad decisions, but Ida never asked for it either. I wish I'd told her that. That I don't blame her or whatever. I just left my phone number and put the ball in her court. I wish I had told her that I didn't come here to make things hard or pass blame."

"These things tend to work themselves out the way they should. Just don't set yourself up for regret. If you think you left things unsaid, maybe find a way to say them."

Tamsin destroyed the lemon wedge and the tea went cloudy. A bell rang in the kitchen, sending Deb scampering for Tamsin's last lobster roll.

CHAPTER TWENTY-FOUR

Tamsin lay another armful of paintings flat in the back of the Cherokee and dropped her clean brushes in the cup holder. It seemed such a sophomoric thought, trying to reconnect with her father by painting the scenes as he had known them. The buildings held no secrets and told no truths. They obscured no lies or uncovered old mysteries. They simply were. Her father was right: it was people who gave these things meaning. The little green cottage of her childhood, once the scene of happy memories, was nothing more than wood and plaster, no matter how she painted it.

She slammed the tailgate and, turning, came face to face with Ida.

"Whoa. I didn't expect to see you before I left. I was going to write you a note or something."

Ida shifted her weight, her hands shoved deep in the pockets of her skinny jeans. She listed to one side, compensating for the weight of her messenger bag. Whatever she carried, she brought with intent and though it weighed her down, she shouldered it well.

Ida lifted her chin. "You have things you want to say? I have questions."

To Tamsin, Ida looked like a slightly younger version of herself. Brown hair, though Ida's hadn't yet started to brittle with age. Hips that would hold onto every cookie she ate if she didn't run from them. The skinny jeans, Doc Martens, and weathered leather jacket told only part of her story. Ida lived by her own rules in a town that had strong opinions about who she ought to be. Ida lowered the messenger bag to the ground gently and folded her arms as if waiting for something, anything, from Tamsin.

"*You* have questions? Of course you do." Tamsin hadn't considered the gaps in Ida's timeline and how many answers it might take to fill them.

"What do you want from me?"

"Absolutely nothing. Maybe a few answers. If you have them."

Ida raised an eyebrow. "I don't owe anybody anything."

"No, you don't. I feel like I owe you something, because I found you first. Maybe just…" Tamsin shrugged. "I don't know. You never deserved to be abandoned. There are no hard feelings from me. We aren't what he did. We can't change the past."

"I know all this stuff. Except the stuff about you. I appreciate that, I guess. Where did you get the drawing? Did you have it all this time?"

"Did you know he's not with us anymore?"

"Five years ago. Dad told me. Connor. Are you going to answer my question?"

"I am. My mom died earlier this year. I found the drawing in the pocket of his coat last week while we were cleaning out her house. We didn't know about you. I didn't know anything about this until I came here."

"Who's we?"

"Me and my sister. Margaret."

Ida unfolded her arms and stuffed her hands in the back pockets of her jeans. She loosened, shifting her weight, but her eyes never left Tamsin's. "Sorry for your loss."

"I heard you say your mom is sick. I hope she gets better soon."

"She won't. She has stage four cancer."

"I'm sorry."

"Me, too." Ida shrugged it off. "I'm sorry about our father. You're the one who knew him. He came around for a while, but then he just stopped."

"When he was here with you, he wasn't where we thought he was. At least now we know all the truth." Everyone but Margaret.

Across the street, the door chimed at the strudel place. A customer stopping in for an after-lunch snack or a cup of joe.

"Do you like wine?" Ida asked.

"Yes. Why? Is it genetic?"

Ida lifted her messenger bag a few inches off the ground. "You said you were leaving, but if you can stay one more night, we can polish off these bottles I ganked from Connor."

"Yeah, I can stay one more night. I was planning to until…"

"Until you chickened out about talking to me at the bakery?" Ida was playful, but Tamsin went on the defensive anyway.

"I didn't chicken out. I decided it was up to you what you wanted to do with the facts. It wasn't up to me to force you into some conversation that maybe you didn't want to have."

"If you say so. Wine, then?" The bottles clanged together when Ida lifted the bag.

Tamsin smiled at the flash of a memory. She had an unspoken rule with Owen. When things got tough or they argued, they split a bottle of wine and talked it out. "Definitely. Plastic cups okay with you?"

"First time I got drunk I was fourteen. At Loblolly Point. I drank half a bottle of Manischewitz out of a Dixie cup. I can handle whatever this place left for you."

"C'mon." Tamsin nodded toward her room, locked the car door, and Ida followed, dropping her bag on the bed. It was a bag like Ansel's. They really did belong together. Tamsin sat in the uncomfortable metal chair at the café table and shook off the notion of playing matchmaker. She'd done enough damage in this woman's life already.

"I figured somebody like you existed out there somewhere." Ida dug a bottle of wine from her bag and held it between her knees while sifting through the contents of the front pocket. "I have a corkscrew in here somewhere."

"Don't worry about it. I came prepared." Tamsin pointed to the top of the dorm fridge. The bottle opener rested on a tray with plastic cups. Always carry a bottle opener. Owen never left for a trip without one.

Ida grabbed it from the fridge and poured liquid sunshine into two plastic cups. Tamsin accepted one.

"Cheers," Ida said, extending her cup.

"Cheers."

"I thought there may be even more than one person like you out there. If it's memories you want, I have a few but not many. I mean, I must have known him well at one time, because I drew that picture. It's all just random things. I remember eating watermelon out on the rocks and spitting the seeds into the water. Stuff like that."

"What did you want to know?"

"I don't know. Medical history? Curiosity? Whatever you can tell me, I guess. I don't remember him being around that much. I only knew him as a guy my mother slept with, who came around sometimes, but they didn't stay together. I didn't know he had a whole other family. I just assumed he was unattached. I think it'll be a while before it really sinks in that I'm the illegitimate kid that resulted from an affair. How old are you? If you don't mind me asking."

"I'm forty-two."

"I figured something like that."

"You?"

"Thirty-three."

"My father sold the house when I was thirteen and Mags was eleven. So you would have been four."

"What house?"

Ida knew less than Tamsin thought. Being the bearer of information carried a lot of responsibility, and she would have to tell the story twice, but it couldn't be worse than telling a hundred people that Owen died. "The green cottage you grew up in on North Road used to belong to my family. My grandparents lived there, and we came here for summer vacations. We inherited it when my grandfather died. You would have been about four years old when my father came home to us from an art show and said he'd decided to sell the cottage because it was expensive to have two houses, and he could use the money to follow his dream of doing art full time. We all supported him, because he was a very good artist, and it was his dream. Now I know that was a lie. I found the deed. He gave it to your mother's mother for a dollar, and she gave it to your mother."

"To buy her silence?"

"Or to give you a stable home and take some weight off your mom. It's hard to say what motivated him. I'm going to take the sympathetic view."

"And you knew nothing about me or my mom?"

"Nope. My sister remembers things being tense. She says that Mom was always hiding something. I didn't want to see it. I just accepted that he had work and art that took him away until Mags visited me when I was in college. She was about to graduate from high school, and I took her to a campus party. She got drunk and started asking questions about where Dad was when we were little and why he sold the house here. I got mad at her for implying that my father had done something wrong, and she got mad at me for denying what she swore was true. I guess I glossed over it. Shellacked it. I didn't want to hear it. She never mentioned it again, until a week ago when we cleaned out my mom's house."

"Your mom lied to you? Did she even know about me? She never said anything?"

Tamsin swirled her wine in her cup. Poor Margaret, being lied to by her mother, now her sister. It was one thing for Tamsin to keep her grief to herself, but it was something else entirely to hide a family member. Every day that went by would increase her sister's rage when she learned the truth. She wasn't looking forward to the conversation. "If our mother knew the real reason he was gone so often and for so long, she never told us. And when he sold the house, she just accepted that he was using the money to support his painting hobby. I assume he visited you after that? I feel like I was sixteen or seventeen when he stopped traveling."

"That sounds right. He came around for a few years after we moved into that cottage. He would show up for a while, then leave again. Eventually, he just stopped showing up. My mom never talked about it, and I never really asked. There was never a big goodbye or anything. He did send letters and cards at Christmas. Birthdays."

"Do you still have them?"

"I wish. I wasn't very good at taking care of things as a kid, but I do have this." Ida pulled an old photo album from her bag. "I thought I'd show you photos and maybe that could fill in some holes. Unless seeing them would make things worse."

"No, I'd like to see them." Tamsin set her glass on the tiny table and moved to the edge of the bed, next to her half-sister.

Ida opened the album on her lap and flipped through the pages. The photographs were a parade of saturated primary colors, just like the ones Tamsin had from the eighties. Huffy bicycles and lunch in the backyard. Camping trips and plastic Halloween costumes that came with those thin plastic masks that cut your face. Delirious Christmas mornings with no hint of her father because he was with Tamsin and Mags in Pennsylvania.

Ida stopped at the first photograph of their father. He was wearing a blue sweater, a slouchy, grandfatherly looking thing made of loose knit stitches with pockets that sagged even when they were empty. It made him look older than his years. He had his arm around Ida's mother, who looked younger then than Tamsin was now. Love hadn't entered her mind—whether her father had loved Ida's mother and if he loved Ida the way parents do. She thought of the woman at work who went through a horrible divorce and how much she missed her kids when they were with their father. Did her father miss Ida in a constant desperation? Did he sneak off to make phone calls, to see if she got home from school okay or ask what they had for dinner? Did it tear at his soul that he didn't have those answers and that he couldn't even ask those questions? Was it easier to walk away, to tear out the stitches and let the seeping wound bleed until it scabbed over, than it would have been to keep up the lie or tell the truth? And what made him finally choose?

Tamsin took her phone from her pocket. "Can I take a picture of this? To show Margaret?"

Ida slid the book from her lap onto Tamsin's. "Go ahead. Any of them you want."

"Thanks. Is there anything you want me to tell Mags?"

"Tell her I didn't ask for this either." Ida split the last of the wine into the two glasses. "Can I ask you something personal?"

Tamsin couldn't think of anything more personal than family. "Of course."

"Did you sleep with him?"

"Ansel? Andy?"

"Yes. Did you sleep with him?" Ida's tone demanded an answer. Tamsin figured she already knew the truth.

"I did, but I didn't know your history. I had no way of knowing. I'm sorry. Trust me, I wouldn't have. I don't do things like that. If I knew he'd dated you…I haven't been with anybody since my partner, Owen, died five years ago. I thought there was a connection between us, and I let it get out of hand."

"What did he say? To get you to bed?"

"It wasn't like that. He has this way of—"

"Getting under your skin. Like he's known you forever. Looking at you like you're the most interesting person in the world."

"That about sums it up, yeah." Tamsin turned the album page and took another photo of her father and his other family with her phone. "I was angry with him, but it's fading now. It was bad timing. He was trying to tell me that he'd stumbled on the connection between you and me when you came in and after that I called him a liar. I figured there was no way he couldn't know. I really don't think he was trying to hurt you at all."

"Andy's pretty stupid when it comes to looks. He can figure out your childhood trauma in five seconds, but he can't see what's right in front of him. Any resemblance between us would be lost on him. We're just his type, is all. And he never knew my mom that well, so based on a newspaper clipping, he wouldn't have seen a resemblance or anything. He had no reason to think we had anything to do with each other." Ida finished the last of her wine. "Your mom never said a thing, huh?"

"Not a word. She always had a reason for him leaving."

"I wonder what our moms would make of us sitting here, talking to each other."

"I'll never be able to ask mine, but it's not too late for you to ask yours."

Ida looked into her empty cup. "Nah. The best gift I can give her is peace."

CHAPTER TWENTY-FIVE

The car was packed and covered in morning dew. In days it would be frost. Tamsin did one last scan of the motel room. She opened her wallet, left a decent tip for the housekeeper, hoping it would make up for the sand in the shower and the paint brushes she'd left in the sink all week, and checked on the snow globe pin zipped into the change pouch. Still there, safe and sound. That's where it would stay. She pulled the door shut and said goodbye to the bay. The air swept off the water, sweet and cold.

Her father's coat crumpled in a ball on the passenger seat, Tamsin aimed Owen's Cherokee for home. Margaret's voice haunted her over the sound of talk radio. Selfish. Impulsive. Reckless. Irresponsible. Tamsin would have to weather the usual storms and worse when she told her sister the truth about the drawing, Ida, and their father.

Her sister's voice lived in her head. *Oh, so you couldn't stay to help pack up our mother's house, but you had plenty of time to run to Rockport to uncover the family mystery that you know has haunted me for decades, and you didn't even bother to loop me in?* There was no good way to explain the last week over the phone. Halfway to Boston, she couldn't wait anymore. She pulled off the highway and into the parking lot of the Northshore Mall where she called her sister.

"Mags, it's me."

"Tamsin? Are you still in Rockport."

"I'm just north of the airport in Boston. I was thinking of coming to you for a day before going home. I haven't bought a ticket yet or anything, and I can't stay long."

"Why? Is something wrong? Not that you're not welcome it's just that it must be costing you a fortune, and you probably have to get back to work, and you never just *come* here."

"I have plenty of money. And can I worry about work, please?" She closed her eyes and took in a deep breath. A car door slammed, and a mother yelled at a child to stand near the car. "Please trust me when I tell you that my life is fine. I have one more day, and I want to stop by before I have to go back to work. Is that so terrible?"

Silence. The telltale sign of Margaret trying to figure out how to be offended. "I don't see why not. I may not have the guest bed made up for you yet. The boys have school, and it's crazy this time of year."

"It's fine. I can make the bed. I'll get an Uber like last time. Want me to text you before I get there?"

"Yeah, let me know what time you'll be here. Text me an ETA."

"Hey. Is it cold there? Like really cold?"

"Chilly. Why?"

"Just wanted to know what to bring."

"Gotcha. This is really weird. Is there something going on?"

"Hold your horses. Everything's fine. I'll see you in a few hours."

Tamsin opted for a blue and gray Boston hoodie from a store in the airport and a bloody mary from the bar across from it. Her father's coat was draped over the back of a tall chair at the bar, and her feet fought for comfort on the chair rail. Her purse rested in her lap with the new sweatshirt. Tamsin dug into it to pay the bartender. It was a wearying wait for the plane to board, watching dueling television sets dice the news into angry fragments on one wall and sports commentators on the other, slicing up sports as if it were anything more than a game of chance complicated by skill and athleticism. A group of people at a distant table cheered. Owen would have rolled his eyes. Nudged her knee. Made a joke. Tamsin smiled at the thought of him, folded a little white napkin from the bar into the shape of a swan, and watched the departures board for her flight to Minnesota.

For someone who hated leaving the house, she'd been in a lot of airports lately, watching weary departures and anxious arrivals. Just one more flight from Minnesota to Boston and a five-hour drive home, and this would all be over. She pressed a button on her phone to see the time, unlocked it, and opened her text messages with Marlow.

I have to fly from Boston to MN then back. And drive home. Time is tight. U think they'd say yes to another day?

While Marlow typed her reply, Tamsin's flight appeared on the departures board. She grabbed her things and made her way to the gate.

You're kidding, right? Doubtful. Not if you want a job when you get back.

Tamsin typed and walked. *I'll have to keep the visit short then. Thx.* She joined the line of people clutching coats, waiting their turn to shove them into overhead bins.

She snagged a window seat, and as the plane carried her higher, she watched cars blend in with the pavement and buildings melt into the trees. The walls that separated Rockport from Philadelphia and Minnesota fell away. She sipped a tiny cup of diet cola knowing that she couldn't land unprepared. There'd already been enough upheaval. What they all needed now was clarity. Approaching the topic of their father's affair the wrong way could do irreparable damage to her already strained relationship with her sister but nothing she could think of, no set of rehearsed lines, sounded good enough. It wasn't until she tipped the Uber driver and pressed her sister's doorbell that she knew what to say.

Once Margaret had tucked in her boys, and Philip had retired behind the closed door of his office, Tamsin pulled a bottle of duty free wine from her purse and handed it across the kitchen island to Margaret.

Mags used a fancy battery-powered opener that sucked the cork from the bottle and deposited it on the counter. Tamsin shared a smile with the ghost of Ansel.

"So what's with the surprise visit?" Mags pushed a glass to Tamsin.

"I have news. It's big."

"You're pregnant."

"If I were pregnant, would I be drinking?"

"I don't know about you lately, Tamsin. You've been doing strange stuff. Running off to Rockport without telling people where you were going?"

"That's what I'm here about."

"Rockport?"

Tamsin took her phone from the back pocket of her jeans. She opened the photo gallery and scrolled to the picture of her father in his slouchy blue sweater with a young Ida on a tricycle. In the background, in the doorway that led to a house she didn't know, leaned a woman in tan knit pants. It looked like a happy family on a Saturday afternoon, and Margaret took it in with a look of confusion that faded to understanding, then anger. Tamsin's phone hit the counter with a rubber thud when Margaret had her fill of the scene.

She raised an eyebrow. "I don't know what that is."

"I can tell you what it is. If you're ready to know."

"I suppose." Margaret moved her wine glass back and forth across her perfectly smooth granite countertop.

"When you were seven and I was nine, Dad had an affair with this woman in Rockport." Tamsin unlocked her phone and the picture reappeared. "This little girl is our half-sister. Her name is Ida."

"What kind of name is Ida?"

"Really? That's your reaction?"

Margaret turned off, her focus set on some distant point down the hall. Processing, maybe. Tamsin glanced behind her to make sure they were still alone and kept her voice down so the boys and Philip wouldn't hear. "I met Ida in Rockport. But before I tell you about her, I wanted you to know what happened to Grandad's house."

"Is it gone?"

"No. It's still there. After Dad inherited it, he sold it to this woman's grandmother for a dollar, and she gave it to her daughter. Ida was raised there, and Ida's mom later sold it. It's owned by an older couple now who only stay there in the summers."

"That house should have been ours, and he gave it away for a dollar? What a piece of shit."

"That seems shallow and harsh and unfair. I know you don't mean that." Even though she knew Margaret would have a strong reaction, hearing her say that about her father—their father—stung. Their father had become two different people in Tamsin's mind, the loving father who walked through the woods with her and taught her to ride a bike and a separate man who betrayed them. Tamsin had always been closer to her father. Her fondness was harder to break. "There's a lot we don't know, Margaret. It's a lot to unpack. I know what he did to Mom was horrible. It was unfair to us and to Ida. It's possible that giving the house to them was the only way he could think of to do right by Ida and her mother."

"So you went out there and dug all this up? For what?" Margaret's whisper shot up an octave. "To come back here and tell me that there's some abandoned woman in Rockport who wasn't given the childhood she deserved by our father? I don't want to deal with this right now. I have a lot going on, and I just don't want to deal with this."

Tamsin shook her head and shifted her weight. She stepped back from the kitchen island and turned so she had a clear view of the hall. Margaret was enough to deal with. She didn't need to bring two boys and brother-in-law into the conversation. "All I can do is give you the facts. It'll take a lot of time for them to settle, you know? To figure out how this changes things. But it doesn't have to. You said something wasn't right, that they'd been hiding something. Now you know you were right. But it doesn't have to change your life."

"It's not about being right, Tam. He cheated on our mother. He lied to us and left us hanging. Mom didn't know where he was half the time, and if she did, she didn't tell anybody. She had to save face all the time with her friends and her parents, making apologies for him missing things when he went to shack up with this woman and this kid he had. Nothing about this is right."

"I know. It's not right, but it isn't the end of the world. What seems horrible right now might not seem so bad once you've thought about it for a while. I mean, he wasn't perfect, but you already knew that. Nothing changes, except that there's this half-sister out there. And it isn't her fault, either. I don't want to look back at my childhood, which was a happy one, and look for the flaws. I just don't want to. I was a happy kid, and nothing changes that."

"You were happy because you were blind, Tam. You chose not to see what was right in front of you."

"You didn't seem miserable. You had everything you wanted."

Margaret's nostril flared, and she gripped the edge of the counter, an obvious effort to release some steam while keeping her voice down. "Everything except my father, because I didn't know where the hell he was half the time."

Tamsin took her phone from the island and tucked it back into her pocket. Margaret wouldn't want to see more. "Did you and Mom ever talk about this?"

Margaret turned her back on Tamsin and left her wine on the counter. She rearranged dishes in the dishwasher, some task of tidying up that either busied her hands or calmed her mind. "Never," she said. "Not once did I broach this topic with mom. I didn't want to make her drag up old excuses or feel like she had to explain it to me. By the time I became an adult, I was just as mad at her as I was at him."

"Why? That doesn't make any sense. He cheated on her. You can't blame Mom for this."

"She was complicit. She didn't leave him. She didn't put up a fight. She didn't pack up our toys and take us away or kick him out or serve as any kind of role model for self-respect. That's not how you should act if you are trying to raise two strong girls." Margaret stopped and wiped her nose on her sleeve. "I don't want to talk about this right now. She hasn't even been gone half a year."

"The timing is crap. I'm sorry for that. I keep thinking about what this must have done to her and how much strength it took to keep up the façade." Tamsin set her glass on the counter next to Margaret's and refilled them both. "I think she did okay. We came out pretty strong." At least Margaret did, anyway.

"Did we?"

"We didn't?"

"Maybe *you* did." Margaret closed the dishwasher drawer and glasses clanged together. "You made it through losing Dad, who was like some icon to you. You made it through Owen. I don't know how you still live in that same house."

"If I'd sold this house, I'd have lost the last piece of Owen I had left. He's in every corner, you know. You just get through it whether you want to or not. You just keep going. That's it. You'll get through losing Mom."

Margaret stood across the kitchen island from Tamsin and leaned across, both hands on the granite. Her voice lowered to a near whisper. "I might be that kind of strong, but I'm not the kind of strong I need to be to face the other stuff. I should be able to walk away, and I can't."

"What other stuff? Walk away from what? Is something wrong with Philip?" Tamsin matched her sister's whisper, but Margaret didn't respond. She covered her mouth with one hand the way she did when she was a kid and scared, looking fragile and small.

"Mags. Are you blaming Mom because you can't walk away from your marriage? Christ. Most people would say they're sticking with it for the sake of their kids, which is exactly what Mom did, but you're blaming her for not being a good example because you hit a rough patch with Philip?"

"It's not like that, Tam. And keep your voice down."

"I am keeping my voice down. Does he beat you or hit the kids? Because I'll go up there and beat the shit out of him with this bottle as soon as we empty it."

"No. Don't start stuff. I don't want to open a giant can of worms until I have all of the information."

"What information? You yell at me all the time for not telling you the details of my incredibly boring life, but you have something major like this, and it drips out of you like the most annoying bathroom sink in the history of running water."

"Shh. I think he's cheating on me."

"No wonder you're so pissed at Dad."

"I can't prove it yet. When you're in my position, with no resources of your own, you don't go accusing your spouse of something like that until

STICK FIGURES FROM ROCKPORT

you have enough proof to stack the cards in your favor. I can't just take the boys and run. I have nothing. And it's not that easy to walk away from all these memories. But if that's all that's keeping me here, that's not enough."

Clinging to memories. Tamsin knew the clench of it well. "I wish I'd known. I can't imagine how you must feel."

"I know. You never married Owen. Just the thought of severing ties and doing all that paperwork. It feels like a terminal illness. Like an impending death. It's hard to admit that it's all about to end."

Tamsin pushed away from the counter. "I don't think being unmarried diminishes the pain of loss. And your divorce isn't anything like a death, Mags."

"I'm not diminishing your experience."

"Oh, you're not? You just stood there and said I couldn't possibly know how you're feeling because I never married Owen, but you're pretty sure what you're going through feels like someone's dying."

Margaret put her hands up in surrender. "I don't want to do this right now."

"Like I do?"

"I have to get to bed so I can get the kids out the door in the morning for school."

"I get it. What are you going to do about the divorce? Are you getting a lawyer?"

"Private investigator."

"How are you going to pay for that?"

"A credit card. I took one out in my name."

"Thank God for paperless billing."

"Right? I used your address, so it doesn't show up on a credit alert."

Tamsin reached across the island and gave her sister's shoulder a nudge. "Now who's not being forthcoming with the information?"

"I'll pay for it. Or he will, when he starts paying alimony."

"Let me know what you need. What I can do."

"Thanks. What are we gonna do about Ira?"

"Ida. I don't know. There's nothing to be done. She knows how to get in touch with me. I said I'd like the three of us to get together some time, and she sounded like she wasn't opposed to it, but she said something about not being ready to join a Ya-Ya Sisterhood. Are you pissed?"

"That I didn't get to meet her? Nah. I'm curious about her, but I'm not pissed."

"She looks like us."

"I'm not surprised."

"And I slept with her ex-boyfriend."

"Tamsin!"

"Well, it just kinda happened. We were both his type."

"I hope you were safe."

"Yes, Mags. We were safe."

"See? You're really strange lately."

Tamsin loaded their wine glasses into the dishwasher. She'd only told her sister half of the truth, but telling her about the child her father abandoned was easier than coming clean about the grief she couldn't release. "Maybe I'm finally becoming myself. One little step at a time."

* * *

Tamsin fed her nephews cereal in the morning, put on her business smile for Philip, and when she and Mags were alone in the house, she unlocked her phone and pulled up the photo gallery.

"This sweater. Do you remember it?" Tamsin pinched and zoomed.

Margaret took the phone and squinted at the photo. "Is that blue or black?"

"Blue. I remember it. I wondered if it was in Mom's stuff."

"Everything's in bins in the basement." Margaret opened the basement door and flipped the light switch. Tamsin followed, her socks slipping on the unfinished stairs. In the damp and cold, she faced a wall of giant bins.

"What's in these?" She knew she opened herself to the typical response from her sister. An accusation that she'd know if she hadn't run off to Rockport and left her to do all the work. If Margaret thought it, she kept it to herself.

"Clothes, photo albums, papers. Stuff I feel like I should hold on to for a while." She pulled a bin off the stack and tossed the lid aside. "This is everything of Dad's."

There wasn't much. The gilet lining that went with his old coat, which Tamsin set aside. An old pair of pants. Some shirts. In the bottom of the bin, she found the navy blue sweater. The tip of one sleeve was still dusted with yellow paint. "Can I have this? I want to set it aside for Ida."

"You want to give her something of Dad's?" Margaret threw the lid on the tub and placed it back on top of the stack. "Why do you think we owe her something?"

"We don't owe her anything. She may not even want it. But it's not about her, it's about us offering it to her."

"I know I said I was okay with this last night, but I'm not ready to incorporate this other woman into my world."

"I don't think this has anything to do with being ready. The timing sucks, sure."

"I really wish you'd let me in on all this. I don't have the energy to argue with you right now, so don't give me a bunch of crap, but you knew. I don't know how you knew, but you knew."

"I found a drawing in the pocket of Dad's coat. It was in an envelope with a Rockport postmark."

"And instead of telling me like an adult, you took off alone. Like I had no right to be involved in this at all."

"I needed to do this. You always have to control everything and tell me I'm irresponsible and incapable. You have to do everything first. When I realized you were right, that there was some family mystery, I had to solve it. I had to figure out why. Not just what was imperfect about the past, but why I worked so hard not to see it."

"You see things that way because everything *always* has to be perfect with you, Tam. And if you can't make it that way, you pretend it is anyway."

"Just once, instead of telling me who I am and being wrong, why don't you ask me and try to understand me? Of all people, you'd think my own sister could make an attempt to understand me."

Margaret pushed a plastic bin further back on the shelf. "I didn't ask for any of this, so you're going to have to give me time to deal with it."

"It's funny you should put it that way. When I asked Ida if she had anything for me to tell you, she said to tell you she didn't ask for this either."

CHAPTER TWENTY-SIX

Tamsin let her suitcase fall from the back of Owen's Cherokee. The grinding of its plastic wheels on the sidewalk didn't sound any more appealing on the way to her front door than they did on the way to her mother's. The bag banged against the wooden steps, slammed against her heel, and came to a stop. She expected police tape. Chalk outlines. Black dust left from taking fingerprints. Some kind of stomach-churning emotion. But there was nothing. The only evidence left of an intrusion was the sheet of plywood covering one window. She'd have to call Renee, take her some cookies or something, have a few drinks, and pay her back.

"Poor, sad house." Tamsin patted the door frame and fumbled the key into the lock. "I shouldn't have left you alone like that. Now we've been invaded and you have this giant, ugly Band-Aid." She and Owen spent a Memorial Day weekend repainting those windows, joking about lead poisoning. She knew what he would say. That's what insurance is for. "It's been ten years. Paint was starting to peel anyway."

Inside, a note from Renee lay on the floor. *Hey. Welcome back. I know you said not to clean, but I didn't want you to come home to a pile of glass on the floor. I swept it into your kitchen trash. I hope you don't think I was invading your privacy or anything. I can only imagine how horrible it must feel to know someone was in your house. And don't even think about trying to pay me back. Hugs, R.*

She could count on two hands the number of people who'd been through the house since Owen died, and the allowable timeline for bereavement had passed. Now this. How many people trampled her area rugs? What path did they take through her house? The police needed a list of what was missing. She abandoned her suitcase by the door. Her father was still on the mantel. There'd be plenty of time to make peace with the urn. She turned her back on it and went room by room with a notepad and pen from the junk drawer in the kitchen. The officer's business card on the kitchen counter went into her pocket. The clock radio was missing. It wasn't worth anything, and there were more in the basement. Hopefully.

In the dining room, she tossed her father's green coat on the back of a chair. The DVDs were gone from the cabinet in the living room. Just a stack of five-dollar films she'd curated from lonely Target runs. Foreground noise that she told herself was background noise. Nothing meaningful or irreplaceable. The back patio looked untouched. Adirondack chairs were still there. What would a thief want with Adirondack chairs, anyway?

She straightened pictures as she moved up the stairs to the guest room where she slept. Eighteen hundred sleeps and Tamsin still didn't think of it as her bedroom. The drawers of her grandmother's dresser were open, her clothing balled and wadded, strewn on the floor. She threw it all into the laundry basket. Spare change was missing from a small dish on the nightstand.

Down the hall and into the bathroom with the laundry basket, she dumped it into the washer. Blue laundry detergent oozed into tub, and she pushed the lid down, pressed the buttons, put the washer through its old familiar cycle. An old bottle of medication was missing from the cabinet. Ibuprofen from Owen's broken finger seven years before, a certain disappointment to a teenager looking for a high. Owen's razor was still there. Everything in its place. But the door to the bedroom was open. The one she'd shared with Owen. That door was never open. Never.

She reached into her pocket for the snow globe pin but remembered it was zipped in her wallet with her loose change. Without comfort, she folded her arms across her stomach and crossed the hall, crept over the threshold and into the den. The only room left to explore outside the inner sanctum. The overhead light glowed a faint bluish tone, an efficient bulb throwing off inefficient light until it warmed up. Chargers for cell phones and laptops were missing from the desk drawer. The pine-scented candle Owen gave her for Christmas the first year in the house was gone. Clean wood visible within a halo of dust. She expected to feel raw, wounded, but it was the scent of the candle that she liked, and it was replaceable. The absence of rage or sorrow, the lack of memories clawing to the surface, reaching out to hold on made her feel worse, somehow. She wanted to feel anything but hollow.

The door to the closet was closed. The old house had settled and leaned and the door preferred to be closed so she kept it propped it open with a cast-iron piggy bank, now gone. Inside, paper and envelopes, pens and cleaning supplies. Extra towels and washcloths that didn't fit in the hall. On the top shelf she kept her old laptop.

Five years before, a man in a cell phone store pointed to a folder icon on her laptop. He told her to take the computer home, connect to the internet, and backup everything in that folder to the cloud. Every voicemail he left her, her calls to him, his voice notes, and ringtones. His downloaded social media profiles and all of his photos. Candid pictures he'd taken of her gardening, laughing with friends, cooking, and shoveling snow from the porch. If she took the laptop home and backed up the files, he'd said, she'd have them for eternity, even if something happened to the laptop. Because the laptop was fallible. Floods and fires could destroy it. It could be lost in a move or destroyed in a hurricane. Or it could be stolen. She never had the heart to face them, to even risk hearing his calls about leaving work early and stopping at the store. Hoagies or pizza and did she want any wine or beer. All of it reduced to icons in a folder. She'd discarded the man's advice and placed the laptop on a shelf that, now, was as empty as the space in her chest where her lungs used to be. Knowing it was gone, possibly forever, made her think of everything else that she cherished.

She took a sharp, stinging inhale and dropped the notepad and pen on the desk on her way to the bedroom. The door was only partway open, stuck in the backswing by the gravity of the old house. She pushed the door, and the thud of the doorknob hitting the wall echoed.

The sheets were the same. The pillows the same. The last time she was in that bed, sunlight hadn't crept across the comforter yet, and her head was on a pillow that, now, was missing its pillowcase. Tamsin filled in the blanks. A teenager stuffing her chargers and change into it, brushing along the picture frames as they ran down the stairs, laptop under one arm.

Owen's wardrobe stood open. Inside were shelves. Socks and shorts and a fine layer of dust. A small clay dish, the survivor from a broken set of pottery they bought on a trip to the mountains, sat empty at eye level. Owen's flash drives had been there, but now they were gone. Every photo of every adventure they'd taken together, organized in folders by date. Canyons and forests and long drives up the coast. Video clips of them singing in the car, making up songs about food and the sights. All gone. Unless the police had them, she'd lost her chance to live those times again, through his eyes, forever.

The top shelf. He'd never used the top shelf, far enough out of reach to lose things. Months after he died, Tamsin went through the house and hid things too painful to see, and she stored them there. Snow globes. One for each adventure they'd taken. All there. Untouched. But what else was

STICK FIGURES FROM ROCKPORT

missing? What else did they rip at the seams?

She tore shirts from their hangers, bits of dust floating into the light. His pants fell to the floor. She dug into the pockets, pulling balls of lint and the ghosts of receipts from the pockets. Looking for nothing, but eager to find everything not scavenged by thieves. Socks and shorts and T-shirts landed in piles. She tore to shreds the last mail he opened, some bill paid long ago by his settled estate. She fell into a windsor chair by the window, clutching the dusty, dark blue trousers that were draped over the arm. The last thing he wore on his last day alive. Not dirty, set aside to be worn again. Tamsin pulled the pants onto her lap, yearning to sob into the hem of one leg, begging for some part of Owen to comfort her in the release, but the tears wouldn't come. Those pants weren't who he was. It was the person he dressed up to be for the work week. Owen was the jeans and the T-shirts and the shorts on the floor. Why had she done it? Because thieves hadn't? Because no stranger could do worse to her than she had been doing to herself for years? For the rest of her life?

She threw the slacks onto the pile and tugged his old Georgia Tech shirt from beneath a hoodie. Dark blue writing on gray. Tamsin stood, the shirt balled in her fist, hovering over the mayhem and pushing aside the emotions one at a time. Guilt. Shame. Giving names to the emotions only worsened the chaotic pile. Owen's shirt didn't smell like him anymore. None of it did. Not his jeans. Not the sweatshirt he bought at the Grand Canyon or his dress shirts for work or his socks. One by one, she picked up the pieces, smelling them, hoping that one would still have something, some essence of Owen. Some hint of that smell of a person. The way soap and shampoo and aftershave blended together with pheromones and whatever else made Owen smell like Owen, but it was gone forever, replaced by the smell of the house and cedar.

The reality of what she'd done, his clothes scattered, his perfect folding undone, his mail destroyed, hit her like a truck. The piles had to be put back. By the armful, she pushed clothes onto the shelves, unsorted and unfolded. When the shelves were full, she threw handfuls on top, forgetting the trinkets she had stashed there when they became too painful to see. A snow globe of London toppled. Her snow globe. The one that came in the little red box with two plane tickets to London on a warm Christmas morning. She reached out her arm, tried to catch it, her fingers brushing the glass as it fell to the floor. But it smashed on the hardwood and white plastic beads rode the tsunami and washed between the floorboards. She didn't hear herself scream.

Tamsin kicked the clothes out of the way and ran for towels, kneeling on the floor and soaking up glycerine and water. She dabbed at the wet corner of the area rug and, from behind a wall of tears, picked tiny white beads from between the floorboards with her fingernail, collecting them in a washcloth. They piled up like her shame. Lying to Mags about why she went to Rockport. Hiding the stick figure drawing. Sleeping with Ansel. The state of her house, like a shrine to a person she couldn't be with anymore. A temple dedicated to a life she couldn't have and couldn't bear to lose. Her father's indiscretion. And so much anger at him for forcing her to accept what she never wanted to see. So many white beads in the floorboards.

No more. No more lying to herself, lying to Margaret. She threw the washcloth and broken glass into the bathroom trash can, and for the first time since she woke next to Owen alone, she rested her head on her old pillow. This time, she soaked it with tears. No dreams waited for Tamsin. No hopes, no longing desire. No dreams deferred. Everything she aimed to achieve had been done. But the cost of living behind a closed door meant losing the person within. She'd pushed everyone away. Her sister, her friends. She would have to clean this mess herself.

The view from her old side of the bed was as familiar as if she'd woken up there that morning. The streak of yellow paint on the ceiling. The ding in the plaster from some resident past. What would a future resident make of the white plastic beads in the floorboards she couldn't rescue? She rolled to her side, toward Owen, toward the gentle rise and fall of his back with each breath. The mattress, the old comforter spread before her like an expanse of sea to the horizon. Pushed up by the ripple was a key.

The opaque blue keychain from the repair shop in town, the color of blueberry JELL-O with faded white lettering, held the key to Owen's old truck. The barn and Owen's tools. Tamsin grabbed it, squeezed it in her fist, and ran.

CHAPTER TWENTY-SEVEN

She thundered down the stairs and past the picture frames, through the living room, and shoved her feet into the wellies she kept on a mat by the back door, wiggling her heel into place. The door slammed behind her as she crossed the porch. Gravel crunched beneath her feet, threatening to twist her ankle. She dug her keys from her pocket and fumbled one into the barn padlock with shaking hands, tugging down on the bulk of metal warmed by the sun.

The barn smelled like no other place Tamsin had ever been. Like charred wood, oil, and gas. Generations of carriages, tractors, and cars had passed through it. She slid the door open, all the way, so sun could reach the truck. Relieved, she faced Owen's dream.

When they first moved into the farmhouse, the land was untended and overgrown. Owen called landscaping companies and winced at the quotes, unable to justify the expense. On a snowy Valentine's Day, he rolled two dreams into one and bought the Willys Truck he'd dreamed of owning as a kid. He'd missed his chance to restore it with his father, but he could use it to clear the land and revive its broken spirit. It took an hour to drive it home in blinding snow with no heat. The truck was rusting, running rich, its paint scratched and faded. It was uncomfortable, and to Tamsin it was nothing more than a hobby Owen loved. He'd expected it to be a toy, but it became a companion, a friend he drove to work and the store. He'd enjoyed the waves and smiles from strangers and cared for it as if it were a pet.

One Sunday, he started an oil change and realized he needed a filter. He ordered a few from Amazon and died before they arrived. When the box showed up two days before the funeral, Tamsin opened the barn door enough to toss it in. Years later, the cardboard had degraded and a mouse had moved in, but the filters inside were none the worse for their time on the concrete floor. She opened the passenger side door of the truck and tossed the box onto the seat.

His tools were lined up on a workbench next to the truck, just as he had left them one hot Sunday in July. Wrenches and pliers and old screwdrivers. Humidity had eaten into the surface, turning them to rust. He would have cared for them, wiped them down and put them away, but his work came to a halt, and here they sat. Another thing waiting for him to return. Decaying. Returning to the earth.

Beneath the truck sat an oil catch can, waiting for oil. For Owen. Tamsin slid into the driver's seat and wrapped her arms around the steering wheel.

The truck didn't care how long it took or who would finish the job. The truck didn't know whether one hour or one decade had passed since Owen stepped away, washed his hands, and suffered a ruptured aortic aneurysm in his sleep. But it didn't stop her from feeling as if she'd let the truck down.

"I'm so sorry, old buddy. He would have wanted more for you than this. If Owen knew you'd sit here for so long, he would have begged me to finish the job or sell you to someone who would. I wonder sometimes what he would have done if he'd known. If he had a deadline, you know? Would he have hung up his pants or cleared off the DVR?"

Tamsin let go of the steering wheel. The seat's rusty springs cried out when she leaned back, taking in the view through the windshield. She ran her finger along the narrow dashboard and wiped away dust. She smeared it on the knees of her jeans.

"I think I was cleaning the fridge when these oil filters arrived. He had a half-eaten hoagie in there. Woulda been gross if I'd saved it forever, but it was hard to throw it away. Like, as long as it was still there, he might come back to eat it. Throwing things away, letting life reboot, and fixing you would have meant accepting that life had to go on, and I didn't want it to. If Owen knew he was going to have that aneurysm, he wouldn't have cleaned the fridge, but he would have found a good home for you. He wouldn't want you to locked in this barn alone forever."

Tamsin dug her cell phone from her back pocket. The rusty springs of the seats creaked beneath her shifting weight. "Here's what I'm thinking. I'll figure out how to change your oil, and then I'll park you outside so you can air out a bit. I'll find a way for you to get to a new home. A happy home where you can make some new memories and fulfill someone else's dream. What do you say?" She ran her finger across the screen of her phone, unlocking it. "This must be on the internet somewhere. What do I look for? Willys Truck oil change?"

She called Mags instead.

"Do you know how to change the oil in a really old truck?"

"No? Philip takes our cars to that Jiffy place, or I stop there on the way home from work. It's easier than having all that used oil sitting around. Why are you changing oil? Are you home?"

"Yeah. I got home a few hours ago, I guess. Did I tell you my house was broken into while I was up in Rockport?"

"No. But you don't tell me anything."

"Renee from next door called while I was in Rockport. Long story short, they caught some kids who broke into a bunch of houses, and they admitted to it. The cops came here and found a mess. Renee came over. Patched up the broken window and cleaned up the glass. I had to go through the house and make a list of everything that was missing. They got everything important. My old laptop that had Owen's voice messages and thumb drives with all our pictures."

"Oh, Tam. I'm sorry. Maybe they'll find them. Did you call the cops to tell them what was missing?"

"Not yet. I was going through the house, making the list they asked for, and I ended up in the barn with Owen's old truck. This truck's been sitting here in need of an oil change for half a decade."

"Out of sight out of mind, huh? I guess you're finally doing something with it?"

"Yeah. It's time to finish it. I'm sitting in the driver's seat, and I can just hear Owen, you know. What he would say. He would say that I should have taken care of this years ago. That he would have wanted me to sell it to someone who would love it, not leave it to rot in this old barn. Did you know that I haven't touched anything of Owen's since he died? His toothbrush is still in the holder. His stubble is still stuck in his razor. His dirty clothes are in the laundry basket. I shut the bedroom door and only opened it a few times before today to hide stuff in there that I didn't want to see because it hurt to look at it. You didn't know that, did you?"

She didn't often leave Margaret speechless. The silence was broken by the sound of a beeping microwave through the phone, a meal to be eaten or a snack to be had. Then Margaret came to life. "You never told me any of this. I didn't know. I would have come."

"I didn't want you to." Tamsin could hear Mags huff through the phone, the start of a protest as old as their sisterhood. "I knew if you came here and saw how I lived, I couldn't lie to you anymore. That you would force me into some kind of counseling. Tell me I should move out of the house I love and let go of Owen."

"That's ridiculous. I mean, I would have suggested you move. I've said a thousand times that I don't know how you can still live there. But all you'd have to do is say no. I wanted to be there for you, and you brushed me off. You always do that. Like it's no big deal, whatever you're going through."

"No, Mags. Saying no wouldn't have been enough. You would have pushed because you were doing what you felt was right, and I would have been angry because you were trying to take away the only thing I had left to hold on to. Plus, no one wants to hear someone talk about their grief. People don't want to be reminded that we all face the same odds." Tamsin folded back a flap of the damp cardboard box and extracted a huge oil filter. "But that's only half the truth. I didn't want to move on. Love can be so selfish. If I let go of Owen, I would let go of the love and comfort I got from him, and I wasn't going to spend one bit of energy on anything that would drive his memory away. I wanted him back. Without him, I didn't have anything to live for."

"You do, though."

"Not really, Mags. Remember that limo ride back from the cemetery after Grandad died? Dad sat there with Gran, and she talked about everything she wanted to do. Her bags were already packed, and she was headed to her sister's in France. Kept talking about seeing Luxembourg. Then Dad died, and Mom moved to Minnesota to live near you and her grandkids. She started a book club, for Christ's sake. I lived my dream with Owen. I didn't save anything for later. I'm forty-two. There's so much time ahead of me, and I kept thinking there was no life left to live. But now I'm looking at this truck thinking that Owen wouldn't have wanted it to sit idle like this and for the first time, I can hear him in my head, telling me that he doesn't want that for me, either. He would want me to treat his truck like it had a future, and he would want me to treat myself the same way."

"That's absolutely true. He would want that for you. That's what everybody wants for you."

"I know. I think I've known that the whole time. I just couldn't accept it, because it would mean losing Owen's voice in my head. And the funny thing is, in Rockport, I could barely hear him at all."

"Maybe that distance helped."

"It did. Without Owen in my head to keep me in the past, I finally saw why I lied to myself all these years. I know you're really ticked off at me for not telling you about Ida, and it wasn't fair of me to drag the past into this, but I figured I would lose control of finding her. I needed to solve this myself because my own truth was so wrapped up in it. It's stupid and silly, but that's what it was. I'm sorry, Margaret."

"I get it. I won't mention it ever again. If I'd known it meant that much to you, it wouldn't have bothered me. It just seemed sudden and—"

"Painful."

"Yeah. What about the house and the break-in? Are you okay? Do you want me to come keep you company?"

It was time to clean out the closets. Put a new coat of paint on the walls. It was time to give Owen's clothes to charity and reclaim the empty spaces. It was time to make new memories with her sister. "Not yet. Soon? Is that okay? You would come?"

"Tam, I would have been on the first flight there, and I never would have left if you told me that you needed me."

"Okay. I'll call and let you know what happens with the cops."

"And the truck."

"I will. Oh! I'm probably going to lose my job tomorrow, too. I think they're selling the company. Even if they don't offer me a pink slip, I think I'll volunteer to take one. It's time I spend some time on me."

"Will you be okay? With money?"

"Yeah. I can't stay unemployed forever, but I'll be okay."

"I'm sorry I piled all my divorce stuff on you. I didn't know all this was going on. I can be selfish sometimes."

"No worries. I get it. As for Philip, it'll take a while, but you'll come to terms with what you'll lose. All those memories that keep you glued there are just ghosts of the past. You can't force them to stay. The good times are still a part of you, and when you're ready to move on, you can choose which ones you want to keep and which ones to let go of."

"That's good advice. Should I point out—"

"No." Tamsin smiled and dropped the oil filter back in the box.

"Okay. Call me?"

"As soon as I hear something." Tamsin ended the call, climbed out of the truck, and patted it's fender. "Maybe I don't need advice. Maybe we can figure this out for ourselves. Can't be that hard to change some old oil."

CHAPTER TWENTY-EIGHT

All of the doors in Tamsin's world were damaged, and the farmhouse was no exception. Bare wood peeked through a ding in the frame where the medics bumped the stretcher when they wheeled Owen out of the house. She wasn't able to fill it or paint over it, no matter how hard Margaret tried to convince her. It was the last impact he made on the farmhouse they cherished.

Poking her finger into the divot, she wondered if she'd remember what it felt like in another five years. If she would be able to call it to remembrance along with the smell of the barn and the sound of rain on the porch during a storm. Would she have the strength to love someone else, and if she did, would the new memories push the ones she loved out of reach? Maybe the new owners would fix the ding. Tamsin had to move on, either way.

She tugged the door open, releasing it from the jamb. A sticky wall of summer air was on the other side. A moving van pinged its cool-down in the driveway, and two strangers peered past her, to the boxes and bins stacked in clusters. One was tall and thin, the other burly and tanned.

The latter pushed past her. "Are you expecting more movers? That's not all gonna fit in this truck."

The tall one stood firm on the porch. "Is it okay to back the truck up to the door?"

"Sure. You can back up to the porch. This doesn't all go, though." Tamsin's eyes were fixed on the tanned one. He moved around the boxes. They were labeled by room. Life in bullet points scrawled on box flaps. "Just the furniture with Post-its and the boxes in these two rooms. The rest stays. It goes to charity. The real estate agent will take care of it."

"Downsizing, huh? My mom just did that. Dad moved to Detroit with some woman he met on the internet. Seventy-two years old and he's meeting people on the internet."

"Crazier things have happened." Tamsin took in the smell of exhaust. The beeping truck cut its engine at the bottom of the porch steps. "What did she do?"

"Who?"

"Your mom? What did she do when your dad left?"

The tanned one lifted two boxes and crossed the threshold onto the porch. "She threw everything out. Moved to Florida. She always wanted to live in Florida."

"Good for her. A whole new life." Tamsin stepped aside. "If you don't need me, I'm going to run out to the barn. Pack a few last things."

"No problem." The two men grabbed and hoisted boxes and tubs. No emotion weighed them down. "We've got the address. We're supposed to follow you, though, right? Something about narrow streets and where to park?"

"Yeah. I might be a little slow on the hills, but I can do the speed limit." Tamsin took her father's coat from the back of a kitchen chair. "Oh, that box with all the fragile tape? It's really, really fragile. It's my snow globe collection."

She carried her father's coat across the gravel drive and into the barn. It looked like it belonged there, tossed across the seat of Owen's old truck. She loaded boxes into the back, tools and Owen's books about restoration. Spare parts she might need. She patted the tailgate on her way to the driver's seat. "Let's get you out of here and close up this old barn. What do you say, buddy? Let's go on an adventure."

Owen's truck pulled out of the barn and down the gravel drive for the last time. Tamsin stopped where the driveway curved between two trees, leaving the keys in the ignition, and taking her phone from the seat. She scrolled through photos to the one she took the day they moved in. Owen on the porch stairs, caught with one foot in the air. He carried a box that still sat on a shelf in the basement. It held drinking glasses then. Next week, the future owners would find spare bathroom tiles in it. She could still remember the way Owen moved. The flex of his calf muscle. The curve of his shoulder. He would be proud of her. Happy for her. And pleased she decided to keep his old truck.

Two strangers hauled memories from their dream house, and she waited in the shade. Soon, she would have to let go.

CHAPTER TWENTY-NINE

Margaret arrived in Rockport just as ice began to pelt the windows. The sound of mother nature's clock, the second hand ticking out of time.

"What horrible weather!" Margaret left her suitcase on the mat inside the door and tugged a hat from her head, her hair full of static.

"You're the one who wanted to see Rockport in winter." Tamsin draped Mags' coat and hat over a chair in the living room, but her sister wouldn't give up her scarf yet. A Christmas Tree in the corner flashed in primary colors. Outside, the wind picked up, howling across the chimney.

"This place looks totally different."

"It was warm for a few days after I moved in, so I bought a ladder and some paint and now it's red."

"It's a nice change. Inside, too. I don't remember the living room looking like this. It's so bright and white. You can tell this house doesn't have kids in it."

"Yeah. I wanted bright and airy. There's so much wood with the hardwood floor and the exposed ceiling."

"And you're cooking." Margaret gave up her scarf, leaving it on the chair.

"Chowder. I've been trying to assimilate. Having a new kitchen has been a little liberating. It's fun to be in there. Plus it's gorgeous. Come on, I'll show you. The people who had the place before me did a lot of work."

On the other side of the central fireplace, behind the living room, a small kitchen faded into a keeping room where family once sat to be warmed by the kitchen. Margaret stopped in the doorway. "This place was covered in toys. We used to put our bikes in here. It looks so grown up, now."

"It was probably pretty grown up when we weren't here, too, taking over everything."

"We left stuff everywhere, didn't we? Mom mentioned this house a few years ago. Her memory of it was totally different than mine. It seemed small to her. To me it was cozy. Dark, though. And cluttered."

"Do you remember playing in here on the floor when it rained?"

"Yes. What was that light box called? With those pegs?"

"Lite-Brite."

"The paper was kinda thick, so it would slip when you tried to push the pegs in. We'd dump the pegs on the floor, and they'd roll everywhere because the place was so uneven."

"Grandad would yell when he stepped on them."

A knock at the front door called Tamsin to the living room. She spoke to Margaret over her shoulder. "Living here all the time now, I can't imagine squeezing three more people and two kids with all their stuff in here. But it sure was fun."

"So many great memories."

Margaret was interrupted by a squeak from the door's ancient hinges. Before Tamsin reached the door, a gust of cold blew in with Ida, ice in her hair and a wet paper grocery bag under one arm.

"Bad out there, huh?" Tamsin closed the door behind her, and Mags hovered in the kitchen doorway, behind the half wall that separated it from the living room.

Ida dropped her coat and hat on the mat by the door and secured her grip on the paper bag. "Not my favorite walk, but it's not the worst, either. You'll see this place completely covered with ice someday and wonder how we ever thaw. I told you to stock your fridge, right?" Ida fell into a chair and unlaced her Doc Martens. "You put up paintings since I was here last. I have one like this. There's a small one in town like it, too. I think it's in that tea place."

Behind the sofa was a painting nearly four feet wide. A dirt road cut through a field of purple lupine to a cottage on a hill.

Mags stepped around the half wall. "Those were all his practice pieces. I have the final one. It's massive. Since Tamsin couldn't help me move it before she left, I had to rent a truck to get it home from Mom's house, then beg a neighbor to help me get it in the door."

"I'll be apologizing for that for the rest of my life." Tamsin walked past Mags and into the kitchen. The soup needed stirring more than the pot.

Ida followed, wet paper bag in tow. "You must be Margaret."

"I am. You must be Ida. Tamsin didn't mention the tattoos. Is it hard to own a bakery with tattoos?"

Ida dropped the bag on the kitchen counter. "I haven't found them to impede the baking process, no." She pulled containers from the bag, stacking them on the counter. "I brought a bunch of yummy things. I couldn't resist. Nothing smooths a rough introduction like lots of sweet stuff. They're the only things that keep children's birthday parties from going all *Lord of the Flies*. Cookies. Sticky buns. A dozen macarons. Extra wine. Bread to go with the soup. I didn't make this. I bought this at the market this morning. They cut little fins in it to make it look like a whale. You should see their lobster breads. Adorable. Here's something new I made—whiskey fudge. You'll have to tell me what you think. And a cake."

"You had me all the way back at cookies. Then wine. How did you fit all this in that bag?" Margaret peeked through the clear lid at a large chocolate cake.

"Chocolate with chocolate mousse and raspberries. It's new, too. I work on new recipes in the winter. Once the tourists are gone, it's nothing but birthday parties, anniversaries, and a few holidays. And the Super Bowl. That's a big one."

Mags popped the lid from the cake box. "You're right about sugar smoothing the landing. Why don't we skip the chowder and dig into this cake with forks?"

"Nice try, little sister. You can't have dessert first." Tamsin ladled clam chowder into bowls and slid them down the counter. Ida and Mags carried them to the table in the old keeping room.

"I'll be honest." Mags's chair scraped the wooden floorboards. "I've been dreading this. I know it was my idea, but it's not quite a vacation, you know? I was really close with our mom, and she never talked about this. We don't even know how much she knew. Our parents lied. It isn't just about what our father did behind our mother's back or what mistakes he might have made. There's no sense of peace to this for me. Either she knew, or she didn't and never knowing how this affected her keeps me from having closure on her loss. And Tamsin was Daddy's little girl. I can't imagine what this did to you."

Tamsin dumped oyster crackers from a bag into her soup. "He's not the man I thought he was, but that doesn't mean that I love him less or that the memories have to change. The fun times were still fun. The lessons he taught me are still important. That's separate from the unanswered questions. Were they trying to do the right thing? Did Mom know? Did she put her head in the sand? Did she treat the situation with compassion?"

"Did Mom show compassion? What about Dad? This is all his fault."

Margaret's spoon fell into her bowl. "Look what it did to Ida."

"What's that supposed to mean?" Ida fished clams from her soup. "You know he didn't give me these tattoos, right?"

If Margaret heard the attempt at levity, she ignored it. "You've had this whole thing thrown at you. Some half-sister shows up, stalks you, moves to your town, and buys your childhood home. Which was also our grandparents' house. This is really kind of uncomfortable, isn't it? We should admit this, shouldn't we?"

"I'm the one who told her the house was for sale. Rockport isn't my town. I don't own it. It has plenty of strange history for me, too. The only reason I'm still here is because I haven't thought of anywhere else to go yet. You can live here too, ya know."

"I have no intention of living here."

"Suit yourself, then." Ida returned Mags icy glare. "This had nothing to do with me. It still doesn't. I came to terms with this a long time ago. The man I knew came and went. He was more like an uncle than a father. There was no affection between him and my mother. No sense of duty or family obligation. Whether he came here for my mother or me, I have no way of knowing, because he left one day and just didn't come back again. My mom died three weeks after I met Tamsin, and I never had the heart to ask about the past, because I didn't want to throw in her face the fact that she never gave me a father or make her think I didn't value my step-dad. I didn't want to make her think she wasn't enough for me. I don't know what that man's motivations were, and I'm okay with that. Half the time, I don't know why I do what I do. Maybe I'm lucky, because I have just enough distance to see this for what it was."

"Oh, I saw it for what it was." Margaret dumped oyster crackers into her soup and poked at them with her spoon. "Maybe not the individual trees, but I saw the forest. I was just a kid, and I could tell something wasn't right.

Tamsin is the one who had blinders on. Pretended everything was wonderful and refused to see the truth. Our father cheated on our mother, and it's not easy to come to terms with that."

"Blinders? I chose to remember the good things, Miss Negative." Tamsin fished bacon out of her bowl.

Margaret pushed her bowl aside. "It was selfish, Tam."

"How was I selfish? Seeing the good in life is not being self-absorbed. Why can't I be happy with what life hands me? We weren't born in a ditch. We never had real problems. Why do you want me to join you on this terrible childhood crusade, anyway? I was happy, and I don't have regrets. If you weren't happy, that's your problem, not mine."

"It's not a crusade, it was a reality. Our mother was miserable, and you refused to see it."

"Crap." Ida dropped her spoon in her bowl and ran from table to the living room. "I have something for you, Tamsin. Speaking of regret, Ansel gave me this letter two weeks ago, and I haven't seen you. I shoved it in my coat pocket and almost forgot it." Ida dropped the letter between Tamsin and her empty bowl where it sat like a lead weight.

"I can't believe the two of you dated the same guy." Margaret's gaze was fixed on Ida, and Tamsin braced for the judgments of their half-sister's tattoos, messy hair, and Doc Martens. "How old is this guy anyway? Passing notes like it's high school. Can't he just text you like a normal adult?"

Ida snapped back. "He's an archivist. A cerebral kind of intellectual guy. He writes letters, not text messages. You know, like adults do." She waved off a raised eyebrow from Mags. "If judgment makes you happy, so be it."

"I apologize for Margaret's misdemeanors." Tamsin turned the envelope over. It was sealed. Ansel's perfect penmanship spelled out her name on the front. "She can be a little rude because she had a very traumatic childhood."

"Funny. Are you guys getting back together?" Margaret reached for the note.

Tamsin swatted her away. "It's none of your business but no. It was a passionate fling, but those never last. Plus, I'm working on me right now."

The exchange lightened Margaret's mood. "Isn't that awkward, though, that you were with the same guy?"

"Not for us," Ida laughed. "For him, yeah."

"Oh, come on! Read it." Margaret reached across the table for the letter, and Tamsin tucked it into her back pocket for safe keeping.

"Who's acting like they're in high school now?" Tamsin stuck her tongue out at her sister. "It's private. We didn't leave things on the best of terms, and he probably doesn't want things to be weird. I haven't even seen him since I moved here. Ran into him ten times a day while I was visiting, but I haven't seen him in months. He's gotta be avoiding me."

Margaret gave her a skeptical look, her eyes narrowed. "Aren't you curious?"

"Sure. But I'll read it on my own terms, thank you very much."

Margaret took their bowls to the sink and returned with an open bottle of wine. "Speaking of notes, what ever happened to the stick figure drawing I heard so much about? Do you still have it, Ida? I never got to see it."

Ida accepted a glass of red. "It's at home, in a box of things I've kept from over the years. I cussed through an entire batch of cookies when I saw it. I wished you had the nerve to talk to me, but then I realized how unreasonable I looked when I tore Ansel a new one. It took guts for you to walk in and drop that in the tip jar like you did. I don't remember drawing it, but it brought back all kinds of memories. Like that coat and crawling on the rocks, looking for barnacles and snails. He always smelled like cigars and had paint on him somewhere."

"Did I tell you about the dream I had? I was on the plane, on the way home from helping Mags—Margaret—clean out Mom's house. I had this strange dream about being little, walking through the woods, through leaves that were covered in little paintings. I collected a bunch of sticks, and when I reached up to hand them to someone, it was Dad, and they turned into paint brushes. He put them in the breast pocket of that coat. I never even knew that coat had a breast pocket. I dug it out of the overhead bin, and that's where the letter was."

Ida swirled the wine in her glass. "Do you think he wanted us to know? Like he was talking to you from beyond the grave?"

Tamsin loved the thought of it. "Maybe. I don't know what's out there, but sometimes I feel like there are signs. I'd like to think that he had a hand in protecting what the thief didn't take. Maybe he was out there helping some of it get back to me. I'll never get those flash drives back with the pictures Owen took, but the laptop was important to me. We always look for someone to blame when something goes wrong, why not look for someone to give credit to when it all goes right?"

Margaret finished her glass and went in for seconds. "Maybe he wanted all of this resolved. Maybe Mom went up there and yelled at him, and he tried to set it straight. So maybe he helped get your stuff back, too."

"That's a really nice way to think of it." Tamsin slid her glass across the table for more. "He was always trying to teach us lessons. How to let go is the hardest one of all."

"Even when you want to." Margaret leaned back in her chair, far from her wine.

Ida reached back for the open box of macarons and slid them across the table to Margaret. "Here. They don't solve everything, but God knows they don't hurt."

Margaret accepted the box of pillowy cookies. "What flavors are these?"

"There's chocolate and strawberry. These peach ones are mimosa."

"So good." Tamsin reached into the box and took one.

"These are chocolate bourbon."

"You're amazing. You know that?" Margaret jumped at the bourbon. "Really, though, you guys have very different memories of him than I do. He never would have appeared to me in a dream. Tamsin was always running around outside with him. He'd sit there and paint, and she'd romp through fields and mud. I was inside, hiding from bugs."

"I remember him telling me these crazy stories about adventures he went on." Ida brushed crumbs into her hand. "We used to climb around on the rocks. But mostly I remember these imaginary worlds that he made sound so real. He told the best stories."

Tamsin took another macaron. "Funny how we all see the same man so differently."

"Shit. I have something for *you*. How could I forget?" Margaret jumped from her chair and dug through her suitcase. Sweaters and jeans landed in the floor in a pile.

"For me?" Tamsin turned in her chair to observe Margaret's mess.

"For Ida. It's not much. I wanted to wrap it up, but I was afraid the TSA would rip the package apart. We're not one hundred percent sure, but Tamsin and I think this is the sweater he was wearing in the picture Tam showed me on her phone."

"This is for me?" Ida took the sweater into her lap. "I can't believe this survived. And that you'd give it to me."

Margaret gave her a genuine smile. "I don't have any particular memory of it. If it means something to you, you should have it."

"Other than a few paintings and that stupid stick figure drawing, I don't have a lot that reminds me of him."

Tamsin offered the last of the wine to Margaret and Ida, who both turned it down. She poured into her glass and reached for the second bottle on the counter. "There was the house."

"True. That was a pretty big thing. I didn't associate it with him at the time. I can thank him indirectly for the bakery, too, since Mom helped me buy it with the profit from selling this place."

"What did it look like when you lived here?" Margaret changed her mind and opened the second bottle.

"It doesn't even look the same. I moved out of here just after I turned eighteen. Not long after that, Mom sold the place and moved to Maine. A lot changed since then. All the rooms are different colors, and it seems smaller. This fireplace is the same, though. I remember Mom hating having a fire in it because the thermostat was on the adjacent wall, and the heat wouldn't kick on. It made the rest of the house so cold."

Margaret refilled Ida's glass. "I remember Grandmom saying the same thing. And it was so cluttered when our grandparents lived here."

"It was sparse for us. We didn't have a lot. Mom ran the laundromat and cleaned houses for extra money. She volunteered at the Arts Alliance to help my uncle. I guess that's how she met our father. There wasn't a lot of money for extra stuff. I didn't have a pony or inherit a million bucks. Just a few pieces of costume jewelry. That's about it."

Tamsin wiped water spots from the base of her wine glass. "We didn't inherit much either. Mom threw a lot away about a month after Dad died. I was so mad. She just nonchalantly threw it into conversation one day that she threw it all away. We never got a chance to go through it. Like the meaning she gave to those items was all that mattered, and we had no right to our own memories. We had a huge fight, and I demanded to know why, and she said she threw it all out because she didn't need stuff lying around just for the validation. It didn't make sense at the time, but after Owen died it did. Then when I saw that she kept his coat, I realized how wrong I was to assume she hadn't thought of us at all."

"What do you mean, you understood after Owen died?" Margaret cocked one eyebrow.

"Everything has new meaning when they're gone. Remember those snow globes Owen gave me for every trip we took? It was just junk. Packaging that came with the gift he gave. They became these pieces of empirical evidence that Owen had loved me. At first, I needed to see them every day. They were proof that he existed, that I wasn't crazy, and I didn't make it up, how much he loved me. But it hurt so much to look at them that I ended up hiding them in his wardrobe. It was the opposite of how Grandmom and Mom were. Remember?"

"They gave everything away. Grandmom went to Europe."

"And Mom started over. Everything had to be new. They had new lives that were so much more fun than the life they had when they were married."

Ida rose, and her chair wobbled as she stood. She brought the cake and three forks to the table. No knives. No plates. "We're way too young to be without our parents and to be losing our partners like that. There's a lot of loss at this table. Seems to me that we know something a lot of people don't and maybe we should try a little harder to hold on to what we have."

* * *

Tamsin folded her jeans and set them on the chair by her bedroom window. Downstairs, Ida slept on the sofa. Better than a tipsy uphill climb on the ice toward her apartment above the wine shop. On the other side of her bedroom wall, Margaret ran water in the bathroom sink. Tamsin slipped into her pajamas and peeked outside. Ice clung to panes of glass. The sky was black but for diffused pinpoints of light, reflecting from houses along the street and across the harbor. The storm slammed the coast with ice and snow and wouldn't tire for hours more. Cold air pushed in between the cracks, and she tugged the envelope from the pocket of her jeans before stretching out in bed.

She considered waiting to read until Mags went home, to delay whatever emotion might be sealed within and to defer the fallout. The memory of Ansel was still hers. At times it was sweet like honey. The moments she was lost in, like a freefall from a cliff. A liberation. Until the sweet turned sour and shame oozed through and stained her skin. Hot water wouldn't wash it away. Not wine nor whiskey. Although Owen's voice was still distant in Rockport, Tamsin knew he would want her to move on. He wouldn't have wanted her to stop living. But Ansel wasn't hers, and she wasn't even herself. Yet. She peeled the tape away from the envelope.

"Tam,

I'm deeply sorry for the way we left things. You were right. There are things left unsaid between us, and I regret that I never told you what I had to say before you left.

Ida came by. Your doing, I'm sure. She apologized and so did I, but I need you to know that there'll never be anything between her and me, and if I had my way, you'd never have left. We'd have worked it out. I'd have gone to you with no regard for the consequences and begged you to listen. And if I had my way, the consequences would have been grand.

I dig too much into people, I know. I push them away by asking too many questions, and they aren't even the right ones sometimes. I wish I'd met you before I learned the hard lesson, that I need to ask people who they are and who they want to be. If I'm lucky, someday you'll tell me.

I have avoided the Neck, giving you space to find yourself here without traces of me, but I would love to see you. Perhaps a drink or dinner to find out what our last chapter might be. Regrets, you know?

At the very least, I need to know that you found the truth you were looking for. Stop by any time? Even if just for a quick visit.

~ Ansel."

The note refolded itself along the crease. She returned it to the envelope and closed it away in her nightstand drawer. Perhaps she could fall into a routine with someone else someday. Wash away the black-and-white and find vibrant color between the absolutes. Different stubble in a razor by a different sink.

The wind-driven ice pounded the windows, obscuring the endless sound of water pounding the rocks. Tamsin let her eyes close and dreamed of spring.

* * *

The sun rose with the morning, peeling away the top layer of ice, letting it thaw and drip and run to the earth below. Shovels scraped against pavement and wooden porches, making room for deliveries and customers. Tamsin scraped away just enough frozen snow to allow for a graceful exit, and the three sisters walked down the street toward the water. One drowning in a blue sweater. One swimming in a green coat with brown collar. Another wearing an oversized sweatshirt with a whale on the front, borrowed and purple. The moon was still up, tugging at the tide.

Tamsin dug a quarter from her coat pocket, dropped it into the binocular viewer, and peered across the ocean. She spun the viewer toward Margaret, letting her sister enjoy the view, and squinted into the new day.

"I know you two were curious what was in that letter." She turned from the sun, toward the land. Toward the voices of men who arrived, unpacking their supplies, preparing to remove storm shutters from buildings they secured in the days before. Metal ladders scuffed on concrete, ratcheting upwards.

JENNIFER M. LANE

"You don't have to tell me." Ida looked like a child in the oversized sweater, her cell phone in a front pocket dragging it down to her knees on one side. "It's none of my business. I support whatever you two want to do, you know. No jealousy here. He broke my heart, but we weren't together long enough for me to cling to it forever."

Tamsin shrugged. "It's cool. He said he talked to you, and that you two were okay. He regretted that we didn't stay in touch and wants to get together sometime."

"What an asshole." Time gave up on the viewer, and Margaret pulled away from the horizon. "I'm sorry, but he is."

"He's not an asshole." Tamsin watched the men work, removing screws that held sheets of plywood from the windows of a historic building. "At least I don't think so."

"I have to agree with you on that." Ida shrugged inside the sweater. "He's not an asshole. Maybe things don't always turn out the way he wanted, but his heart's in the right place most of the time. He asked me if I would mind if the two of you hooked up again. I said I wouldn't, but I didn't encourage him in one direction or the other. I don't want you to think that."

"No, I know." More men arrived with ladders and coffee, taking their places in the ritual. Ansel was among them, there to save history. He dropped a toolbox and raised a ladder. Tamsin turned her back to him and faced the sun. "I don't want to wait for things anymore. I don't want to just get through life. Moving here is my second chance, you know, and I want to take my time to get it right. Take control of what happens from here. I don't want to go with the flow anymore."

Ida tugged her hands inside the sleeves. "Good for you. Just don't be too independent. Trust me, it's not as fun as it looks. I never wanted nothing from anybody. Never wanted to lose myself in anyone else."

Margaret turned away from the ocean. "Seems like a lonely way to live."

"I grew up with a label, being an illegitimate kid in a conservative artsy town where everybody knows everything. Whether it was true or not, I felt like people expected me to wear that stain. I decided I was going to live a private, independent life, on my own terms. I wasn't giving anyone a reason to look down on me the way they looked down on my mother. In the process, I may have missed out on some pretty amazing people."

"You two are figuring out all this big stuff." Margaret stood between her sisters, watching the waves push islands of ice against the rocks. "I'm just getting started. You know, I've never been good enough. I spend so much goddamn time worried about whether or not the people around me were good enough, and it was all a front. I wasn't a good enough daughter. Haven't been a good enough sister. If I'd been a good enough wife, I wouldn't be paying for a divorce lawyer with a credit card. If I were a good enough mother, I'd be with my kids, not staring out at this water wishing I could walk on it, wondering where I went wrong. I just want to find a place where I'll be good enough."

Tamsin nudged Margaret's shoulder. "If you find it, you let me know."

"Yeah. Me, too." Ida shoved her hands into the pockets of her jeans. "Three first class tickets to wherever that is."

"What's that sound?" Mags squinted at the horizon.

"It's my phone. My calendar." Tamsin dug her phone from her pocket. She swiped the screen and silenced the notification. "I ordered one of those little plaques for the house. Like the ones people put by their house number that say when it was built. They said it would be ready in four weeks and today is four weeks. I put a note in here to call for an ETA."

"Is the cottage on the historic registry? Is it even that old?" Ida glanced behind her, at the men removing plywood from the windows so the restaurant could open to the world. "Ansel would be thrilled."

"No, nothing that exciting." Tamsin turned toward the ocean, knowing she could weather whatever storms it sent. "Just a little nameplate, like you see on little cottages around here. I decided to call it *Afterlife*."

ABOUT THE AUTHOR

A Maryland native and Pennsylvanian at heart, Jennifer M. Lane holds a bachelor's degree in philosophy from Barton College and a master's in liberal arts with a focus on museum studies from the University of Delaware, where she wrote her thesis on the material culture of roadside memorials. She resides with her partner Matt and a tuxedo cat named Penny.

Visit The Author's Website
jennifermlanewrites.com

OTHER WORKS BY THE AUTHOR INCLUDE

Of Metal and Earth
Blood and Sand